SONGS OF SPRING

The powerful conclusion of her Great War saga...

Christmas 1917, and as the Lilley family gathers at the Rectory in the Sussex village of Ashden, the mood is far from festive. Caroline's parents refuse to support her love of Belgian Army intelligence officer Captain Yves Rosier, and she is forced to leave abruptly. Phoebe falls in love with a divorced music-hall singer, and she too incurs her parents' disapproval.

The new year brings fresh tragedy, and Caroline returns to Ashden as the war ends. The Rectory opens its doors to a new world, its inhabitants strengthened by the grief and happiness shared during the long years of war.

SONGS OF SPRING

SONGS
OF SPRING

by

Harriet Hudson

Magna Large Print Books
Long Preston, North Yorkshire,
BD23 4ND, England.

British Library Cataloguing in Publication Data.

Hudson, Harriet
    Songs of spring.

    A catalogue record of this book is
    available from the British Library

    ISBN   0-7505-1602-X

First published in Great Britain 2000
by Severn House Publishers Ltd.

Copyright © 2000 by Harriet Hudson

Cover illustration © Melvyn Warren-Smith by arrangement
with P.W.A. International Ltd.

The moral right of the author has been asserted

Published in Large Print 2001 by arrangement with
Severn House Publishers Ltd.

*All situations in this publication are fictitious and
any resemblance to living persons is purely coincidental.*

Magna Large Print is an imprint of Library Magna Books Ltd.

Printed and bound in Great Britain by
T.J. (International) Ltd., Cornwall, PL28 8RW

Acknowledgements

Songs of Spring concludes my quartet of
novels on Ashden Rectory during the First
World War, in which the earlier titles were
The Last Summer, Dark Harvest and *Winter
Roses*. I am very grateful to those who have
helped me during its creation and pub-
lication; in particular I would like to thank:
my agent Dorothy Lumley of the Dorian
Literary Agency, my editors Marisa
McGreevy and Hugo Cox of Severn House,
Jane Wood, Marian Anderson, Norman
Franks and Mary Lewis.

One

Agnes stretched luxuriously. She would make the most of her extra half-hour in bed while she still could, for the precious gentle mound in front of her would next summer become another small person demanding her time. There would be no extra half-hours, even if she was entitled to them as parlour maid. Myrtle, the housemaid, had been eager to help look after the new baby, when Mrs Lilley had said there was no question of Agnes's leaving the Rectory.

Where would she go anyway? Jamie and she had no home together as he'd been away at the Front all their married life, and she wasn't going to live with his parents, thank you very much. Her own parents didn't have room for her and the children, but from the Rector and Mrs Lilley there was always warmth – in their hearts at least. Practical warmth was harder to come by in this December of 1917; coal rationing meant cold bedrooms in order to keep the rest of the Rectory reasonably warm. The

9

eight hundredweight a week allowed for houses over twelve rooms didn't go far here, and many rooms had been shut up tight for the duration of the winter.

'Cold hands, warm heart,' as Mrs Dibble valiantly maintained, and 'You should thank your lucky stars we work in the warmest room in the house' – the kitchen.

Funny how things changed... Once Agnes had been terrified of old Dribble Dibble, the housekeeper, once there had been *rules*, and the worst you had to worry about was whether your black was ironed well enough for the afternoons, and whether the drawing-room fire would choose to smoke the room out today. Now, in the fourth year of war, there was Jamie to worry about, far away with the 7th Sussex on the Western Front, and looming beyond that, when – if ever – this war would come to an end and who would win it?

Life in this once sleepy Sussex village of Ashden had changed beyond what anyone could have imagined in 1914, and she sometimes worried about what kind of life would await two-year-old Elizabeth Agnes as she grew up. Agnes cocked an ear. Where *was* she? There was a suspicious quietness in the tiny boxroom adjoining Agnes's, which meant Myrtle had probably already dressed her, and together they had staggered down the back stairs to light the stove ready for Mrs Dibble. Mrs Dibble terrified Agnes no longer: Mrs Dibble no longer carolled hymns throughout the day, and Mrs Dibble no longer moved briskly and purposefully, as though she were commanded by God to organise the whole world as well as the Rectory. Not since the summer, when it had happened...

Margaret Dibble was up early this December day. She had to be, for this was the day she had set aside to make the Christmas puddings. Puddings? What a joke. She didn't laugh though. She hadn't laughed at anything since her son Fred had been murdered out on the Western Front – that's the word she used, for all the Rector's kind talks. Not even Elizabeth Agnes could make her laugh, and not even her own grandchildren. Which is why she had to force herself to make the puddings today. It was the only way she could acknowledge she was still part of this gloomy old world. She and Percy had lived all their married lives in the Rectory, and so to them the Rectory *was* the world. If it continued to have its

Christmas puddings, no matter what, Margaret would have done her bit to cock a snoop at the Kaiser, who'd brought all this on us.

'I've brought the brandy, Mrs Dibble.' Mrs Lilley appeared in her kitchen, waving a small bottle, and vanished again.

Now *that* wouldn't have happened before the war. Firstly even Mrs Lilley would have thought twice about coming into the kitchen, without at least knocking, and secondly, Percy would have been in charge of the brandy like he was of the wine – what there had been of it. But since 1914 there had been no brandy at all, and Mrs Lilley had been forced to beg some from Lady Buckford, the Rector's mother. This year even her reserves were at rock bottom, like everything else, but as Mrs Dibble had said: 'If there's no brandy, the pudding won't keep.'

Thanks to that Kaiser and his submarine blockade the brandy was almost the only proper ingredient she did have. In the early days of the war she'd had her own private little stores of food tucked away, but they were all gone now, and she was down to pleading and queuing at the village shops like everyone else. She'd had one piece of

12

luck, however. Under a Ministry of Food scheme she gave food-economy demonstrations in Tunbridge Wells, and when it had come to showing them how to make a wartime Christmas plum pudding she'd managed to keep some of the fruit back for the Rectory.

She'd had to demonstrate the Food Controller's recommended Christmas dinners for them, and a sorry business that was: it was a pretty kettle of fish when the Lord's birthday would be celebrated with rice soup, haddock, roast fowl, plum pudding (if you could call it that), and caramel custard. It *sounded* all right, but when you saw the reality – and the price of it – you could have wept. Then there was cake. Who would have thought that English teatime would be as good as abolished? Restaurants could only serve you two ounces of cake, and that wasn't worthy of the name half the time. You could serve as much as you liked at home, but with milk controlled and now sugar rationed, let alone the perpetual battle for decent flour and the price of eggs, teatime was vanishing like a mirage in the desert.

Still, it was all to help the soldiers on the Front, she told herself. Poor devils, like her Joe. He was in a so-called pioneer battalion,

13

the 5th Sussex, but from what his wife said he was out *in front* of the front line making tunnels and digging the trenches.

'Finish the tennis court, Percy?' Margaret looked up from her organising of ingredients into pudding basins, as his lugubrious face appeared through the tradesmen's door.

'I never thought I'd see the day I had to dig it up to grow vegetables.' Percy looked as downhearted as she felt, and that succeeded in rallying her.

'It's that or starve. We've got to get potatoes somehow.'

'I bet the blooming Kaiser isn't eating potatoes.'

'No. He's too busy eating my sultanas,' she snapped.

Plough up Britain, that was the new order from Whitehall. Everything, not just wasteland, but parks, lawns and private gardens were to be dug up; no more colourful cottage garden flowers, it was all vegetables from now on. Even Sir John and Lady Hunney of the Manor had dug up a lot of their grounds. Not that there were any proper farmers any more to help them tend them, and Margaret couldn't see the august Lady Hunney out there with her fork and spade. Then last week some of the Land Girls lodging up at Castle Tillow descended on the place like a plague of locusts.

Margaret didn't recognise Ashden any longer. The village was full of foreigners. Half of the old village were away at the front or dead, and a load of strangers had taken their place. The Towers was now army officers' quarters, the Land Girls had replaced the Norvilles at Castle Tillow, and Ashden Manor was an officers' hospital. Sir John worked most of the time in Whitehall – something to do with the Army – and Lady Hunney had moved into the Dower House.

Where was it all going to stop? At the Rectory, Margaret had vowed. There'd be little change here beyond what the thieving hands of this war had already taken from it – if Margaret Dibble had anything to do with it. Makeshift puddings, or no makeshift puddings, she forced herself to pick up the wooden spoon to stir her unappetising mixture. This year, there was no one here to do it but her. That Kaiser had a lot to answer for.

'Wonderful news, Mrs Dibble.' Mrs Lilley shot through the door again shouting in excitement, and triumphantly waving a

15

letter. 'Caroline is coming home for Christmas!'

Margaret beamed. 'That's what I call *good* news, Mrs Lilley.' Her spirits were suddenly lifted, who cared about food shortages? Miss Caroline would make the Rectory come alive again. She could see her bright inquiring eyes and curly brown hair now, popping her head round the door. 'Are those raspberry buns I can smell baking? I'm starving.'

Mrs Isabel was still at home, the eldest of the five Lilley children, but though she'd changed for the better now she'd taken over running the village cinema, it wasn't the same as having Miss Caroline around. Mrs Isabel's husband, Robert Swinford-Browne, was away in Flanders flying balloons, which still sounded funny to Mrs Dibble, although Percy told her it was a very dangerous job because they were so easy to shoot down. Why send them up then, she'd asked?

'To see what's going on,' Percy explained.

'Like spies? The Unseen Hand?'

Percy had been stumped. 'You can't call 'em the Unseen Hand if they're floating around in big balloons.'

The news about Miss Caroline pleased Margaret for Mrs Lilley's sake too. Her

16

presence would make a *real* Christmas.

'Any chance of Miss Felicia coming home or Master George or Miss Phoebe?' Margaret was sorry she'd asked because Mrs Lilley looked downcast again.

'We don't know yet. It all depends what's happening at the Front. The fighting in France is continuing much later in the year than before, so I suppose the offensive might go on all over Christmas, and of course, there's always some fighting somewhere. Caroline says she hopes to bring with her that nice Belgian captain she works with. You remember he was staying with the Hunneys last Christmas and came over here quite often.'

Another bedroom to air, another mouth to feed. Still, she'd manage, Margaret supposed, though she didn't approve of those Belgian ways of his. Agnes and Myrtle had thought it a fine joke for Miss Caroline and the captain to cook servants' luncheon and then serve it to them, but it was stepping too far out of line for her.

She picked up the wooden spoon again. Once upon a time Miss Caroline would have been here to help stir the puddings. It was a tradition in the Rectory that all the children would have come to take their turn, but Miss Caroline had always clamoured to have the first stir. Now, four of them were over the hills and far away, and Mrs Isabel was too scatty and preoccupied with herself to think of such trivial things as Christmas puddings.

Perhaps Mrs Lilley saw her doleful face, for she hesitated before leaving. 'I've never dared ask you before, Mrs Dibble, but I wonder as Caroline isn't here whether I might stir the pudding this year?'

Margaret could have cried with pleasure, as she handed the spoon to Mrs Lilley. 'Three times round for the Three Wise Men,' she instructed, as though everyone in the Rectory didn't know it perfectly well.

Times changed, but the world went on and soon Miss Caroline would be home again.

Caroline groaned. Surely it couldn't be time to get up yet? Last night there had been another terrible Gotha air raid over London, and though no bombs had fallen on them in Queen Anne's Gate, the warning maroons, the noise, the searchlights, and the uncertainty of waiting for the all-clear had kept them awake well into the early hours. London was now mainly spared the attention of Zeppelins, but in return they had been presented with an even worse hazard, the Gotha aircraft which regularly appeared with their cargo of bombs, dropped to devastating effect. Londoners regularly took to the underground stations for shelter at night, and a whole organisation was springing up to put order into the ensuing chaos down there.

Thump on the door. 'Hot water, Caroline.'

She was now officially a Waac – and so was Ellen, her old friend from Dover days. How long ago those now seemed. The difference between them was that Ellen's job was to look after the housekeeping in their lodgings at Queen Anne's Gate while Caroline was clerk assistant to two army captains, Luke Dequessy and Yves Rosier. Ellen had thought this a cosy number after a year abroad as a VAD, from which she had returned with pneumonia. Because of the nature of their job, Yves and Luke had needed someone discreet, and at Caroline's suggestion Luke had pulled strings to get Ellen transferred. Her cooking was erratic, to say the least, but her liveliness and good humour made up for it.

'Secret Blooming Service Bureau.

Blimey!' Ellen had been overawed when first approached, and had gleefully signed the Official Secrets Act. 'I won't tell a soul how many spuds you eat for supper, Caroline,' she had promised.

'And particularly not Mrs Dibble, when you come to the Rectory again.'

There was another reason for discretion. Caroline had decided – against Yves's wishes – not to tell her parents that she and Yves were lovers. It would hurt them too much if Father and Mother knew that their bed at Queen Anne's Gate was a double one. Three years ago the idea would have seemed unimaginable, but the war had changed everything. It was necessary to look to the present as well as the future, when one could not know how little of the latter remained. The older you were the more difficult it was to keep up with the times, Caroline realised, especially for her parents, living within the confines of Rectory life.

Yves was not only a Roman Catholic, but married, and when – if – this war was ever over, as a captain in the Belgian Army would be honour bound to return both to his country and to his wife, even though his wife had refused to consummate their marriage. Even worse awaited him if the war went against the Allies – but that she dared not contemplate. Surely the vast sacrifice of human life in the last three years could not have been in vain?

As a Belgian Army intelligence liaison officer operating between London's Secret Service Bureau, army intelligence at GHQ Montreuil and King Albert of Belgium at La Panne, Yves was all too often away, although London was his base. Luke, in the British Army, liaised between London, army intelligence in Folkestone and GHQ. The three of them, Yves, Luke and she, shared a small office in Whitehall Court, where she acted as assistant to both of them, a difficult task at times, especially at present. Yves had confided to her that King Albert was not always convinced that Belgium's best interests lay with fighting with the Allies, which was the reason he had always insisted on being in sole command of his own army.

Their rooms in Queen Anne's Gate were far from ideal, especially for Ellen. They were lodged in a large nest of servants' rooms, at the top of the house, the rest of which was given over to offices. This meant a steep climb for them, especially for Ellen since the only kitchen was in the basement, though they were as a gracious gesture allowed to use the only bathroom which was on the second floor. The bath was an august and temperamental beast, however, and on cold mornings hot water brought up from the bathroom in ewers was a welcome substitute.

'Where's Yves?'

Caroline hurtled breathlessly down the staircases to the kitchen to grab some breakfast more speedily – oh, for Mrs Dibble's array of dishes awaiting them in pre-war days, plain cheap food though it was. On the other hand, she told herself valiantly, looking at today's meagre spread, she wouldn't go back to those days now. They remained a happy memory in her heart, like Reggie, her first love, born of her girlhood, not her maturity. She was twenty-five now, and had she married Reggie she would still be in Ashden. She loved Ashden deeply, but not as a prison, and with all the feudal duties and burdens that even now after three years of war lingered on, that's what it would have become for her as the squire's wife.

'He and Captain Dequessy left early.' Ellen sat down to pour herself some tea from Caroline's pot.

This sounded bad. Had some new

problem arisen? Caroline hadn't quite yet worked out the correct balance between her three roles: clerk-assistant to two army captains, and those of lover to one and friend to the other (and moreover friend might become sister-in-law if Felicia married him).

'Did they say why?'

'Only that they wanted you to have some more sleep after last night.'

Caroline felt somewhat annoyed. She had a job, just as they did, and here was Yves making concessions to her that he would not have tolerated in anyone else. When she arrived at the office, having run most of the way across the park, there was no sign of Yves or Luke in the office, and she slipped behind the desk in her cubby-hole to attack her work. Today's batch of intelligence reports was already waiting for her. It still amazed her to think that she, Caroline Lilley, rector's daughter, had managed to land up in the Secret Service Bureau, although of course to the outside world she was just a Waac.

Her irritation vanished as usual when she looked up to see Yves coming through the door. Her heart still lurched when she saw his tall, awkward figure, and the scarred face, which looked so austere and yet so quickly changed, when his eyes lit up with warmth and tenderness – as they did now.

'Caroline, I am glad you are here.'

'What's wrong, Yves?' She was alarmed.

'I have to leave for La Panne immediately – Luke gathers that there is a crisis developing, and I should be there.'

'How long will you be away?' Normally Caroline did not ask such unanswerable questions, but today she could not help it. Despite the bleakness of the war situation, and of the December weather, she had been eagerly looking forward to their spending Christmas together at the Rectory. Christmas might provide, with her father's quiet good sense, a beacon of light for the unknown horrors of 1918. Last summer had seen the usual public optimism that the next offensive would be decisive, as the High Command always maintained. In July the troops had gone into battle at Ypres in the belief that to take the Passchendaele Ridge meant the end of the war, and in late October, the Canadians had, suffering enormous casualties, gained a toehold there. Yet there was still no end to the war. On and on it went. Even the recent success of the big tank offensive at Cambrai had not offset the spur offered to the enemy by the collapse of Russia after the abdication of the Tsar and the Italian retreat to the Piave line.

Yves, of course, realised the reason for her question, and came over to her desk to talk to her quietly. 'I will return in time, *cara*. We will spend Christmas together, never fear. I have no choice but to go now.'

He told her that King Albert had been impressed by Lord Lansdowne's courage in writing to the British press that he believed the Allies should negotiate peace terms now. The Belgian government was split on whether to seek a separate peace for themselves now, or to pursue the 'Death or Glory' policy the Allies would undoubtedly favour. 'The Allied plans for 1918 need the Belgian army to stand firm,' he explained.

'Plans?' she echoed hollowly. '*Are* there any?'

'Certainly there are!' Luke had come in without their noticing. 'Lots of them. Everyone has his own, that's all.'

'*My* plan,' Caroline announced firmly, 'is to spend Christmas at the Rectory, preferably with both of you, even if–'

'Felicia doesn't come,' Luke finished for her, as she barged into dangerous waters. 'If she doesn't, I'll volunteer to stay here,

25

though. Someone has to man the barricades.'

He was right of course. War no longer stopped for Christmas – if it ever had. Trains carrying troops one way might indicate a lull in German strategy; carrying them the other could signpost a coming offensive, or, almost worse, prior knowledge of Allied plans. Every day Field Marshal Haig had the benefit of new intelligence gained from the increasingly successful secret organisation La Dame Blanche, operating within Belgium, and which took its name from the ghost of the White Lady said to herald the downfall of the Hohenzollerns. If only the legend would prove true!

This autumn it had risen, phoenix-like, from the ashes of its predecessor, which had been controlled by Caroline's former army intelligence boss in Folkestone, and which had been betrayed from within. The new La Dame Blanche offered their services not to Folkestone, but to the Secret Service Bureau, whose organisation in Holland, run by Captain Landau, had leapt at the opportunity.

The network of agents was increasing rapidly, after an initial problem had been solved – partly thanks to Yves. La Dame Blanche had insisted not only that they should organise themselves on military hierarchical lines, but that they should be a recognised part of the British Army. The latter requirement was the hitch, but it looked now as though Yves and Landau had managed to achieve a good old English compromise, whereby they declared oaths of allegiance, and were issued with identity discs, which were to be buried in the ground until the war was over. Everyone seemed happy at the moment.

Caroline looked on each new batch of intelligence as another hammer in the enemy's coffin; after all, her sister Felicia's life might depend on some stray snippet of information that allowed C, as the head of the SSB was known, to deduce German intentions.

Felicia and their Aunt Tilly, her father's younger sister, ran an advanced first aid post on the Flanders front, and had been heavily engaged all the autumn, for the fighting had been aggravated even more than usual by the winter rains and mud. The offensive was over, but somehow Caroline thought it unlikely that her sister would take leave at Christmas this year.

'I don't know why I set such store on Christmas,' Caroline remarked, cross with herself for caring so much.

'You're a rector's daughter,' Luke pointed out. 'It's the family business.'

Surely it was more than duty that called her back? Something more even than Ashden. It was the image of the Rectory itself. In her mind's eye, it never changed: Mrs Dibble always stood at the kitchen table stirring Christmas puddings, Mother was working in her 'glory-hole' boudoir or floating round the Rectory organising her family in her own disorganised way, Father sat in his study, his door and heart ever open for his family's problems.

Another factor, she recognised, was that in her disappointment over Yves' absence, though she tried to live in the certainty of the moment, she knew that the inevitable final farewell to Yves would have someday to be made. That was what made these temporary separations all the more difficult to bear. However hard she tried to convince herself that the war effort was gaining from what deep inside she saw as a waste of precious fleeting time for herself and Yves, the mutiny inside her rumbled on.

'I have to leave now, Caroline.' Yves came

round to her side of the desk, bent over and kissed her.

Why had he done that? she instantly panicked. He *never* kissed her in the office. Was he going back to his wife already? Happiness, like raisins, never came unadulterated – perhaps that's what made it happiness? With much effort she managed to joke: 'I hope the Germans know it's Christmas too.'

'I'm not sure Ludendorff does, but I do.'

She promptly stood up and saluted him. 'Then *au revoir, mon capitaine.*'

As soon as he had gone, the office seemed desolate with just herself and Luke. She could hardly see over the top of the pile of reports today. Gathered from different sources, they all needed to be checked for duplication. This had proved a major problem, since if GHQ or C received two or three reports each with the same information, they were naturally inclined to believe it true. In fact, owing partly to the complications of the many smaller organisations that existed in Belgium, partly to the 'letter-box' system they used to smuggle the reports over the frontier to Holland, and partly to the increasing use of pigeons to carry intelligence, the agents often overlapped, with the result that one report could find its way by several different means to London. If that information was wrong, and false credence was given to it, it could have devastating consequences.

'For want of a nail, the shoe was lost...' as Benjamin Franklin once said, and Luke said all the time.

Caroline took a deep breath and picked up the first report. Luke glanced up and saw her face.

'Don't look so glum. You're in luck. Yves has given me strict instructions to cheer you up while he's away.'

Margaret plodded steadily back through the Rectory garden. The sooner the war ended and she could get a new coat, the better; this one was only fit to be torn up for dog blankets, and even Ahab would turn up his nose at it soon. She'd been queuing for an hour at the butcher's. She thought longingly back to the days before this war had started: when Mrs Dibble of the Rectory telephoned, the orders were round here before she'd hung the receiver up. Now there were no more delivery boys. They were too busy delivering bullets and shells to the enemy.

Her face sank into its now customary lines

of bitterness. Christmas and no Fred. Christmas and no Joe. At least Joe was alive – somewhere. Italy, his wife Muriel had worked out from their private code. She wouldn't even see his kiddies this Christmas, as Muriel was taking them to her parents.

Margaret knew only two things about Italy: firstly it had come down in the world since the time of Julius Caesar, and secondly you got there by crossing over the Alps. Hannibal had done it by elephant, but she presumed even Field Marshal Haig must have thought of some better method by now. Though judging by the mess on the Western Front, she couldn't be too sure. She tried to picture Joe on an elephant – ridiculous, maybe, but it put off having to tell Mrs Lilley the bad news.

It was all very well the Government telling everyone to eat roast fowl at Christmas, but were they going to provide them? The most she'd been able to wheedle out of Farmer Sharpe was the promise of one capon. How was that going to go round goodness knows how many at the family table and nine or ten in the servants' hall? What's more, Wally Bertram said he could only let her have two pounds of sausage meat and a small joint of beef. He was getting above himself. Meat was so scarce, he claimed, that he was only opening in the mornings now. In Margaret's opinion, he wanted his afternoon nap. What happened to service for the customer?

The net result was that she was going to have to tell Mrs Lilley that Oscar would have to go after all. She remembered the day he arrived as if it were yesterday. Percy had shouted in the middle of her pastry – if you could call it that. 'Daisy!' (That was Percy's pet name for her.) 'Look what I've got.'

She'd looked up and shouted right back. 'What's that dirty animal doing here?'

There, trotting along at Percy's side at the end of a piece of string, was a pink piglet. In *her* kitchen.

Percy was disappointed at her lack of enthusiasm. 'Seb Mutter gave him to me for helping him muck out his sties. The Government says we should all fatten up our own pigs, so here he is.'

The piglet had given a confirmatory squeal, before she hustled both of them out, with orders to build the animal a sty of its own. The Rector had named him Oscar after that playwright, because he seemed to have literary leanings. On his very first day in his new sty he was found to be eating his way through a copy of *The Strand Magazine* with evident enjoyment, while leaving the rest of the pile, composed of parish magazines, untouched. The heap was in the adjoining workshop and Percy had left the door open by mistake.

Oscar had grown not only in size but in the family's affections. Not to mention Elizabeth Agnes's heart. Every day she trotted down to see Oscar. If the next time she saw him he was in the oven – even Margaret flinched at the consequences. Now there seemed to be no choice.

She pulled herself together, as she entered the kitchen. She stopped short in shock. There at the table Agnes was sitting over a cup of tea chatting to *Lady Buckford!*

'Good morning, your ladyship,' Margaret managed to say through stiff lips. When the Rector's mother had come to live with them, there had been ructions and the whole household had been upset. Now it had all settled down, and she and Lady Buckford had come to an understanding. But that didn't give her the right to push herself into her kitchen.

'Have a cup of tea, Mrs Dibble.' Agnes leapt up hastily, seeing Margaret's reactions. 'I hope you will forgive this intrusion,'

Lady Buckford said, sounding more like she assumed it rather than hoping, in Margaret's opinion. 'But it is kitchen business.'

'Yes, your ladyship?' Margaret did not give an inch.

'My son, Lord Buckford, tells me he has leave over Christmas, and will naturally be spending it in Wiltshire with Lady Gwendolen. However, he proposes to call here on Christmas Eve with his gift to me.'

'Yes, your ladyship.' Margaret was busily calculating whether an earl could be fed on vegetable pie, should he stay for luncheon.

'His gift is two large turkeys, three capons and a goose from the Buckford House Farm. They are all at your disposal.'

Margaret was flabbergasted, unable to say a word even of thanks, but Agnes promptly burst into tears.

'What are you crying for, girl?' Lady Buckford was taken aback at this reception of her news.

'Oscar's safe.'

The days were passing slowly, and Caroline had to restrain herself from pestering Luke for news. If there had been any, he would have told her, good or bad. Her greatest fear

– unlikely though it was – was still that Yves had gone himself into occupied Belgium, either on a mission (and there had been talk of dropping agents in) or to see his wife. If he did so and were caught, he would be shot as a spy. He never spoke of Annette-Marie. Caroline would hate it if he did, but she hated it when he did not. She told herself that to have his arms around her was enough, for war brought a time span of its own, but now that she lacked them, anxiety was biting deep.

In the week before Christmas Luke suddenly announced: 'I'm taking you out tonight. Theatre and dinner. Yves' instructions.'

'You mean he's not coming back for Christmas?' Caroline was immediately suspicious. She knew that Yves was worried because the enemy had been putting a lot of effort into propaganda in the Flemish-speaking part of Belgium, which considered itself hard done by compared with the French-speaking areas. There were some deserters from the free Belgian army, and, worse, inside occupied Belgium much more co-operation with the Germans. *Had* Yves gone in himself to find out the truth of this?

'I don't mean anything of the sort, and I'm

surprised at you. Where's your stiff upper lip?'

'Wobbling. The gum they sell nowadays isn't up to much.'

All the same, she was pleased at the break, even if Luke's choice of theatre wasn't hers, and even if there was yet another of the thick fogs that were characterising this December. They went to the Comedy Theatre in the Haymarket to see the Charlot revue, and when they came out into the darkness of wartime London, she found her spirits had lifted. Fun and froth were no bad thing when you wrestled all day with reality.

Soho was no longer the home of so many small Italian-run restaurants, for many of their owners and their sons had returned to join the Italian army when Italy declared war against Austria-Hungary. However, Luke had winkled out one still run by the owner's wife and daughters, which pleased Caroline greatly for with Yves she usually went to one of the coffee bars or restaurants around Piccadilly Circus, which had been virtually taken over by the French and Belgian military. On special occasions they went to Gambrinus, Belgian-owned, but less 'discovered' by the troops. The restaurant was packed with uniforms of course, which was hardly getting away from work, but so was every restaurant in London, and a small intimate restaurant was much nicer than the large hotels. Moreover the food would be better, even if they did have to gobble it because of the ten-thirty closing time imposed by wartime law. The Italians were more efficient at making do than big hotels who specialised, it seemed to her, only in providing *less*, as a way of coping with food shortages.

Not everyone was in uniform. She glanced round the crowded room, seeing one civilian at least, though he was dining with a khaki-clad Waac. Whom she recognised.

'Phoebe!' she yelled joyously before she could stop herself, to the great interest of the restaurant.

What on earth was her sister doing here when she was supposed to be driving motor transport on the Western Front? Mother hadn't said anything about her getting leave.

Phoebe promptly turned bright red in the face. A suspicious sign, thought Caroline warily. She excused herself to Luke, and rushed over to hug her youngest and, in the past, most troublesome sister. Phoebe did not look pleased. 'Caroline, this is Billy

Jones. Billy, one of my *elder* sisters,' she introduced him crossly.

Billy Jones? *Now* she recognised him, from his pictures at any rate. He was the popular Cockney music-hall star, and presumably Phoebe had met him in her work for the actress Lena Ashwell, who organised concerts and plays for the troops in France, and used WAAC transport. The first thing that struck Caroline was how small he was, as he stood up to shake hands. He was even shorter than Phoebe. The second thing was that she rather liked the look of him. He had twinkling brown eyes and a small moustache – and he looked comfortably at ease with Phoebe as if he'd known her some time.

'Pleased to meet you, Miss Lilley. Why don't you join us?'

She realised that Luke had already come to her side, and of course, she belatedly remembered, he had met Phoebe at the Rectory last Christmas.

'We've been to the Charlot revue,' Caroline opened the conversation while her mind threw up one question mark after another.

'Nice revue, bad news for music-hall,' Billy pulled a face. 'People like more variety now. More legs and dancing and more foreign fancy acts. Home-grown cockney singers are out of fashion.'

'Not you, Billy,' Phoebe said.

He reached out and squeezed her hand.

Caroline could not resist asking the obvious question. 'Do Mother and Father know you're here?'

Phoebe and Billy exchanged a quick look. 'No, it's going to be a surprise,' Phoebe said defiantly. 'I'm going there for Christmas and Billy is coming too.'

'Oh. Does Mrs Dibble know about it?' Phoebe was all too apt to disregard the practicalities of life.

'No, but she'll cope,' Phoebe assured her happily. 'You won't warn them, will you, Caroline?'

'I won't say a word,' Caroline promised. Where, she wondered, though dared not ask, was Phoebe staying tonight? After all, she was still a child. Well – twenty, she rapidly calculated, but she'd never had much common sense and had leapt from one disaster to another in her emotional life. Please, oh, please, she made a silent prayer, let this not be another.

'Mother says you two are living together,' Phoebe said brightly.

'That's not quite as it sounds,' Luke said easily, before Caroline could reply in heated terms. 'There are four of us. Yves Rosier, myself, and our batwoman Ellen, and, as your mother says, our assistant Waac Sergeant Lilley.'

Phoebe giggled. 'What *fun*.' She shot Caroline a curious look.

Victoria Station was pandemonium with noise and thousands of uniformed bodies, as the leave trains came in and disgorged their passengers, mingling with the thousands attempting to reach their homes in time for Christmas. Not one of them was Yves. Caroline had heard nothing from him, and here she was alone to catch the Tunbridge Wells train, as Luke wasn't coming either. Felicia had elected to stay at her post so that Tilly could come home. Much as Caroline loved her aunt, she minded this very much, although she knew she was being unreasonable. At least Isabel would be there – Isabel was always at home, and despite her mannerisms and annoying little ways, the thought of seeing her brought one warm glow at least. Phoebe would be there, but no George who was flying with 56 Squadron on the Western

Front, no Felicia – and now no Yves. Santa Claus was being extremely remiss this year in his gifts for Caroline Lilley.

As the train chugged its slow way through East Grinstead towards Hartfield and then Ashden, she tried valiantly to cheer herself up. There would be no transport to meet her, for Poppy, their old horse, had long since died, and probably no familiar faces either. Mother and Mrs Dibble were too busy nowadays to stroll up to meet anyone for the pleasure of their company. Caroline hauled down her suitcase, and tried to convince herself she was going to enjoy the walk. Despite the biting cold, it was a homecoming – and it was Christmas.

She handed her ticket to Mr Chappell, the stationmaster (no porters nowadays), and walked through into the ticket office, which seemed as crowded with uniforms as London. And then she saw an apparition: a Belgian khaki uniform, and *Yves was inside it*. She threw herself into his arms.

'*Cara*, I could not get to London in time, so I came direct to Tunbridge Wells. Are you cross with me?'

'How could I be cross? I'm just so happy to see you.'

Everything would be wonderful now. How

could it fail to be? Even the icy rain had stopped when they got outside. She was coming alive again, like the ground after a long winter. Never mind that in the Rectory they would have separate rooms; Yves was safe and that was all that mattered.

She felt as though she were walking along Station Road in a dream. Sometimes she had nightmares of this long road, with the Rectory at the far end which she could never quite reach. She would now that Yves was at her side. They strolled past the Towers, now an army officers' home but formerly the home of Robert's parents, the hated Swinford-Brownes. Isabel's parents-in-law were now living in East Grinstead; there had been a terrible accident in William Swinford-Browne's munitions factory last year, and since then, few Ashden girls travelled to work there, preferring to work on the land or in Tunbridge Wells. One of the girls killed had been a former housemaid at the Rectory. Someone had to make munitions, the girls argued now, but it wasn't going to be Swinford-Browne, if they could help it.

They walked past all the dear familiar fields and at last reached the Gothic Horror, the Swinford-Browne cinema that Isabel now ran, which was advertising the Christmas fare of *Gertie the Dinosaur*. Almost home. The gates of the Rectory were open, the driveway was short, looking strange now the grass had been ploughed up for vegetables. At last she was ringing at the front door. Who would open it? Phoebe? Isabel? Mother?

'Surprise!' George yelled, jumping out at them.

Two

'No muffins,' Caroline cried disbelievingly. 'But Gwen Wilson *always* brings them round at four o'clock, and you can't tell me she's gone into the army.' Gwen, the baker's sister from Lovel's Mill, was fifty, and as well rounded as one of her delicious products; her sturdy trouser-clad figure, the clang of her bell and her call of muffins, fresh muffins, had become the symbol of winter to Caroline during the dark afternoons.

'It's the war,' Isabel inevitably replied. 'Don't you read the newspapers? New regulations for bakers.'

'In London I don't stop for tea, but at Ashden I expect muffins. Muffins,' Caroline declared grandly, 'are a bastion against war. They should be the last thing to fall victim to shortages.'

'Try Mrs Dibble's oatmeal cakes with saccharin jam instead.'

Caroline laughed. She knew she was being ridiculous to mind so much, but she had wanted Yves to experience all the joys of Rectory life so far as was possible in wartime. Ah well, if it came to a choice, she would rather have Yves than muffins.

At least those first few precious moments standing in the Rectory hall, the centre of the warren of rooms around and above it, had not been denied her. Down those stairs the five Lilley children had clattered and shouted, rejoiced and wept, and here, God willing, they would all gather again once this war was over. To save paraffin for which agricultural use now had priority, the stove was not on, but it seemed to Caroline it hardly mattered; they were enclosed by the old familiar sights and sounds, and that was enough.

'I'm home,' she had declared with great satisfaction, then immediately regretted it as she realised what those words would mean to Yves, who had no home to which he could return – yet.

'Follow me, captain!' George had seized Yves' luggage, saluted smartly, and charged up the stairs to the room Yves had been allotted. Caroline had followed, humping her own suitcase (typical of brothers) into her own bedroom.

And there had been Isabel, waiting for her.

Most unusual. Normally old lazybones Isabel would wait until one sought her out – unless she wanted something, Caroline remembered suspiciously.

'You're looking very pretty, Isabel. Is Robert coming home on leave?'

Isabel, the oldest of the four Lilley girls, would be twenty-nine in January. She had always been attractive, with her fair curls and large grey-blue eyes, but now she looked positively blooming.

'No, but I've something even better to tell you. I made Mother and Father promise not to let the cat out of the bag first.' Isabel paused impressively. 'I'm going to have a baby. Isn't that marvellous?'

'Isabel!' Caroline catapulted herself into her sister's arms. 'That's wonderful news. I shan't miss the muffins one little bit now.' She disengaged herself and glanced at Isabel's figure which was as slender as ever.

'It's very recent, about two months, but it's certain. Nearly anyway, Dr Marden said. If so, it will be born in July.'

'You didn't want children at one time,' Caroline asked curiously. 'Are you sure you can cope?'

'Times change,' Isabel replied vaguely.

They did indeed. Isabel, from being the

wayward, self-centred elder sister of her youth who would beg, borrow or steal whatever she wanted, was now a reformed character, according to Mother. This was quite obvious today, although Caroline was amused to see there were still a few signs of the old Isabel. There had been not a word about how Caroline was faring – but that was Isabel and always would be.

'There may be a war on but tea's still going to be served the way it ought to be, Myrtle,' Margaret said sternly. 'You put a decent cloth on that table. No making do with yesterday's. Field Marshal Haig won't be having to do with dirty cloths and nor will we.'

It was bad enough having the dirty mud-coloured 'wartime bread' that the Government had forced on the bakers. Once upon a time the best of the grain made flour for human beings, and the rest was given to the animals. Now their flour was a concoction of some of the best, some of the animals' food, and the remainder any other cereals they could rake up. The Ministry proudly pointed out this meant they could probably avoid rationing it, but, if you asked Margaret Dibble, the taste of it did a good job rationing itself.

'Off you go, Myrtle. Don't stand there like a Lord Tom Noddy.'

Chastened, Myrtle scuttled off to the linen closet, while Agnes put the cups and plates ready. No sitting down watching for Margaret, however. Usually she took a cup herself about this time. Not today, as she presided over the rituals she had followed for so many years. She'd seen nearly as many Christmases here as the Rector himself. The war had put an end to many of the old ways. She and Mrs Lilley had had to put their heads together three days ago on St Thomas's Day over what to do if the needy of the village came a-goodening. No one could be refused a gift if they came on Goodening Day. Nowadays not many came. It wasn't that there were less needy folk in Ashden, but that they kept themselves to themselves more, knowing that food shortages affected rectories as much as the smallest cottage. Once upon a time she'd made an extra twenty or so small plum puddings, and the good Lord alone could count the mince pies. This year, only Sammy Farthing had come, and that was only because his neighbour Nanny Oates, with whom he shared many meals, would be coming to the Rectory on Christmas Day, and Sammy liked to lay in stocks in case his daughter-in-law forgot about him.

At least the mince pies were as they should be – or nearly – whatever deficiencies the stuffings, cakes and puddings might have. Percy's potatoes went to help make pastry, a plentiful supply of apples from the orchard, and a lump of suet and scrag ends of beef obtained with a little pressure on Wally Bertram ensured that her mother's old recipe for mincemeat could be adhered to. *And* the mince pies were the proper Sussex oval shape, not round like this modern fashion. Margaret was justifiably proud that her mince pies were striking another blow at the Kaiser, and a good job too.

It would be a small Christmas for her and Percy this year, even though Mr Peck and Miss Lewis, Lady Buckford's staff, swelled the numbers. Myrtle would be off home after church, and Agnes too maybe. Lizzie would be here of course, bless her, and baby Frank. Not so much of a baby now. He'd passed his first birthday, and was into everything. Margaret supposed she should go to midnight mass like the Rector wanted, but she hadn't felt the same about the Church, not since Fred had died. The

Rector never pressed her, he said she'd come in her own good time. If so, that wasn't yet. This was the first Christmas without Fred and how could she go and give thanks as though nothing had happened?

There was a knock on the kitchen door, and when she opened it Margaret found not only an unexpected, but an astonishing visitor. It was the Honourable Penelope Banning, Lord Banning's daughter. Whatever was she doing here? She'd no idea there were to be Rectory guests for tea, and even if there were, she didn't expect them to visit the kitchens, especially through the tradesmen's entrance.

'I'm sorry to barge in like this,' – she didn't look sorry at all in fact – 'but Mrs Lilley said you wouldn't mind. I wanted to tell you myself, so that if I can't find Lizzie you can pass on the news.'

Lizzie? News? It had to be bad, for that was all there was nowadays. But what did Miss Penelope have to do with Lizzie? She'd never met her, to Margaret's knowledge. Miss Banning had been Master Reggie's friend first, then Miss Caroline's, but since the war began they hadn't seen anything of her to speak of, her being out east as a nurse. *East!* A terrible thought struck her.

'It's good news in a way,' Penelope said hastily, seeing dawning realisation on her face. 'I wanted to tell Lizzie that Frank Eliot is back in this country. He's in hospital with dysentery at Shooter's Hill, south of London. The hospital where Caroline and Felicia did their training.'

The world was going cuckoo. Margaret just couldn't take it all in. Frank was the father of Lizzie's son, and hadn't been able to get home since he was called up eighteen months ago. He'd seen she was all right for money and written regularly, but the letters didn't arrive the same way. They came in bunches, and they hadn't heard from him in months. Margaret fixed on the immediate puzzle. 'How do you know about Frank, Miss Penelope?'

'I was a nurse on the hospital ship that brought him back from the Mediterranean. He was part of Allenby's army.'

Now that was a name Mrs Dibble knew well – everyone did. Two weeks ago General Lord Allenby had marched triumphantly into Jerusalem, where he had given a speech in every language under the sun to make sure this was a happy day for everyone – especially Jerusalem. It was the first success the British army had had for goodness knew

51

how long, and it was fitting, Rector said, that at this time of year it was Jerusalem to be freed from occupation by the Central Powers and Turks.

'Frank's a fine man, Mrs Dibble,' Penelope continued. 'I came to know him quite well after we discovered we had Kent and Ashden in common.'

Before the war Miss Penelope wouldn't have had a chance to chat to Frank Eliot, even if she'd wanted to. He had been manager of the hop garden for the Swinford-Brownes, and being a foreigner to the village he'd always been regarded with suspicion. It's not that Miss Penelope would have thought him out of her class, but that their social circles would never have collided. War was a funny thing.

'How is he?' Conflicting emotions battled within her. She had grudgingly come to like Frank after Lizzie moved in with him without the benefit of the Lord's blessing, but Lizzie had to remember she was still married to Rudolf, German or not. He'd left at the beginning of the war, and they'd heard that he was still alive.

'He's improving, I'm glad to say, but he needs a few more weeks in hospital.'

Well, Lizzie would have some good news

for Christmas after all, for surely they wouldn't send Frank back to the wars at his age, having been so ill? He must be nearly forty, if not over. Then she remembered what *they* had done to Fred, and misery overwhelmed her again. *They* could do anything they chose.

After Penelope had left, Margaret decided to have that cup of tea after all – to get over the shock, if nothing else. Not that you could call it tea nowadays it was so weak, more like water bewitched, as her mother used to say. Perhaps, she thought as the kettle boiled, she would go to church this evening after all, just to please Rector and Percy. Even the turkey and capon stuffing looked much more interesting, even if it was mostly oatmeal and herbs. Unbidden, she suddenly found herself first humming, then singing: 'Jerusalem! ... *Jerusalem!*...'

'Mrs Dibble's singing!' Caroline went to the drawing room door to make sure of her facts, and returned contentedly to Yves.

'She has not the most tuneful of voices.'

'It's dreadful, but that's not the point! It's that she hasn't sung since Fred died.'

'I understand now.' Yves crossed to sit beside her on the Chesterfield. 'Caroline, I should not attend mass at St Nicholas this evening.'

'Because of your being a Roman Catholic?'

'No, because of you. I should not take communion without telling your father how things are between us.'

'We've discussed that,' Caroline said gently. 'What's the point of hurting them unnecessarily when we don't know how long we'll be together?'

'It worries me.'

'Please come.'

Reluctantly he agreed, to her great relief. St Nicholas and midnight mass *were* Christmas. Within the timelessness of its thick grey walls, the meaning of Christmas, even in these dark days of war, came home, and how could she bear it if Yves were not at her side?

Late that evening, in the familiarity of the scene of the villagers walking along the path to the church, each clutching a candle or torch because of the blackout, it was hard to think of the suffering of the men in the trenches. It was too big and too terrible a concept. She could only see it through the faces of those around her in church who had lost sons and fathers, faces like Mrs

Hubble's and Mrs Dibble's, and those of her own family.

The church seemed full of ghosts, for most people here had been touched by the tragedy of war. For the Lilleys it was Felicia who was in their thoughts. Felicia had never told their parents how dangerous her job really was, always implying that she and Aunt Tilly worked at a baseline hospital, but somehow as time went by, Mother and Father seemed to have gathered the information without being told, perhaps from the newspapers, perhaps from people's comments, or perhaps by parents' intuition. Tomorrow they would at least have Aunt Tilly with them, for she was recovering apparently from some slight illness at Lord Banning's home in Tunbridge Wells. Simon Banning, Penelope's father, was a good friend of Caroline's, and she suspected that he had designs to change Aunt Tilly's single status once this war was over. Designs he might have, but fulfilling them could prove harder, and Caroline and Penelope watched the progress of the 'game' with great interest.

As they emerged with their candles into the darkness after the service, ahead of her in the procession out of the church were the

Hunneys. They still sat in the Hunney pew, as for centuries past.

Father had wanted to abolish the two remaining private pews now that the Norvilles had gone, but one hint of this to 'Maud' as she was disrespectfully known at the Rectory and even he had quailed. The Hunney pew remained.

Sir John was with Lady Hunney tonight, and also Daniel, now stomping around on his wooden leg without a second thought. All her life Caroline had battled with the domineering, awe-inspiring Lady Hunney, but now she seemed diminished in size, a woman, not the monster of Caroline's memory. The shoulders were as stiff, but appeared bowed, although no hint of this was evident in her greeting to Caroline.

'I am glad to see you, Caroline – and you too, Captain Rosier.'

Even as she was murmuring good wishes, Caroline could feel Reggie between them. His death, oddly enough, had brought his mother and Caroline together, just as his life had separated them. She was reluctantly now speaking to her daughter Eleanor, whom she considered had disgraced the family by marrying the vet Martin Cuss, but Martin was still beyond the Hunney pale.

He was in the Royal Veterinary Corps, but had managed to wangle Christmas leave. He and Eleanor weren't spending it in Ashden, however, but at his parents' home in Dorset, suitably far from Lady Hunney.

The bells were ringing now – so Christmas had truly begun. With so many men at the front, it was a struggle to keep the bells going, but wives had nobly stepped into the breach, and the memory of Mrs Bertram being lifted high into the air by mistake in her training days, black boots kicking wildly under the heavy skirts and petticoats, still made Caroline giggle.

'What's the matter, Yves?' Caroline asked anxiously, when they had finished the mince pies and hot chocolate provided for their home-coming. He was looking bewildered, a little lost.

'It is so different. In Belgium we would have been exchanging presents at this moment.'

'Can't you wait?' she teased him. 'Look, you can see them all in a heap under the tree. They'll still be there tomorrow.'

'I will try to be less impatient.'

'I knew you'd be feeling like this. So this is a little pre-present.' She put a small package into his hand. 'It's perfectly hideous, but I did write it myself.' It was a short poem of love, decorated with dried rose petals she'd saved from the summer. She stopped him as he was about to unwrap the tissue paper. 'Don't open it now. Take it to bed with you,' she dropped her voice, 'and think of me.'

'I do not need *aide-mémoires* for that.' For a moment she thought there were tears in his eyes. 'But I have no pre-present for you, and I love you.'

'*You* are my present.'

'Where on earth did you get the turkeys from, Mother?' Caroline clapped as Father ceremoniously carried in the Christmas festive fare, with George behind him blowing a child's trumpet, and the rest of them singing the Boar's Head carol. Even Grandmother sang – she seemed unusually benevolent this year.

'We have to thank your grandmother for it. *And* three capons and a goose. One for Mrs Dibble to cook for themselves and the rest for tomorrow.'

'Well, I do thank you, Grandmama. What fun to have turkey.'

'Oscar thinks so,' chortled George. 'Percy would have been after him with a cleaver otherwise.'

'If that pig has any sense, it will teach itself to truffle-hunt to earn its keep,' Laurence declared, setting down the bird and brandishing the knife.

'Unless the war ends,' declared Elizabeth. 'Even the Kaiser couldn't be so cruel as to deprive us of Oscar.'

'He'd always be part of us, Mother,' George consoled her gravely.

'George!' Caroline warned – before she realised he was no longer a mischievous schoolboy, but was a lieutenant in the Royal Flying Corps, *and* one whose cartoons of life in the air were rapidly becoming as popular as Bruce Bairnsfather's of trench warfare.

He winked at her to show he'd understood exactly what she was thinking.

There were only ten of them round the table this Christmas. Conscious of the expected battle for food, the Hunneys, the Bannings, and Aunt Tilly would not be joining them till the afternoon. Caroline was almost glad of this, because it made the family circle more intimate, and this now – so far as she was concerned – included Yves. Phoebe seemed to think the same way about Billy, for she kept an adoring eye on him throughout the lunch. He had been awkward at first in the Rectory, being no churchgoer and clearly unaccustomed to family gatherings, at least at Rectory tables. He seemed to have found his feet quickly and firmly – indeed, almost too firmly.

Caroline smiled to herself as she thought of her mother's whispered comments yesterday evening. 'He's very *unusual*, isn't he?'

Compared with Ashden folk, Caroline supposed he was. 'Probably there's something about him that reminds her of Harry Darling.' Phoebe's sweetheart had been wounded at Loos, and died in hospital.

'Besides the cockney accent and lack of table manners?' Elizabeth asked drily. '*And* his age. He must be over forty and she's only twenty. Suppose she wants to marry him? What would your father say?'

'I imagine Father would want Phoebe to be happy, first and foremost.'

Her mother had a final shot however. 'Certainly, if Billy were like Yves. You must enjoy working with him.'

Did she imagine it or was there a slight emphasis on the *working?* 'Yes,' Caroline had answered uneasily.

She decided she liked Billy very much. He had a presence that rivalled even Father's in company, as he reeled off jokes and anecdotes of music-hall life, while Phoebe giggled at his side.

'You seem to lead a very full life, Mr Jones,' Lady Buckford remarked glacially, after one outrageous story. Obviously Billy Jones was still beyond the limits of tolerance that Grandmother was prepared to consider as part of her war effort.

Billy grinned. 'Now I do. They never let the likes of me out of the East End before they were needed in the trenches, your ladyship.'

'From what I gather, you left the East End some time ago, Mr Jones.'

'But not for your drawing-room, eh?'

Billy was running straight towards the portcullis at the end of Grandmother's drawbridge, marked 'No entry, fear of boiling oil', and his ease of manner wouldn't be enough for Grandmama to show mercy.

'I spy a currant in here,' announced George hastily, investigating his slice of pudding. 'Has it escaped from somewhere and if so, do I have to hand it back?'

Margaret Dibble looked at her diminished family, Percy, Lizzie and little Frank, all doing their best to jolly her along so that she would forget Fred. She'd tried to make an effort, but was it worth it? Why should she bother? The reins should be handed over to the younger generation now. She was fifty now, and the grey hairs were coming. Even old Peck and Lewis were looking to her as though she was solely responsible for cheering everybody up. Lizzie at least was happy that Frank was back, and was planning to leave the baby with her tomorrow while she went to visit him.

Mind you, Lizzie might *look* happy, but inside she was a worrier like Margaret, though unlike Percy. She had a lot to worry about too. It was all very well and nice Frank coming home to be with his baby, but how was she going to choose between him and Rudolf? Someone was going to get hurt.

'How about one or two of your songs, Louise?' Percy said in desperation to Miss Lewis. Louise Lewis, the highly respectable personal maid to Lady Buckford, had turned out to have hidden talents. She had been giving singsongs on the Rectory piano for the wounded officers from Ashden Manor hospital. 'Carols, of course,' Percy added quickly, his eye on Margaret, 'seeing it's Christmas.' There was an old piano in the servants' hall. It wasn't up to much, but it served its purpose.

'Why not?' Louise said. 'And I'll tell you what. Let's ask Billy Jones to come and give us a song, seeing that it's Christmas.'

Margaret stared at her as though she'd suggested flying to the moon. In normal times she would never have dared ask the Rector if one of his guests could come to the servants' quarters to give them a song, but suddenly she too thought: why not?

'I'll go.' Resolutely, defying umpteen years of protocol, Margaret marched into the drawing-room where it seemed an army of people had now gathered and were drinking tea. The Hunneys and the Bannings had arrived, and there propped in a chair looking very pale was another familiar face.

Caroline was the first to notice her entrance. 'Look who's arrived, Mrs Dibble. Isn't it marvellous to see her?'

Yes, it was, Margaret decided, though Miss Matilda (she always refused to be called your ladyship as she was by rights) didn't look well. Seedy, almost yellow in the face she was. Too many late nights in that hospital of hers, Margaret thought knowingly.

'Pleased to see you, Miss Tilly, and how's Miss Felicia?'

'It's me let the side down,' Tilly rasped, 'not her.'

She was a shadow of her old self, Margaret thought, alarmed, and Lady Buckford was fussing over her like a new-born lamb, for all they hadn't spoken for years. That was because Miss Tilly had let the side down then too, by being a suffragette. Funny to think she, Margaret Dibble, being over thirty, would probably have the vote next year if this bill went through parliament, and it was all because of Miss Tilly.

'I beg pardon for interrupting, Rector,' Margaret remembered her mission, 'but I speak for us all in the servants' hall in asking whether Mr Jones might favour us with a song there at his convenience.' She looked uncertainly round. 'Seeing as how it's Christmas.'

'Right you are.' Billy leapt up to come straight away, but he couldn't do that. Margaret knew this was the time that the Rector started the traditional Christmas game of the Family Coach.

'Any time would suit us, Rector. We're only a small group, as you know,' Margaret said, alarmed at the inconvenience to the Rector's programme.

Caroline saw a glance pass between her

father and mother, but even she was surprised when her father said warmly: 'I've a better idea, Mrs Dibble, if your family agrees. After we've played the Family Coach, why don't you all come to join us? We'll have tea and entertainment together, if Miss Lewis would oblige us on the piano and Mr Jones is agreeable. And of course if you yourself have no objection, Mrs Dibble.'

Objection? Margaret was dazed. Never would she have thought it proper for servants to sit with family drinking tea and chatting, but now the Rector suggested it, it seemed highly sensible. Seeing that it was Christmas. It took an hour and a half with so many players for the Family Coach to reach its destination. Father allotted everyone a role, refusing to be put off by his mother's bleak face. Fortunately, Grandmother's rivalry with Lady Hunney meant she could not afford to refuse to play. Every year Father chose a different story to relate as narrator, to invoke a different set of circumstances, and this year, following last year's triumph of 'The Hunting of the Snark', he had chosen *Through the Looking-Glass*, Lewis Carroll's sequel to *Alice in Wonderland*. The coach rattled its way through the battles of Tweedledum and Tweedledee, and the Lion and the Unicorn, and past the White Knight, and by the time it had arrived back through the looking-glass they were ready for the tea which father summoned.

'Dear Lord,' he finished in his customary prayer for the year ahead, 'as we rattle through this topsy-turvy looking-glass war, into the year ahead, full of uncertainty and fear, may we overcome with Thy help all such monsters and obstacles before us.'

After tea had been cleared, the servants self-consciously filed in, automatically gravitating to the back and sides of the room. By now they included Agnes and Elizabeth Agnes, since Agnes had decided to make her visit to her parents short and sweet – if that was the word for the gloomy hell-fire atmosphere of her childhood home.

'No,' said Laurence firmly. 'Sit *with* us, if you please.'

Even the tradition of family prayers every morning had long since gone by the board, Caroline knew, for everyone breakfasted at different times, so this mixing of the two components that made up the Rectory was indeed breaking new ground.

Caroline saw Lady Hunney exchange a

quick look with Lady Buckford, obviously to gauge the reaction of the other at this novel procedure. Fortunately neither of them dared to be the first to make an objection, which would afford the other the opportunity to display Christmas goodwill. Baby Frank broke the ensuing ice by trying to clamber onto Lady Buckford's lap, sending Lizzie chasing after him.

'I will hold him, if I may,' Lady Buckford said graciously. 'It is a long time since Lady Matilda could be held in my lap.' She glanced at her daughter, with whom she now had an uneasy relationship again, after Tilly had been cast from the house in 1914 for her suffragette activities.

One up on Lady Hunney, Caroline thought appreciatively. Her ladyship retaliated by bribing Elizabeth Agnes's attention with one of Mrs Dibble's few precious home-made jelly sweets. No truffles and chocolates this year.

'How's Felicia?' Daniel Hunney asked nonchalantly, coming to sit next to her (for that express purpose, Caroline suspected).

'Aunt Tilly says she's well, though she's insisted on staying at her post.'

'What's wrong with Tilly?' he asked, keeping his voice low.

'I don't know. Simon says some kind of pneumonia, but she looks odd, doesn't she? I'm amazed Tilly's held out so long in those appalling conditions.'

'I'm amazed at both of them.' Daniel frowned as he looked at Tilly, but he said no more and Caroline dismissed the odd niggle from her mind. Felicia was deeply in love with Daniel, but there was a bar to their marrying – which Caroline had correctly deduced had to do with impotence due to his war wounds. Luke Dequessy was equally deeply in love with Felicia. What a pickle it all was, Caroline thought despondently. Herself and Yves, Felicia – war had a lot to answer for, and whom or whether one could love was the least of it.

After Billy Jones had sung several of his own Cockney songs and then Albert Chevalier's 'Wot Cher' and 'It's a Great Big Shame', Percy disappeared, at Father's suggestion, to make some of his famous punch. It wouldn't have quite so much 'punch' in it as usual, since the brandy had all been used in the puddings, but he said he'd see what he could do. When pushed, Percy was as adept at 'making do' in his field, as Mrs Dibble was in hers.

'Caroline told me you believed the days of

music-hall were numbered, Mr Jones,' Laurence said. 'Why do you believe that?'

Billy shrugged. 'The old tunes and songs spring from everyday life, that's why. Now the war's on, there isn't one. So we sing war songs or little bits of nothing.'

'What about a nice love song?' Margaret asked belligerently. '"My old Dutch". That's a good one.'

'Then I'll sing it for you, madam.' He made her a deep bow, and she gave a mental sniff just to show she wasn't going to be smarmied.

When he finished, another volunteer took his place. 'I too will sing you a love song, Mrs Dibble.'

Caroline's jaw dropped, as Yves went to the piano and whispered to Miss Lewis. *Could* Yves sing? How odd that after all this time, she hadn't the least idea.

It was soon apparent that he could. He stood, in the grand manner, one hand on his heart, the other on the grand piano, singing majestically: 'Under the old apple tree, When the love in your eyes I could see...'

The old apple tree. Caroline had to struggle to keep back tears. It was in their orchard of apple trees she had met Yves again, and mistaken him for Reggie, for it was in that same orchard that she and Reggie had become engaged, once upon a time and long ago. To sing this song was Yves' way of reminding her that he, as Reggie, loved her and that he was not jealous of old ghosts.

'I've just come to say goodbye.' Phoebe had taken advantage of the Rectory tradition that if one's bedroom door was open, one was available to anyone who wanted to pop in.

'You're off to France already? I thought you said it wasn't till Friday, and this is only Wednesday. It's Boxing Day. You can't go yet.'

Phoebe beamed happily. 'Billy hasn't got another tour in France until March, so we want a day or two together before I have to leave.'

'Oh, Phoebe, I do worry for you.' Caroline spoke impulsively before thinking, and her sister immediately flared up.

'Why worry? Billy and I are going to marry ... and that's that.'

'But you're under age, and anyway, isn't he married already?'

'He divorced his wife, if you must know. And after what I've been through, Father must realise that I know my own mind.'

'Has he spoken to Father?' *Divorce?* He'd have a fit.

'No. Billy thought we should wait until my twenty-first birthday in June, though goodness knows what difference that makes. Anyway,' she added defiantly, 'that's why we're off. Dearly as I love the Rectory, staying here does have certain disadvantages – doesn't it?' She fixed large challenging eyes on Caroline.

'You mean you're lovers?'

The horror on her face must have been all too plain, for Phoebe retorted furiously: 'No, in fact. And how can you talk? I bet you're sleeping with Yves.'

'Yes, but–' She broke off, seeing Phoebe staring aghast over her shoulder, and turned round. Her mother was standing in the doorway, and had obviously overheard and been appalled by their conversation.

'Is this true, Caroline?' she asked jerkily.

Caroline groaned. Of all things to happen, of all ways and times for her parents to find out, this was positively the worst.

'Yes, Mother, and I'm very happy.'

'I can't believe it, Caroline. I realised you were growing fond of him, but never dreamed you would let it go this far. You deliberately kept it from us, letting us believe you just worked for him. What's your father going to say?'

'Nothing, I hope,' Caroline said wretchedly. 'You know it would hurt him and–'

'*Hurt?* My dear child, it's rather more than that, and if you're hoping I won't tell him, you're very much mistaken. I *can't* keep it from him, even if I wanted to. He is a priest of God and you are his daughter. How could he condone sin in you, even if he forgave you? To say nothing of the *risk*,' Elizabeth added practically.

'There is no risk,' Caroline assured her unhappily, watching the storm cloud rush down the staircase. How could her mother be so understanding in some ways, so intolerant in others?

'What is the matter, Caroline?' Yves answered her knock on his door, and drew her inside. 'You're trembling.'

'Mother knows about us.'

He held her very close. 'Then I will go to see your Father now, and talk to him, as I should have done long ago.'

'No–'

He kissed her, and the door closed behind him.

She sat on his bed feeling sick. How could the happiness of Christmas have vanished so completely? She struggled to think clearly, and some minutes later she managed it. She should be with them, not leaving it to Yves to face Father alone. If she was the independent mature woman she thought she was, and not the innocent girlish victim her mother clearly believed, she must follow Yves down those stairs to defend herself, however much she wanted to hide under the bed and pretend it hadn't happened. Her mind made up, she walked, legs trembling, down to the study. As she approached, she could hear the rise and fall of voices, her father's even tones, and Yves' less controlled voice. She went straight in, and both men stopped in mid-flow. Her mother stood by the window, white-faced and alien.

'I want you to know, Father, that it was against Yves' better judgement that we kept our love from you. He wanted to tell you, I stopped him.' Bravery was easier to plan than carry out.

'Then I am deeply and gravely disappointed in you, Caroline.'

'Yves and I both know our own minds and hearts.' Always before her father had been understanding. She was convinced she had only to find the right words this time and he would see her point of view.

He listened while she talked, with the occasional interpolation by Yves, but all he said when at last she finished was: 'Are you quite determined to continue with this ungodly relationship, Caroline?'

'Yes.'

'Even though Captain Rosier tells me he is a married man?'

'In name only,' Yves pointed out.

'I presume you made your wedding vow under that name?'

'I did, and I am always aware of it. Had I not and if I was not prepared to honour the promise I made then, I would now be free to marry Caroline.'

Caroline was terrified. She had never seen her father's face so bleak. She ran to him, throwing her arms round him and pleading childishly, 'Please don't say I can't come home any more.'

He put her aside gently. 'Caroline. I won't say that. There is room here for everyone, even for those God sees as sinners, but I cannot give you my blessing on this relationship. It follows that, much though it pains me, I must ask you not to accompany

Caroline here in future, Captain Rosier.'

Before Yves could reply, Caroline spoke first, not on impulse, but out of the sure knowledge of her own heart. 'I love Yves, Father, and he is as much to me as Mother was to you, when you walked out of Grandmother's home because she did not approve of your choice of loved one. If you cannot welcome Yves here, then I cannot come alone.'

The last words were almost swallowed in the effort to hold back her tears.

Three

Caroline peered down through the attic bedroom window in Queen Anne's Gate – or rather she tried to peer down. The heavy tracery of frost patterns on the glass prevented her from seeing anything but a faint suggestion of swirling snow outside. Mrs Dibble said it was a 'blackthorn winter' which meant cold and frost in April, not January.

'Are we snowed in yet?' Yves asked sleepily from the bed.

She breathed hard several times on the window pane to try to clear a hole in the frost, and eventually it responded to treatment, or sufficiently so for her to see that snow still lay thickly in the road beneath them.

'I don't know, but I've sent a special prayer for a path to clear wherever your dainty boots choose to walk.'

'They would prefer not to walk at all. Did *le Bon Seigneur* agree?'

'Yes, He sent you a shovel.'

'Captains do not shovel except at week-ends. Captains stay in bed while the batmen shovel.'

'Shall I tell Ellen or you?'

Yves sighed heavily. 'I will arise.'

Caroline looked at him tenderly. His hair was tousled, his chin stubbly, his eyes still heavy with sleep; it was the Yves she loved best – save the very private one whom she shared only with the pillow. The moment his feet touched the floor, little by little Captain Rosier would take over from Yves; the face would subtly change, growing layers like garments donned one by one. First the long johns in this icy weather, then the vest, the shirt, and khaki breeches, until it needed only the uniform tunic for Yves to be slumbering deep inside while His Majesty King Albert's liaison officer assumed command.

Washing and dressing were brief routines at the moment, for though the coal ration-ing system was working well, there was little left for bedroom fires.

'I wish I were a motor car chase in a Harold Lloyd film,' she complained, as she wrestled her way into her blouse and WAAC jacket, and then returned to tackle the time-consuming battle of the suspenders. 'Then I could do this at double the speed.' Hollywood films could speed up the action by the turn of a switch, but human beings took a little longer. She blew on her fingers, still cold from the washing water.

'There'll be ice on the lake,' she said, trying to think of the bonuses of a London winter.

She had been thinking of the Serpentine, but he misunderstood, and in a moment she was warm again from his arms around her.

'*Cara*, do not grieve for Ashden – there are other lakes and we will find them. How long will it last, do you think?'

How long would it last? How many ways to interpret that: the cold January weather, her happiness with Yves, her estrangement from the Rectory? Always in her life Ashden had come first, and London was merely a place where she worked and lived. Now London was her home, at least until the end of the war. What would happen then was as impenetrable a white blur as the snowy, frosty scene outside. There would then be no Yves, and perhaps no Rectory either. The ache in her heart had even made her doubt the wisdom of what she was doing. Yves and she had talked it over endlessly, and each time she had come to the same conclusion, despite Yves' repeating all the arguments against it.

'How can I allow you to cut yourself off from your home, *cara?* It is a small thing for us to be separated for a few days while you visit Ashden alone.'

'It is not a small thing, Yves, and you know it,' she had patiently replied each time. 'I have made my choice, and it is you. In not accepting our situation, Father is rejecting me as well as you.'

War altered everything, save basic morality, and in her view she and Yves had not transgressed those rules. Never in her life had she so irrevocably divided herself from her father, and she still could hardly believe that it had happened. It had, though, so the less she thought about it the better.

'Come on, lazybones, time for work.' She dragged Yves away from the window through which he was peering with no enthusiasm at all.

'If this is 1918,' he said, 'I do not like it.' She agreed with him. Clad in galoshes, mackintoshes, scarves and gloves, and somewhat warmer inside thanks to Ellen's breakfast, they battled their way across St James's Park to Whitehall against a bitterly cold north-east wind and fine driving snow.

All around them white-encrusted uniforms and greatcoats were marching with similar determination. It was, she decided, a whole new army trooping to battle. Their battle, although vital, could never compare with that on the Western Front, however, where troops were captives in trenches and dugouts, without loved ones, and without home comforts. A free Christmas pudding sent to all the troops didn't seem much compensation.

Moreover it wasn't just the soldiers; there were those that looked after them. People like Felicia. She felt humble remembering what the sister they had all believed to be so fragile was enduring.

'Glory be!' she said thankfully, as at last they reached their office. Someone had lit a small fire.

'I bestow upon them the order of Leopold II,' Yves said thankfully, as they collided in their eagerness to reach the warmth first.

'I thought army captains were impervious to cold.'

'That is true – save for those who are not.'

'Luke's back!' Caroline cried, spotting the portmanteau by his desk. 'He must have come straight to the office.' She had been surprised not to find him there when they returned to the office after the Christmas break, and were told that he had taken leave. Then Luke himself appeared through the door to greet them.

'You don't look well, Luke,' Caroline said, concerned that his usual cheerful face was drawn and colourless. Did she imagine it, or had a glance passed between the two men even as she made her comment?

'Bad journey.'

'From Reading? That's where your parents live, isn't it?'

He appeared not to hear the question, for he disappeared through into the small adjoining office, and brought in some hot cocoa for them which Caroline seized gratefully.

At last Luke did reply. 'My journey wasn't from Berkshire. I came from France and there are gales in the Channel, as you probably know.'

'You've been to see Felicia,' Caroline exclaimed. 'How is she?' The moment she had spoken, she knew she had misread the situation, and the excitement was lost in a wave of inexplicable fear. 'You didn't spend Christmas here, did you? You were in France all the time.' Of course. How could she not have realised that before?

Luke nodded.

'And it isn't the gales making you look so ill, is it?' she pressed him. 'It's Felicia.' The words just came, from where she did not know. 'Is she dead?' she asked jerkily.

'No,' Luke answered quickly, quietly. 'She's not. She is very ill though. That's why I went.'

She could hardly take this in. 'How long? Where is she? How ill?' She blurted out the questions like bullets. 'Do my parents know? How did *you* know?' Oh, the hurt. All over Christmas Felicia had been lying ill, while Caroline had been escaping from the war at Ashden.

'She would not allow *anyone* to know, particularly her parents. I heard by chance. Tilly knew, of course.'

Aunt Tilly had been at Ashden at Christmas. 'How could she not tell us?' Caroline cried unbelievingly.

'To spare your parents, Caroline. To spare all of you the worry. It was Felicia's decision.'

'Do not blame her, *cara*,' Yves said quietly. 'She took the same decision as you, to spare others' pain.'

Caroline longed to cry out that this was different, that Felicia was ill, needed them, could not be held responsible for what she said. She could not do it, however, as she realised the hurt inside her was purely selfish; it was on her own account, not on Felicia's. Felicia, unlike Caroline, had always known what she wanted, and if this meant suffering alone, her decision should be respected, however hard to bear for her family.

'Tell me about it, Luke,' she asked quietly.

'She and Tilly were both gassed, Felicia much more seriously than Tilly, in the last stages of the battle for Passchendaele Ridge in November. Tilly recovered well enough to return to England in December, as you know, but Felicia did not.'

'So it wasn't pneumonia.' Of course it wasn't. Caroline realised she had subconsciously realised something was wrong, but hadn't pursued the thought, intent on her own concerns. *November.* All that time, and they had merely assumed Felicia was manning the advance dressing post on her own, and since she very seldom wrote, no matter the season, her silence had not worried them unduly. War, as Caroline had been reflecting earlier this morning, changed everything.

'She's in hospital at Étaples now,' Luke

continued, 'not well enough to be moved.'

Caroline licked her dry lips. 'I heard that serious gas cases died quickly.' She tried not to think of what she knew of the effects of gas. The skin burnt with mustard-coloured blisters, the effects on the eyes, and the choked-up throats that slowly closed for ever. Surely God would spare Felicia's beautiful dark eyes? She fought panic and tried to think rationally.

'That's so, and she's survived the first few weeks.'

'But that means she's improving,' Caroline said eagerly. 'There's no longer any danger to her life?'

Luke hesitated. 'Probably not.'

The sick feeling returned. 'Tell me the truth, Luke.'

'It's true that usually survival of the first weeks means gradual improvement. In Felicia's case, it's more complicated.'

'Because of lack of resistance caused by poor diet and exposure?'

'Lack of resistance in my view, yes, but not for the reasons you think.'

'What then?' She waited, heart in mouth.

'I don't think she has the will to survive any more.' Luke tried to speak impassively, but the effort was obvious.

'Then we will give it to her. Mother and Father and I will go. Phoebe can go, George–' She broke off, seeing his expression.

He shook his head. 'She's quite adamant, Caroline, that she wants to see no one, and that no one was to know, even you. If – when – she dies, everyone will believe she died from a German bullet.'

'There must be *something* we can do.'

Even as he replied slowly: 'There is one way,' she guessed what it was.

'Daniel. You want me to tell him.'

'Yes.'

She dared not think how much it was costing Luke to admit that Daniel might succeed where he had failed, and that all his dedicated determination to marry Felicia was not strong enough to overcome the bond that still held her to Daniel. Even in this extreme situation, Luke's self-sacrifice must be immense.

'I'll see him today.'

'To what do I owe the honour of your company at luncheon?' Daniel laughed, waving a hand round their 'luxurious' surroundings.

Caroline had suggested lunch in order to

give herself time to get over the shock, as well as not to alarm him in advance. She had been somewhat taken aback when Daniel had laughingly suggested they meet in St James's Park at one of the many new open-air cafés which his friend Lieutenant Latham had opened in London. It seemed – in thick snow and ice – not an ideal choice, and she was relieved to find that temporary walls and a roof had been added to provide shelter. With the lake drained and covered with huts for Government workers, it was a good spot to choose. Even so, they were the only customers, and the one-armed soldier behind the counter looked as pleased as punch to see them. Lieutenant Latham had conceived this plan to fight his depression after his disablement, and had staffed the cafés with other disabled servicemen. It was better than selling matches, as so many were reduced to, and judging by the enthusiasm with which this old soldier was humming 'Dear Old Blighty', he agreed.

'It's self-help here,' Daniel explained. 'New idea of Latham's. You don't need waiters, you just go up to the counter and collect whatever you want, rather like being served drinks in a pub, or the War Kitchens. Clever idea, isn't it? Now tell me what you wanted to see me about,' he commanded, once they were established with coffee (of a sort) and a fish-paste sandwich. At least it was one up on Mrs Dibble's leftover mashed-potato and anchovy essence sandwiches, as recommended in the food economy talk Caroline had dutifully attended once in Ashden. 'Something about Ashden, is it? I gather from Mother you and Yves ran into a stone wall. Folk who aren't actually in the war don't understand, do they?'

'You heard so quickly?'

'Your mother was pretty upset, according to Isabel.'

'Ah.' Now she understood. Isabel was on good terms with Lady Hunney and was not the most discreet person in the world.

'Bad news always travels fast,' Daniel said consolingly, then glanced at her face. 'It's not that at all, is it? It's Felicia,' he said sharply. 'Dead?'

'No.' She laid her hand on his arm. 'She's been gassed. She needs you. She's very ill.'

'She's asked for me?' He was poker-faced, and she realised that he was containing shock by sheer will-power.

'She's still in France, at Étaples. She didn't want anyone to be told, but Luke found out and went to see her. He thinks she is dying because she has no will to go on living.' With all that Felicia had achieved, it would seem a crazy thing to believe, for anyone who did not know her.

'Say that again, please, Caroline.'

She did so, and saw him swallow several times as if fighting back emotion. He was silent for a few moments. 'Is Luke engaged to her? Does she–' He broke off. She knew he had been going to ask, 'love him?' but there was no need for they both knew the truth: that whatever her feelings for Luke they were outweighed by her love for Daniel.

'You know that he loves *her*,' was her reply. 'Yet Luke wants you to go to Felicia. He said that you were the only person who might be able to give her the will to survive. And he of all people would hardly say that unless he meant it.'

'If Luke could do nothing, why should I?' His voice was hard.

'You know why, Daniel. And Luke knows why, and Felicia's life means more to him even than his love for her.'

'You don't understand, Caroline,' Daniel said jerkily. 'Even if I go, nothing can come of it. If I go, what then?'

'We've both seen enough of war not to reckon with the "what then?" That's God's department, not ours. Look–' she pointed to the painted café sign above the counter – 'your friend's cafés are called "Fortune of War". Your leg, Felicia's illness, my love for Yves, Felicia's love for you – none of us can legislate for an uncertain future. We don't know when peace will come, and what it will bring. Don't think of whether or not you and Felicia can marry. Think of all the good Felicia can do if she lives. Think of all the lives she's saved in the past.'

'I do. Mine was one.'

Oh for the Rectory. Even if not always warm it had always provided a cocoon against the harsh winds of winter. In London no matter where she went she never seemed warm for more than a moment or two at a time. Except, she thought to herself gratefully, in bed with Yves' arms around her. The severe weather continued, although it was past the middle of January. London froze in sixteen degrees of frost, and the wind still blew. And to cap it all, the authorities still claimed the Serpentine's ice was not thick enough to bear, and skating was therefore forbidden. It had been icy enough for the Peter Pan Cup for swimming in the Serpentine to be postponed, but had not yet reached the obligatory thickness of three inches.

'I have a surprise for you,' Yves announced, seeing her mutinous face on their day off. She had thought without doubt that in return for their enduring such cold, Fate would be fair enough to grant such a small desire as thick ice in Hyde Park. But then Fate was never fair, and she was ashamed of her pettiness anyway.

'If it is an oatmeal cake for tea, I don't want it.'

'It's a toboggan. We'll go to Parliament Hill Fields and slide down slopes, instead of across ice.'

'Oh Yves.' She hurtled across the room and threw herself into his arms.

'Why are you crying?' he asked in surprise.

'I feel so ... so ... childish. And Felicia—'

'*Cara*, you can pray for Felicia, and remember Daniel is with her.'

Daniel had sent her a short note saying he was taking leave to go to Étaples, and since then Luke had been extra cheerful both in the office and at home, to the point of driving them mad.

'But why should I enjoy myself when I know she's so ill?' Caroline wailed.

'You owe it as your duty to me,' Yves pronounced. 'In fact it is an order from a captain to an insubordinate Waac.'

She managed to laugh at that. 'Very well, but only if I can hurl snowballs at you to show what I think of you.'

He made her a quaint little bow, one hand on heart. 'You may vanquish me with snowballs, *cara*, as you have conquered my heart.'

He had only to look at her with his melting dark eyes, only to lay his hand on her shoulder, and her body would tingle, longing to be with him, so that the third Yves, the private one, would be hers alone, looking at her in passion as well as love.

'I suppose,' she said unsteadily, 'we could go tomorrow instead?'

'But why?' He looked anxious. 'Are you not well?'

'Quite well.' Her voice seemed to be a croak. 'I thought – since Luke is at work and Ellen out, we might make hay.'

'Make hay?' He stared at her in astonishment. 'You make teacakes of hay?'

'No.' She was torn between laughter and blushing. 'An English phrase. It means to take advantage of a situation for–'

'For what?' He still seemed perplexed.

'Love!' she bawled at him in exasperation.

Really, men could be so stupid.

His lips began to twitch, his eyes to gleam. The next moment she found herself upside down over his shoulder, staring at his boots.

'*Ma mie*,' he said softly, as he dumped her on the bed, 'I shall make a whole haystack.'

Hampstead Heath railway station seemed full of toboggans and people wrapped up like Eskimos, obviously bent on the same purpose as them. As they approached Parliament Hill Fields, they could see well-worn tracks in the snow, and queues of tobogganers. They must have been the oldest, but it didn't matter a jot.

She lay face down on the toboggan, in a way of which Mother would most surely not have approved, but which was easily the most fun.

'George always used to push me off with a "Steady the Buffs",' she yelled at Yves. 'I thought he was talking about chickens at first, not being brought up on toy soldiers.'

'Then *Vive La Belgique!*' Yves gave the toboggan a mighty push and she was off, flying into a white sky.

She hurtled onwards, exhilarated, as the snow churned up around her and stung at her face. She seemed to be rushing through life itself, unable to control her path, until at last she came to a sliding halt at the bottom of the hill and tumbled off into a soft pile of snow. At the top she could see Yves' tall figure waving, and she waved back, setting off on the long trek upwards, dragging the toboggan behind her. She watched as, his long legs splaying out over the toboggan, he propelled himself off on the same journey. Her heart was in her mouth as she saw him tumble off into deep snow and the toboggan careering on without him. Her ridiculous worry that he would never emerge from the drift was laid to rest as he reappeared, looked round for the toboggan in vain, and set off in leaps and jumps to retrieve it. His lanky figure looked so ridiculous, she was still laughing when he returned.

'What amuses you, *cara?*' he asked breathlessly as she hugged him.

'Nothing, I'm just pleased to see you return from the Antarctic.'

'There are very few polar bears in Parliament Hill Fields.'

'How strange,' she remarked later, as they returned to the railway station, 'to think while I was tobogganing in Ashden Park as a child, you were a young lad doing the same thing in the Ardennes, and we neither of us knew that we would meet one day.'

'Are you glad you came here now, *cara?*'

'Yes. It still makes me feel guilty that everyone can't be here today, but I'm glad we are. We could have a bigger double toboggan one day–' She stopped, realising what she'd said. 'I'm sorry, I'm just talking nonsense.'

His face relaxed. 'Nonsense is necessary from time to time, to make us forget not only today, but tomorrow.'

He was right. She longed for a double toboggan, and for a tandem to ride through the countryside together like Daisy Bell and her swain. She longed for Yves' baby. All three wishes belonged to a tomorrow that would never be. Yves took painstaking precautions to ensure she would not conceive, and each time he did so, wise though she knew it was, that bleak tomorrow grew a little closer. In return, she had his love not only for today, but for ever, even though they would be parted. Sometimes that seemed enough, and sometimes it did not. It was her private war effort to make it appear enough for always, and for Yves not to see the struggle this cost her.

'The maroons!' Caroline groaned. Improving weather at the end of January brought its drawbacks. The air raids would begin once more, and here came the warning! At least they were not yet in bed. In the autumn they had slept badly, half attuned for the sound of the maroons, the Government system to warn them of approaching bombers. This was a belated improvement on the previous methods which, looked back on, were laughable: a bugler standing in the back of an open car, or a policeman on a bicycle, pedalling furiously with a notice to take cover. There had been no raids since before Christmas, however, and this was an unwelcome reminder that spring was on its way with the consequent hotting up of the military war as well as the air war.

They rushed to gather blankets to shelter in the basement cellars. Many people took shelter in the underground railway stations. At the time of the full moon they were usually gathering from early evening onwards, causing problems for late homegoers, as they stumbled over recumbent bodies.

Tonight Luke and Ellen had beaten them to it, and they promptly joined in the consumption of the iron ration cocoa and biscuits that Ellen routinely provided there. Occasionally, if the warning came early enough, they took down their small gramophone and some records to dance to, but jollification at such times took a lot of determination.

London's anti-aircraft batteries and its balloon barrages had done much to allay fears in the inhabitants at first. Now the Gothas and Giants seemed to have things all their own way, and despite the formidable defences erected around London, they seemed to roam wherever they liked.

'I don't hear anything,' Caroline said hopefully after a while.

'Don't leave yet,' Luke said. 'They've got a new technique – they're cutting down the noise of their approach by stopping and starting their engines to circle in silence. *And* they're reducing engine noise. We just have to wait for the guns to start.'

They did, and for two hours they listened to their noise, and those other duller sounds that meant exploding bombs.

'Did you hear,' Ellen asked brightly, 'about that fellow in Piccadilly last autumn who heard the bomb drop on Swan and Edgar's and saw a woman's head rolling towards him?'

'Don't be so gruesome,' Caroline said sternly.

'I'm not. It was one of the dummies from the window. What a coup for the Kaiser, eh?'

The next night the Kaiser sent yet another Gotha and Giant raid across. It meant another night short on sleep as they all trooped to the cellars. It had not been a good day either. When they arrived in the office, there was no fire lit. A bomb had hit the Odhams printing works in Long Acre. Although not many people were working there, the cellars were crowded with people sheltering from the raid. Most of the dead were children, and of the women killed one was their office cleaning lady. That was why there was no fire. Out of respect, they left it unlit for the rest of the day.

The death of Mrs Hopkins depressed Caroline greatly. That unlit fire symbolised for her the whole stupid wastage of human life this war had caused. On the 30th, the day after the second raid, there was more bad news at work too, especially for Yves. The Germans had scored a victory in Brussels in their long-running battle against the clandestine newspaper *La Libre Belgique*. Arrests were not uncommon, but this time they had tracked down not only the two most wanted contributors, code-named Fidelis and Ego, but hundreds of others too, distributors, organisers and printers.

Caroline moped for several days over the general gloom of this winter – until Yves produced a bag from behind his back, and flourished it. She had finished work early since it was a Saturday and returned home to tea to find Yves just arrived – he had been out of the office since early this morning.

'What's that?'

'See!' Proudly he tipped the contents onto a plate on the living-room table.

'Muffins!' she shouted in delight. 'We can have real tea. Where did you get them?'

'*Cara*, I cannot provide the Rectory for you, but I can be second best,' he said seriously. 'Stolen muffins are a small price. I acquired them in the Belgian Embassy. There is good news to celebrate.'

'*Good* news?' Was there such a thing nowadays?

'Sir John told me that Daniel is bringing Felicia home to Ashden hospital.'

For a moment she could hardly take it in. Then all at once the full glory hit her. 'She's going to live!' she cried in triumph.

'She's well enough to make the journey.'

'That *does* mean she'll live. Oh, how wonderful.' She promptly burst into tears.

Yves regarded her anxiously. 'There is more good news too. Can you bear it? On Thursday night Governor von Falkenhausen was toasting their victory over *La Libre Belgique* in champagne when a special delivery arrived. It was a copy of the *next* issue of the newspaper with a photograph of the Governor on the front page and a jeering message. The editor, whom the Germans mistakenly thought they had arrested, has found new printers, and business is to be as usual. Now you can have your muffin.'

'Did you really steal them?' she asked when she could speak again after all this excitement.

'I cheated. I put in an order for them to feed couriers bearing vital intelligence from Belgium.'

'This courier is very grateful.' Caroline promptly bit into one. 'It's real,' she said contentedly. 'Not made of potatoes.'

'Nor am I.' He put his arm round her and kissed her.

'I wish you hadn't done that,' she complained.

'Why?'

'I don't want to leave this fire.'

'Why should you? There is a comfortable sofa here.'

She laughed. 'Suppose Luke comes in?'

'He will not. He is on a special mission chasing wild geese, and it's Ellen's day off.' By this time his lips were on hers, and she wouldn't have cared if the Kaiser himself had come in.

'All this – and muffins too,' she purred, as he took her into his arms.

It was her turn for office duty on the Sunday, and she set out for work early. Today she lit the fire. It was her personal signal to the enemy that the embers of England still glowed, and would burst into flames once more – no matter what they did.

Four

'Watch what you're doing with that milk, Myrtle.' Margaret spoke more sharply than she intended.

'It's not on the rationing list.' The mutter was scarcely audible but Margaret caught it.

'Butter will be, and you already need ration cards for it in London. And to think you were brought up on a farm.'

Myrtle departed sullenly, and for once Margaret couldn't blame her. It wasn't the girl's fault, it wasn't hers either. It was the whole Rectory. It was turning into a mere boarding house, its inmates wrapped up in their own concerns. They came and went at all hours, which meant meals had to be kept hot and set times went down the drain quicker than Sanitas cleaning fluid. Once Mrs Lilley used to refer to the Rectory clock, so regular were its routines. That was the proper way of doing things, to Margaret's mind. Rector ran the village by the Church Year clock and Mrs Lilley ran the Rectory. Tick-tock, tick-tock, time for morning prayers. Tick-tock, tick-tock, time for Fred to clean the lamps. Margaret swallowed hard for she hadn't meant to think of him. Anyway, Mrs Lilley seemed to be more intent on running the war than the Rectory now; she was present in person, but preoccupied most of the time with her work on the Agricultural County Executive Committee under the Ministry. She would be working in her glory-hole or receiving callers in the morning room. It wasn't just village women for her rotas now; she had a little empire of Land Girls, army corporals in charge of soldiers whom the Government were now eager to get working on the land because of the food shortage, and that wasn't all.

Thereby hung a tale. To think the day would come that Ashden would be harbouring the enemy. Prisoners of war they may be, and although she conceded that while they were in the Ashdown Forest camp Germans might as well be put to work, to expect decent folk to pass the time of day with them was too much. Yet she'd actually seen Mrs Lilley talking to a group of them, when she popped into the village yesterday. They were, so Mrs Lettice of the General Stores informed her, on their way to The

Towers to work on renewing poles and wire, and dressing the hop plants. She supposed it was a good thing that the hops hadn't been grubbed up to grow potatoes, but the thought of good English beer being produced by the enemy turned her stomach right over. It was a relief The Towers was an Army Officers' HQ now; they'd be keeping a strict eye open for any sabotaging or poisoning of the plants. This was one year she wouldn't be producing hop soup from the waste sproutings.

Topsy-turviness caused by the war wasn't the only reason for the cloud that lay over the house nowadays. Nor could it be blamed on its being early February, always a dark hour before dawn.

What had gone wrong Margaret didn't know, but Miss Caroline hadn't been home since Christmas, and even then she had left earlier than intended. Margaret had come to the conclusion it was all something to do with that Belgian officer. Most likely Miss Caroline had announced her intention of marrying him, and he being a foreigner was most likely a Roman Catholic. That would set the cat among the pigeons in the Rectory, for that meant Miss Caroline would have to convert her faith, and what would that do to the Rector? Margaret hadn't been entirely happy with this reasoning, and then yesterday Mrs Isabel had talked too freely. She'd wandered into the kitchen as she often did nowadays.

'You sit down, Mrs Isabel, you're doing too much.'

Once upon a time you couldn't have said that about Mrs Isabel, far from it, but now she was changed out of all recognition. Running about all over the place she was, and her having a first baby at nearly thirty. She'd been no more than a big baby herself, married or not, until she took over the cinema.

'It's good for me,' Mrs Isabel laughed, though she sat down at the table all the same. 'Where's Agnes?'

'Still doing the dusting.'

Mrs Isabel had taken to chatting with Agnes. Margaret wasn't sure she approved, but after all, they were more of an age and seeing as how Agnes was having her second the month before Mrs Isabel was due, naturally they were close. All the same

'You have one of these buns,' Margaret continued, concerned how thin the girl's face was getting. When Mrs Isabel shook her head, she decided the time had come to speak out. 'You're looking after two, remember,' she pointed out.

'Good, can we have dumplings for luncheon?'

'Dumplings but not much more, most likely.' There were more dumplings than stew nowadays, even though this wasn't a meatless day. Meat would be on the rations list for them sooner or later, that was for sure. She'd read so much about the new cards and coupons for butter, marg and meat in London and the Home Counties that her mind whirled. It wouldn't take long to reach Sussex, and although Mrs Lilley thought everyone would get more once it was distributed more fairly by enforced rations, Margaret was not convinced.

'You'll have Miss Caroline jealous,' she replied to Mrs Isabel, highly pleased. 'She's always one for a dumpling or two.'

'She'll have to make them herself now,' Isabel said soberly, tucking in to the bun after all.

'She'll be down shortly, I suppose?' Margaret wasn't exactly fishing for information: it just slipped out.

'I doubt it.'

Isabel was leafing through *The Lady*. The family had given up their copy, but Percy insisted on buying it for Margaret – to take her mind off things, he explained vaguely, as though a magazine could take her mind off Fred. Still, she had to admit she looked forward to reading it every week, and there was no doubt it kept you in touch with how best to fight the War at Home. There were times when even Margaret's mother's handed-down resourcefulness failed to cope with what was going on nowadays. What was the use of recipes for nettle soup when no weed would dare show its face in good ploughable land?

'These waistless dresses–' Isabel scrutinised the sketches – 'will be just right for me. Harrods Bargain Floor are advertising serge and silk dresses at forty-nine and six.'

'They won't fit you for long, Mrs Isabel,' Margaret said daringly.

'Oh well, I'll just have to ask Agnes – no, I'll ask Mrs Hazel – to cut a hole in it with a flap,' Isabel said carelessly. 'Mrs H needs the work, with everyone doing their own repairing and turning nowadays.'

Well, who'd have thought Mrs Isabel would ever learn to 'make do', and to cast a thought for poor Mrs Hazel struggling to make a living? In her hoity-toity days, she never saw eye to eye with the village dressmaker.

'Miss Caroline and that captain are busy, I expect.' Margaret meant working together, but Mrs Isabel took it in a different way.

'Don't let Mother hear you say that. There's a silence like the Great Wall of China about it.' Mrs Isabel put down *The Lady* and blurted out: 'I don't think I can stand it much longer, Mrs Dibble. After the row when Caroline walked out, neither Father nor Mother said a word to me about it. I had to pump Phoebe for information. It's too bad. Just when the Rectory ought to be happy because of my baby, Mother's thinking about Caroline, as usual. I *know* she is. I can sense it.'

That was more like the old Miss Isabel. Margaret had been quite taken aback. 'Oh, Mrs Isabel, I'm sure you're wrong.' It was inadequate, especially since Margaret had more than a suspicion that she wasn't wrong at all.

'Phoebe's cheering Caroline on, too,' Mrs Isabel swept on. 'Of all the people in the world to fall in love with, why on earth did Caroline have to pick a married Roman Catholic and make *our* lives a misery?'

Margaret nearly dropped the basin with the dumpling dough. *Married?* She'd always known you couldn't trust the Frenchies, and the Belgians were almost the same thing. Look at that couple who arrived here just after the war had broken out. Tricky customers, all of them. She'd said so then and she'd say so now. And now one had got poor Miss Caroline in his wicked clutches. And to think she'd let him cook in *her* kitchen.

Just then Agnes had arrived, so Mrs Isabel changed the subject. Not consciously, in all probability, but Agnes, married though she was, was the younger generation, and to Margaret's mind it wasn't fitting... She stopped this train of thought. Suddenly she felt very, very tired. Fitting? What a word to use in the middle of this war, a war where they shot you for being born not right in the head, a war that turned women from their homes and sent them out to work, a war that sent menfolk away from their families to live in the mud. What was the point of soldiering on?

Caroline had refused to let Yves accompany her to see Felicia; she would face the ordeal of going to Ashden, without visiting the Rectory, alone. In any case Yves was busy and so was Luke. The opening of February brought spring, and the constant watch for signs of an offensive by the enemy, perilously close. Work in the office had doubled in the last week or so, with increased enemy troop movements being reported by the La Dame Blanche train-watching agents at the important Antwerp, Liège and Fourmies junctions. Wasn't it a good sign, she had asked Yves hopefully, that crack divisions were being taken out of the front line?

'No.' He pulled a face. 'It probably means they are being rested to be ready for a March or April offensive. And they still have nearly thirty more divisions than all the Allies put together. When you remember that last autumn English and French divisions had twelve battalions each, and now only have nine, you can see why the Germans may be ready to strike as soon as possible.'

'Oh.' It was easy to deal with the facts staring at them from white-paper reports, but Caroline immediately translated them into a personal reality. Shortly it was all going to begin again. The balloon would go up, and Robert would be in it. George would be flying on battle patrols, Joe and Jamie Thorn were out wallowing in the front-line mud, Phoebe might be at risk, and everybody's loved ones would increase their odds against survival on the see-saw of war. Thank goodness at least Felicia was safe and Aunt Tilly too, for the doctor had point-blank refused her permission to go back to Ypres. Not that that alone would stop Tilly, nor even the War Office refusal to countenance it (Simon's hand?), but the news that other volunteers had been found to man their front-line post did satisfy her, after intense interrogation of their suitability.

Since Daniel had told Caroline that although Felicia was at Ashden Hospital, now, she would shortly return to the Rectory, Caroline decided to go straightaway.

'Wait and visit her at the Rectory,' had been Yves' advice.

'Not until you can come with me.'

Yves said no more.

The train was as crowded, uncomfortable and slow as ever, which made the journey a physical torment as well as an emotional one. How she had so mishandled her life as to be going to Ashden Station, but not to her home? Caroline steeled herself as she jumped down from the train. Relief that at least the moment had arrived was replaced by a sharp lurch of her stomach. How could the station look so normal? Mr Chappell was collecting tickets, Mrs Chappell was manning the tea counter which Phoebe had set up early in the war, young Joey Sharp – a man now – was home on leave from the Navy, one of the Thorns was boarding the train for the Wells. And here was Caroline Lilley, barred from being part of it all.

'Haven't seen you for a time, Miss Caroline.' Mr Chappell took her ticket.

Was this her replying so cheerily? 'No, duty calls.'

He nodded solemnly and, feeling a hypocrite, Caroline tried to march jauntily off down Station Road, by thinking of something happy. Apart from the prospect of seeing Felicia, she failed dismally. Her conviction that she was right to remain with Yves was weakened by this home-coming that was no such thing. Perhaps her mistake had been to take Yves home in the first place. That, however, meant the 'crime', if crime it was, remained the same and only the need to conceal it was at stake. She had believed she was right to take and give happiness as she could, yet as she passed the first catkins of spring, sudden doubt assailed her. She did not question her love for Yves, but could *true* happiness be achieved with such a Damoclean sword hanging over its future? Sometimes she found herself fostering comforting hallucinations that Yves' wife had fallen in love with someone else, or that she would refuse to have Yves back, and worse, she was ashamed to admit, than those. How long would the war go on anyway? How could one long for its end, yet dread it so much? At the moment it appeared to be stretching out forever and ever. The fighting never stopped, even for winter, but the coming of the catkins heralded major offensives. When she reached the junction of Station Road and Bankside, Caroline went straight across to the main road, trying not to glance at the cottages and her home opposite. How could she pop in to see Nanny Oates on Bankside in these circumstances? It was better that she did not know Caroline had been in Ashden. There was little chance of that, unfortunately, and her heart sank as she was immediately recognised.

'Morning, Miss Caroline.'

Rosie Trott from the Dower House staff shot her a curious look, as she passed on her way to the baker's.

It was inevitable that she would meet at least a few people and news would get out, but Caroline did her best to look as though it was normal for her to be crossing the road towards Ashden Park, not the Rectory. She breathed a sigh of relief as the grey bulk of St Nicholas' hid the sight of her home from her. Why should *she* feel a traitor? It was ridiculous, but she could not rid herself of guilt, and she walked as fast as she could along the drive to the hospital. Through the windows she could see a few convalescent officers sitting downstairs, but there was no sign of Felicia. She would be well tucked away, of course.

Too well, it seemed.

'Miss Lilley has two visitors already,' was the matron's uncompromising stance, as she looked Caroline up and down, seemingly finding her wanting.

'I've come a long way, and haven't long,' she pleaded winningly. 'Is there somewhere I could wait to see my sister, or should I go to the Dower House to wait for an hour or two?'

London-type diplomacy paid off, though Caroline hated resorting to it. The casual mention of Lady Hunney's residence immediately sent a flicker of doubt over the woman's face, and Caroline was led through the all-too-familiar corridors with their wartime clinical smells and sights towards some safe haven where the Matron's other patients would not be contaminated by the sight of a khaki-clad Waac.

'Caroline!'

She stood horrified, unable to move, as the familiar voice cried out. Why hadn't she thought of the possibility of her mother being here?

Seeing her mother's dear, anxious face, now white with shock, Caroline wanted to throw herself into her arms, and for a split trembling second it looked as though Elizabeth would have liked nothing more. Yet how could she make the first move, Caroline agonised? It would be a betrayal of Yves.

'How's Felicia?' Caroline managed to jerk out. 'And everyone?' Inside, every nerve was crying out for her mother to reply: 'Come home and see.'

But she didn't. 'Felicia's better. Caroline—' Elizabeth broke off, her lips quivered, and she walked quickly away.

Her mother walking away? Caroline couldn't believe it. This was some ghastly nightmare. Walking away out of her life? Leaving her there? Without a word? Without love? She watched, rooted in horror as her mother's back, familiar in its old blue serge costume, retreated before her. Then it stopped, and slowly her mother turned round. She was coming back! Cold with terror, Caroline waited. Elizabeth took her in her arms, and kissed her.

'Change your mind,' she pleaded hopelessly, as though already knowing the answer. 'Please do.'

'Would you?' Caroline could not move in her mother's embrace, in case she broke down. The hug grew briefly warmer, then her mother had gone. Trembling, Caroline hurried after the Matron, and collapsed in the room to which she was shown, trying to regain her composure. Five minutes later Isabel burst in. Here were the hugs and the warmth she needed.

'Oh, why didn't you tell *me* you were coming? Oh, how marvellous to see you. Did I tell you in my letter I've got Lord Kitchener?'

If anything could make her laugh, Isabel could – without her sister having the slightest notion of why.

'Ghost or alive?' she enquired with straight face.

'Silly. The new *film,* of course. Don't you hear about anything up there in London?

And *The Gay Lord Quex*. And Felicia's coming home next week. Oh, Caroline, why–?'

'No, Isabel. I can't.'

'I don't understand,' her sister wailed. 'You're working with Yves, so it's all respectable, even if you love him too. You can't help that, even if he is married. From what Phoebe says you're not threatening his marriage. Why–?'

'Isabel,' Caroline interrupted, agonised, 'let's stop, shall we? I'm here to see *Felicia*.'

'Thanks very much,' Isabel grumbled. 'So much for me. Don't you want to know how the baby is?' She patted her stomach proudly. 'You can see for yourself now, I suppose. Only five months to go. And if you still refuse to come here, I'll have to come to see you in London. I miss you,' she added with indignation.

'But the baby, and the trains–' Caroline was appalled at this suggestion. 'You can't possibly do that.'

'Don't you want to see me?' Isabel glared.

'Oh, Isabel, of *course*.' Caroline hugged her, conscience-stricken.

'Well then, I'll come. When the weather's better,' she added practically.

Isabel departed, to Caroline's guilty relief,

for she preferred to see Felicia alone.

She hardly recognised her sister, who was propped up against the pillows with her eyes closed. Her face still bore traces of yellow from the gas, and her breathing was rasped. She was thin, so thin.

Caroline bent over and kissed her, and the eyes flew open. 'I'm glad you've come,' Felicia whispered. 'I didn't think you would.' She coughed, the effort painfully shaking her whole body.

'You did your best to keep us in the dark,' Caroline teased. *Didn't think she would?*

'So have you,' Felicia retorted weakly.

'Ah.' Question answered. 'Do you blame me?'

'No. I saw you in France with Yves, remember? I saw how suited you were to him, as well as happy. A different happiness than with Reggie. If he's your choice, it's also yours to balance family against him. I'm glad that doesn't include me.'

'But Father–'

'Caroline,' Felicia interrupted gently, 'I've been on the Ypres front for nearly three years. I've seen enough death to believe that life should have its turn whenever possible and however briefly.' The racking cough again.

Was it true that Felicia was getting better? Caroline firmly dispelled the sudden doubt. She hesitated, then asked: 'You've lost your faith too?'

Felicia answered readily enough. 'No, but it's buried deep in the mud.'

'I thought once you might become a nun.'

Her sister glanced at her. 'It's still possible.'

'As an escape from choosing between Luke and Daniel?'

She should not have asked, for Felicia was too weak. Caroline was annoyed with herself for her stupidity. So eager to reclaim her sister from death, she was behaving thoughtlessly. Felicia's eyes were closing again, and Caroline rose to creep out, with just a whispered: 'You just told me life should have its turn, little sister.'

The eyelids fluttered in what might have been acknowledgement.

If anything could cheer Margaret up in bleak mid-February it was Lizzie's news. She even found herself humming again this morning – a good sign, Percy said approvingly as he passed through the kitchen to the scullery to trim the lamps. Margaret promptly stopped humming – that had used to be Fred's job.

She forced herself to concentrate on Lizzie. Miss Penelope had telephoned the Rectory to ask for her, Margaret Dibble. She had carefully wiped her hands on her pinny, apologised to the Rector for yet one more intrusion on his telephone, and picked up the receiver. 'Who's there?' she bawled, since you never knew where folk might be telephoning from.

'Penelope Banning,' was the cheerful answer. 'I have a message for Lizzie.'

'Frank? He's not dead, is he?' Margaret braced herself. February might as well bring one more disaster while it was about it.

'Good gracious, no. I'm bringing him home to Lizzie tomorrow. He can't wait to see the baby!'

Margaret couldn't take in all the implications at first, then she had a strong cup of tea, and set off to give the good news to Lizzie. Lucky it wasn't time to serve luncheon yet, and Myrtle could do the vegetables for once. Miss Penelope had continued to take an interest in Frank's progress, which was good of her, and sure enough the next day she turned up at Lizzie's cottage, bumping poor old Frank along Pook's Way in an ambulance. How Margaret had longed to be present to see

Frank meet his son, but Muriel, who was visiting that afternoon, said better to leave them alone.

Margaret had been mutinous. 'Miss Penelope will be there. Why not me?'

'She's a nice lady, you always said. She'll leave as soon as she can.'

Margaret had no answer to that, and was rewarded by Lizzie rushing up to the Rectory that night, clutching her dimmed torch, just to describe the scene to her. 'Oh, ma, he says Baby Frank has got his hair and he can see a moustache already.' She burst into tears.

'Well, I never did. Don't you take on so, Lizzie. I said he was no good, that Frank Eliot.' Margaret was shocked, and fiercely defensive.

'I'm not upset, Ma,' Lizzie snivelled. 'I'm just happy.'

'Mm.' Margaret was still doubtful. 'Well, just you remember I bath that baby too, and I'll give Frank a piece of my mind if he starts criticising the little fellow again.'

Lizzie's sobs turned to howls of laughter, until Margaret grew quite worried about that too. No one would be laughing when Rudolf came home, least of all Lizzie. Still, it looked like the war was going on and on

120

forever, so there was no use worrying over-much about its end when every single day clamoured for your attention. Like what to have for luncheon, for example.

They said in Sussex you could turn anything into a pudding, but these scalded bacon rinds gave even Margaret pause for thought. A nice onion or two and a leaf of sage might do it. She sighed. It was easier to preach food economy than practise it. She looked up in surprise as Lizzie arrived unexpectedly again. Two visits? And she'd said she was working today, Frank or no Frank. What's more, she had a stranger with her, a man in uniform. She didn't recognise it, but then one never did nowadays. What she did know was that unless Frank had lost twenty years or so and sprouted ginger hair, it wasn't him. And he was skinny, so skinny.

'I need your help, ma. Or rather Joachim does. He's bruised and cut his hand on the farm. I thought some of your arnica might help. And rice flour – I'm out of it.'

Poor young man. He looked as though the rice flour inside him was what was needed.

'You would be out of it, girl,' Margaret replied grimly while she was inspecting the damage. Lizzie was no housekeeper.

'There, that'll stop the bleeding, young man. You go and see your medical officer when you get back to camp. Might need stitching up.'

One of them soldiers from King's Standing, she supposed. Dr Marden didn't charge much, but if he could get it seen to by the army, it would be cheaper still.

'I told Mrs Lake you'd help,' Lizzie said with satisfaction as Margaret bound it round with lint.

'And I daresay she was only too happy to let me do it,' Margaret grunted, highly pleased at being needed. 'There you are, young Joe.' She patted the hand gently and restored it to him.

'*Danke schön, Frau* Dibble.'

Margaret froze. 'You from up north, Joe? Scotland maybe?' But she already suspected he wasn't.

'No,' Lizzie laughed. 'He's one of the prisoners of war on the farm.'

Margaret jumped back as though this Joe had a bayonet pointed straight at her. 'You mean I've been helping a *German*, Lizzie Dibble?' she screamed.

It wasn't hard for Joachim to realise what was going on, whether he spoke English or not. He went white, hastily rising from the chair and backing towards the door.

'Ma,' Lizzie shouted. 'He's *hurt*. Of course you'd help him.'

'What you do for one you do for the Kaiser, my girl.' *Her* kitchen had been polluted by a German. 'And bringing him to a rectory, of all places.' Even Margaret could see there was a flaw in her argument, but she didn't care. She was furious.

'That's why I came,' Lizzie said quietly. 'Frank said I should. Joachim's a good Christian.'

'Then why's he fighting for the Kaiser?' Margaret asked – unanswerably, as she thought.

She was wrong, for Lizzie retorted unforgivably, 'Suppose Fred had been a POW – wouldn't you want some nice German lady to be serving him dumplings and binding up his cuts?'

'Lizzie Dibble, how could you?' Margaret burst into tears.

'It's no use, ma, you've got to face it. Fred is dead, and it's not Joachim's fault. He's a soldier just like Fred.'

'Not just like Fred,' Margaret muttered, eyeing him up and down.

'No, he's got all his wits,' Lizzie said, 'but that–'

'That's not what I meant. Fred *always* had a square meal inside him. And I suppose, Joe, or whatever your name is, I'd better do the same for you.'

Mrs Lilley popped her head into the kitchen en route from her outside glory-hole to luncheon. She looked surprised, and no wonder. It came to a pretty pass when a German POW can be sitting at the kitchen table when her own daughter couldn't.

There'd been more ructions, Margaret didn't need telling – she'd heard them. Mrs Isabel had let slip about seeing Caroline at Ashden Manor and Margaret put two and two together. She said Mrs Lilley had been present too. As a result for the first time in her life, Margaret had heard the Rector and Mrs Lilley having what was undoubtedly a first class row. She supposed it had happened before, but never had they been storming at each other without caring who might be listening. Mrs Lilley stormed out of the Rector's study with the Rector's voice shouting after her just as if he was lecturing one of the children – and that only when they were small. There was such an atmosphere, Margaret had held up supper not knowing what to do, until Mrs Lilley had come in, and told her quite calmly she had a headache and would not be requiring supper. The Rector and Lady Buckford ate alone in silence, or so it appeared whenever Margaret went in. Mrs Isabel took a tray for herself and disappeared, most likely to sit with her mother.

Lady Buckford had other things to worry about too, for last night there was an air raid on Dover with a lot killed, and a hospital bombed. Today her ladyship had been very quiet, the poor old soul.

'How's Felicia?' Tilly was lying on a *chaise longue* by the morning-room window. Caroline liked coming to Simon's London house where she had lived for a while in 1915, for it felt like a second home. Deprived of one, she still had this, and to see Tilly here seemed entirely natural. Caroline hadn't seen her aunt since Christmas, and her visit to London provided an unmissable opportunity.

'Much better.' Caroline's fears had been groundless. Felicia *was* much better, so Isabel told her. 'She's going home to the Rectory soon.'

'You too, I hope.'

Caroline sighed. Did the whole world know about her predicament? 'Isabel, I suppose?'

'Your father, in fact. I asked him why you left so suddenly at Christmas, and with some reluctance he told me.'

'Do you disapprove?'

'Of what?'

'Of my refusal to stop loving Yves.'

'You can't stop loving him. Even Laurence would realise that. It seems to me that Laurence just expects you to stop sleeping with him, and preferably, seeing him at all. You must admit, Caroline, it's a shock for a country rector who hasn't seen what we have over the past year or two, and who is busy maintaining old standards in every situation. If you and Yves had planned to remain together at the expense of his marriage, I might agree with Laurence, but as I gather you haven't, I don't.'

Caroline thought very hard. Should she explain the situation fully, for she doubted if Father had. 'Yves' is not a normal marriage,' and when Tilly looked at her enquiringly, she explained.

'Ah.' Tilly reflected for a moment. 'And how old is his wife?'

'Twenty-seven or eight.'

'She might change.'

'Thank you,' Caroline said wryly. Trust Aunt Tilly to go straight to the wound.

Tilly grinned. 'Don't discuss things with me if you don't want unpalatable comments. It's what your father would be thinking.'

'But I *still* don't agree with him,' Caroline burst out, 'and that hurts. Father has *always* been my standard in life; you don't have to trail across the world to see beyond your own horizons.'

'No, but it helps. Can't you get used to the idea that you can still love and respect your father without accepting everything he says?'

'Not yet, but I suppose I will. After all, he disapproved of your suffragette activities, but he still defended you and housed you. Why can't he do the same for his daughter?' Caroline smarted anew.

'Because you are his daughter, made in his image, or so he hopes. I gather your parents have had a mother and father of a row, incidentally.'

'Over me?' Caroline was appalled, though a tiny part of her registered pleasure. The wound of her mother walking away from her was still deep.

Tilly nodded.

'You mean my father relented, but my mother wouldn't?' In Caroline's experience it had always been her mother whose standards were intractable, and Father who had more instant understanding of the situation.

'Wrong. Your mother wants to accept the situation for the sake of seeing you.' Tilly looked aghast. 'What have I said? Why are you crying, Caroline? I thought you'd be pleased.'

'I thought she didn't love me any more,' Caroline sobbed.

Tilly sighed. 'Rubbish. I don't always get on with Elizabeth but I know her well enough to know you could never doubt that, no matter what stance she takes. I think it's Laurence beginning to demonstrate one more unfortunate effect of having my mother in his home.' Tilly had looked after her mother for years, who had never suspected her suffragette activities. When she was sentenced to prison, and the truth emerged, her mother refused to allow her to return, and it had been Father who welcomed her, regardless of his opposition to her militancy.

Caroline sniffed, blew her nose, and decided to change the subject. 'What do you feel about the fact that you now have the vote?'

Tilly shrugged. 'A compromise. We wanted equal footing with men. They haven't conceded the point at all; it's lip service giving the vote to women over thirty, and there's nothing about our being able to stand for parliament. That's still gentlemen only. Patronising old fools.'

'Tilly!' Caroline laughed. 'I'm shocked.'

'You're not. You feel the same, don't you? In the middle of this mess of war it seems almost immaterial; even darling Emmeline has sided with the politicians.' Whereas Tilly and most other militant suffragettes, as well as their non-militant sisters, had gone into war work, Mrs Pankhurst was still heavily embroiled in politics.

'So what are you going to do now? Get married?' Caroline asked.

Caroline meant it as a joke, but Tilly did not take it so. 'You were a suffragette too once, Caroline. Is that the way you think now? That once the war is over, women will return to purdah behind closed doors? Is that what you would do if you remained with Yves?'

It was her own fault. Caroline knew she had brought this on herself, and must bear the consequences. 'I can't remain with Yves, so it's no use even considering that question,' she replied evenly. 'And what will I do? I haven't the slightest idea. Though–' she searched for a painful honesty – 'I most certainly won't look for the first man to marry me.'

'You can go back to the Rectory.'

To creep back into the womb of comfort? Caroline tried for honesty. 'I would *try* not to.'

'Well done,' Tilly said approvingly. 'Nothing wrong with doing so, but it just seems a pity after all you've achieved. I'm sure there's scope for us both after the war.'

'Yes, but–' Caroline hesitated, but if Tilly could intrude on her private life, then so could Caroline on hers. 'Tilly, don't *not* marry Simon just to prove a point, will you?'

There was a silence, then Tilly replied amiably: 'No.'

Five

Margaret tried very hard not to show her irritation. Granted, it wasn't usual for her to be in her own sitting-room and not the kitchen, but this was her free time and today she wanted to be alone, not available for all and sundry to come wandering in.

'I'm sorry,' said Isabel. 'I know how annoying it is to be interrupted when one's reading, but I wanted to discuss something with you and I shall have to be off to the cinema soon.'

She waited hopefully, and there wasn't much Margaret could do except to say, 'Sit down, Mrs Isabel, I'll make you a cup of tea.' Government-controlled it might be now, but even if it tasted like sawdust it was still wet and warm.

'No, don't bother, Mrs Dibble. I can see I'm in the way.'

Margaret was so touched by Mrs Isabel's thinking of her for once that she made the tea all the same. *And* brought out some of the duchess buns she'd reserved for herself as a treat. They didn't need the flour that most cakes did, and so her conscience was clear, and after all, Mrs Isabel was eating for two.

'I know you're busy with your Tunbridge Wells talks,' Isabel said through a mouthful of bun, 'and that's why you've cut down on your cookery demonstrations at the cinema—'

'They've heard all I've got to say,' Margaret interrupted defensively.

'Yes, but with the Government pressing for a cinema propaganda campaign, and the National Food Economy League running this poster campaign and issuing recipe leaflets, I wondered whether you could begin again? With meat rationing coming in for the whole country in April, it's the ideal time. You could display the amount of meat rations on the table, show what you can make out of it, and the same for marg and butter when that gets rationed.'

Margaret sighed. 'I'll do what I can. I suppose we've got to get this war over with somehow. I'll be serving up the same old thing though.'

'That doesn't matter. It will help keep the village together, and anyway, rationing isn't going to be straightforward in the country-side, even if it is in towns. There's going to be a lot of trying to beat it by going direct to the farmers–'

'Are you saying good Ashden folk will be trying to bribe the farmers, Mrs Isabel?'

'Haven't you ever asked for the extra chicken for the Rectory?'

'That's different,' Margaret snapped. Of course it was. The Rector had to keep his strength up.

'If you began your talks at the cinema again, I could tie the films in with them, a Charlie Chaplin tramp film, for example, to make them laugh. That way we could keep the village together, and not looking over each other's shoulders to see what their neighbours are getting. It's worth a try, anyway.'

'I don't know that I've got the time.' Margaret was weakening, though. The idea of the village rallying round her stove was attractive. She'd let it all drop after Fred's death, because she didn't want to see the sympathy in their eyes – if sympathy it would have been. Enough time had passed, though; if she didn't show herself again now they'd think she was ashamed of Fred, and that wouldn't be right.

'Some of the older villagers are going to need the coupon system explained to them.

And there's all this advice about eating slowly so you won't want to eat so much.' Margaret looked at Mrs Isabel, halfway through her second duchess bun. No eating slowly with her. 'I'll think about it,' Margaret promised her in a tone that indicated the discussion was over.

Her lips snapped shut as her eyes involuntarily returned to her book. She didn't want Mrs Isabel to think she was turning her out, yet she longed to get back to it.

Unfortunately Isabel's eyes had followed hers. 'Oh, Mrs Dibble, you're not reading *that* rubbish?'

'Rubbish? What's wrong with it, might I ask?' Margaret bristled, despite the fact that when Mrs Coombs from the Dower House had given it to her, she'd thought much the same.

'This'll give you comfort in your trouble,' Mrs Coombs had said, and how right she was.

Margaret had never had much time for Mrs Coombs, and had been surprised to find she was a book-reader. It turned out she wasn't, but she'd lost her nephew she was so fond of, and someone had told her about this book. Margaret had accepted it, because she couldn't do much else. How could it comfort her though? Fred was dead, that was that, and no book was going to put it right. That had been yesterday, and now she couldn't put it down. *Raymond*, it was called. The author wasn't just anybody, he was a Sir and he was a famous scientist. His son Raymond Lodge had been killed in 1915, but he was alive and well on the other side. His father knew this for a fact, because he was in touch with him through one of these mediums, and from all the things this medium knew about Raymond, she couldn't be making it up. Margaret had heard a lot about mediums and spiritualism; it had been a craze in the last year or two, and the Rector often talked about fakes exploiting the bereavement of others by setting themselves up as mediums, divine healers, psychic healers and what have you. The *Daily Mail* had put a stop to this racket by exposing it in the newspapers. She'd read all about it and thoroughly approved. That was before she'd read *Raymond*. Now she argued that just because there was a lot of imitation sugar around, it didn't mean the real cane didn't exist. It was the same with this book, and she'd just reached the exciting part.

Over on the other side, Sir Oliver reported, a young girl called Feda, in control of a medium, Mrs Leonard, was passing on messages from Raymond, and Margaret had now reached the verbatim accounts of the conversations between himself and Raymond talking through Feda. It all made sense the way Raymond described the other side, and the thought that Fred too was up there having his poor body and mind put to rights, and singing and joking with his mates was indeed comforting. Raymond reported that they even produced cigars and whisky and sodas for any newcomers who requested them, but this didn't last, and a good thing too, or Fred might get seduced into bad ways – if such a thing was possible in heaven.

Early this morning as she avidly read the next page or two as she had her first cup of tea of the day, she had wondered whether this Mrs Leonard could be making things up, but then Sir Oliver wouldn't have published it if he wasn't satisfied it was true. He was not only a scientist, but the head of a university somewhere. Late last night, after she had said her prayers, Margaret had lain in the darkness, her eyes shut tight, thinking of Fred happily carving wooden animals as he used to in the gardens on the other side. He couldn't be healing them for there wouldn't be any to heal in heaven. Or would there? Maybe he helped out on the curing side when all those shot pheasants arrived. True, Sir Oliver had said nothing about animals so far, but then maybe Raymond didn't like them.

'You mustn't read that!' Isabel looked horrified. 'It's just a panacea.'

For the first time in her life Margaret was rude to a member of the family. 'I'll read what I like, if it's all the same to you, Mrs Isabel.'

'But Father says–'

'I'll listen if he can explain how this medium got hold of all the details about that poor young man Raymond. What do you think mediums do? Spend all their time going round the country like the Unseen Hand, questioning the servants on what he likes for dinner, how the poor man died, etc? How do you explain this medium could describe a group photograph of Raymond and his mates which at that time Sir Oliver himself had never seen? There are more things in heaven and earth, Mrs Isabel, as my mother used to say.'

'Shakespeare, actually.'

'And I daresay he got it from *his* mother.' Margaret wasn't going to give Mrs Isabel the last word, not in her own sitting-room.

Isabel flushed, and rose from her chair to leave. 'I'm sorry, I shouldn't have said anything. I was just so surprised.'

Margaret did not reply, but watched Mrs Isabel walk to the door. Then, as she walked out of the room, she delivered her olive branch. 'I'll do those demonstrations for you, Mrs Isabel. We'll call it The Same Boat campaign.'

Everyone was in the same boat in this war, and if Mrs Isabel couldn't see that some of the passengers in that boat were unseen visitors from the other side, what did that matter? They were still there, however invisible to the rowers.

Last week Felicia had moved back to the Rectory, and Luke had stayed there at the weekend. Caroline tried not to mind that Luke was welcome in the home she was forbidden to enter, for after all it had been by her own choice, but nevertheless it was hard. She had gone out with Penelope to see a Mary Pickford film yesterday evening, in order to not be at Queen Anne's Gate when Luke returned, and though she enjoyed it

138

she was disconcerted to find that he hadn't yet come back. Nor was he at breakfast. Luke finally arrived at the office halfway through the morning.

'And before you ask me what time I consider this,' he said disarmingly, before she could speak, 'I went to see Sir John at the Dower House last night, and the train was late this morning. And slow, *and* crowded. Does that satisfy you, ma'am? You won't dock my king's shilling?'

'How is she?' Caroline struggled to overcome her unreasonable resentment.

'Doing well. She's up and about – chiefly because the Dragon Grandmother refused to let me into Felicia's bedroom unchaperoned.'

'Serve you right. The very idea.'

'I haven't seen Felicia laugh so much in years. In fact, I'd *never* seen her laugh like that before. I can't say it amused me. Anyway, Felicia climbed out of bed in her nightie, asked me to help her into her dressing gown and to carry her downstairs. That put Dragon Lady to silence. Unfortunately, as I did so, Daniel came through the front door, which was open for Rector's Hour, and found me bearing her off like young Lochinvar. He was not amused either, though he tried not to show it like the gent he is. Felicia thought that was even funnier, so Daniel forgave me on the grounds that I was cheering her up. We sat either side of her in the drawing room like two gaolers, while Mrs Dibble fussed around with fires, coffee and cakes, and worried about us all staying to luncheon since there were only five chops.

'I must say,' Luke added, 'it must be a strange feeling for Lissy to return to the ways of the Rectory after life on the Western Front.'

'Yes.' Caroline remembered how odd even she had thought it, when Reggie asked her father's permission to climb in her bedroom window as a surprise after coming home unexpectedly for Christmas from the Front.

'Anyway,' Luke continued, 'that gave Felicia a taste for downstairs life, and she even managed to get dressed with Isabel's help the next day. She had great fun trying to find something from her pre-war clothes that didn't make her look like something out of Dickens. Agnes is busy shortening all her clothes.'

Oh, how painful those images of home. 'Can't she buy new ones?'

One of the compensations for wartime life

was that many young women previously dependent on families were now earning a wage. Even the Rectory's finances had been eased this way – much, she suspected, to her father's annoyance.

'You know Felicia. Soldiers' comforts first.'

'What are her plans now she's really improving?' Caroline asked.

'Not to marry me, as you won't be surprised to hear. Not at least while there's a war on.'

'And then?'

Luke shrugged. 'What do you think? There's always Daniel. It's a hopeless situation, Caroline,' he added, seriously for once. 'If she marries me, and Daniel lingers around as the family friend, we risk her as well as myself coming to resent the situation. If she marries Daniel, she has to face the fact she'll never have children or a normal married life. That's presuming Daniel would marry her in the circum-stances. He's kept well away so far, but there's no doubt her illness has brought them closer together again.' He grimaced. 'We make fine couples, don't we? Felicia and I, you and Yves. None of us can wholly blame the war, for that's only played an

141

incidental role. We've done it to ourselves, and I can tell you, Caroline, it hurts.'

'Me too.' It did. She struggled to overcome it, but the question 'How much longer can I have him?' was there in the background all the time. The irony was that the more she worried, the more it might drive them apart. It was an ordeal by fire. If they survived it, they would be welded forever, even if parted. If not... She made a tremendous effort to think positively. 'Tell you what, let's rope Ellen in and we'll all four go dancing tonight.'

'I have a better idea.' Yves, coming in unexpectedly, overheard the dreaded word dance. 'Let's go to eat black eggs and sharks' fins at that Chinese café in Regent Street.'

'I've an even better one,' Caroline retorted firmly. 'Let's do *both*.'

'To answer your question about Felicia,' Luke mentioned, helping himself to stewed seaweed some hours later, 'she has plans of going back to nursing, I believe.'

'Not back to the Front? It would kill her.' Caroline was horrified.

'No. At Ashden.'

'Is that a good idea?' Caroline had meant that if she were near Daniel and again he rejected her, Felicia would be deeply hurt.

142

Luke misunderstood. 'Not in my view. Felicia was the star turn there at Ashden as patient, because she's so famous among the Tommies. Not that she cared about that, but to be there as patient and there to work are not the same at all, and I'm not sure how it would work out. It would mean taking orders again and she's not used to that.'

'She has discipline. She would soon adapt. My worry is that it's a tiring job with long irregular hours.'

'Yes, and furthermore—' Luke said no more, perhaps because Yves looked so forbidding. She had sensed he disliked talk of the Rectory; he would listen politely but then change the subject. It was understandable, for he had much on his mind. Though the main thrust of the terrifying speedy German advance was in the Arras area, Belgian troops were also under attack in several places on the short length of front they held so tenaciously between the sea and the British and French front line. Furthermore, whatever she said, Yves might still blame himself for her rift with her family. Hastily, she changed the subject.

As March had begun, so had increased tension. German HQ, they had discovered, had shifted from Kreuznach to Spa, nearer the Western Front. It could be an ominous sign. Germany had been fighting a defensive war, leaving the grand scale offensives to the Allies who were trying to push the enemy line back. That could not last forever, although sometimes it seemed it would. However, now the indications of a coming German offensive were growing stronger by the day.

The reports they received were usually a few days old, since they had to wait for them to be decrypted and passed on to them from the central office of the SSB. GHQ were first in line for the decrypts, and they came second.

'Another report from Fourmies,' Luke observed.

Yves' head shot up. Fourmies was the important train-watching post inside the French border, and one of the closest to the Front. Significant movements observed there might indicate the enemy had its eye on the Arras-Cambrai section of the Front, rather than that further north near Ypres. And *that* in its turn suggested an early strike since Yves had told Caroline that the ground in the Belgian sector in the Lys Valley would be too wet before mid-April to sustain an offensive.

The work La Dame Blanche was doing was now invaluable. The Allied intelligence services were aware that the enemy was using dummy military installations to blur the picture when RFC reconnaissance planes swept over the lines but trains carrying troops were impossible to conceal, or to deploy on deceptions when manpower must be as critical on their side as on ours. In Britain it was at crisis point, and there was talk of raising the conscription age to 50. The enemy, on the other hand, seemed to be lowering theirs. It was reported many of the dead and wounded were no more than fifteen or sixteen.

When Caroline and Yves reached home that night, they heard the sound of laughing, followed by a feminine squeal. Ellen? Was she entertaining someone in their sitting-room? This was strictly forbidden without special permission in view of their jobs and the use of the offices in the rest of the building. Yves raced ahead, with Caroline after him, to find it was indeed Ellen, although it wasn't exactly a sweetheart teasing her. There lounging on the sofa, reading *Punch*, feet up, puttees unwound and RFC cap flung carelessly on the table, was George, and Ellen, somewhat red-faced, was sitting chastely some way away.

'Admiring your own work, George?' Caroline enquired sweetly. George's cartoons appeared frequently in the magazine.

He grinned. 'If I don't, no one else will. It was Ellen laughing at them, actually.'

'So we heard,' Caroline said drily. 'What was he doing to you, Ellen, or daren't I ask?'

'Entertaining me.'

Caroline decided not to speculate on what form George's entertainment took nowadays. It didn't sound as though it had been restricted to showing her his photographs, half a dozen of which lay scattered on the table. She picked one up, to see a group of three uniformed men, one of whom was George, and three Waacs, with their arms round each other's shoulders, laughing their heads off. Odd to think that George, their baby brother, now had a life of his own apart from them, of which they knew nothing. They feared for him all the time, and yet there were moments like that captured in this photograph.

'To what do we owe this honour?'

'I'm over here on official business, leaving dear old Blighty tomorrow, and heading for my little grey home on the Western Front. I thought I'd pop in in case the balloon goes up and I go down.'

'Don't jest about it.'

'All one can do, dearest Sis. Even you can't ignore the fact I've been on borrowed time for the best part of a year now. It only needs the Red Baron's circus to spot my trusty SE5a and down goes baby, cradle and all.'

'Or down von Richthofen goes.'

'Yes. That would be a lark.' He considered this. 'I'd get another gong for that all right.' He already wore the DSO, a fact he had concealed from the whole family until the summons for its presentation at the Palace had arrived last autumn. 'Father and Mother would burst their buttons with pride.'

'Have you been to the Rectory?' Caroline asked eagerly.

'Just for a day to see Felicia and say hallo. Official business, as I said. I needed a word with Isabel, anyway,' he added carelessly.

'Whenever you use that tone of voice, I know there's something you want to keep from Father.'

'There is, as a matter of fact,' he admitted. 'As well as the business, I wanted to see a chum, so I told the folks I only had a forty-eight-hour leave.'

'A girl sort of chum?'

'You could say that.'

'I do, George.' Good luck to him. He was nineteen now, and with what everyone perceived would be a short life span. Live for the day was the attitude of most young men of his age, and London was full of them. In George's shoes she wouldn't want to go back to the Rectory either, which would be clouded by their fears for him. George had a loaf of bread, a jug of wine, and now he'd found himself a Thou beside him singing in the wilderness. Omar Khayyam's attitude was right, even if Father would not agree.

'What did you want to talk to Isabel about? Babies?'

'Not Pygmalion likely. It was official business actually. The Government has plans to set up a fleet of cine-motor cars and send them round the country with propaganda films, including war cartoons. Like that film of Bairnsfather's, A *Better 'Ole*. They asked me to chip in, so I wanted to ask Beautiful Bella what went down best in villages.'

'I don't understand. What have cars to do

with it? Why not send the films to the cinemas?'

'Because, nit-head, not many villages have generous folk like Swinford-Browne donating cinemas. The cine-motor cars carry portable screens and set them up wherever they can find.'

'Propaganda to join the services, I presume. Don't you think there's been enough of that?'

'No, I don't. The point of propaganda is to get the war won. Everything's propaganda in a way. If you *don't* keep the home flag flying, you're simply doing the enemy's propaganda for him.'

Yves laughed. 'Come and work for us, George.'

'No, thanks. Sitting in an SE5a beats a Whitehall chair any day.'

The next morning, 9th March, there was more bad news. 'The Germans have begun a bombardment all along the Western Front,' Luke reported, torn between anxiety and excitement that at last it had happened.

'The offensive has *started?*' Caroline's stomach contracted. George would be leaving for the Front at this very moment.

'Probably not. This is the preparation for it.'

'It won't be long though. The Germans won't want to risk too many Americans coming into the ranks.'

'That's hardly likely,' Yves commented wryly.

The American involvement in the war was causing much dissension. Few of the 120,000 combat troops in France were yet in combat, despite all Haig and Clemenceau's pleas. The problem seemed to be that the Allies wanted to integrate American divisions under their own command, whereas Pershing wanted to have them under his sole control. The US commander had visited Haig and King Albert in January, and Yves had returned with a funny story. Pershing's train had arrived at Adinkerke ten minutes early, catching the General still dressing; he was only halfway through putting his uniform on. Poor King Albert had been left at Adinkerke station with himself and his officers at full salute for ten minutes. He didn't say a word when Pershing finally appeared.

'You know Pershing. He's immovable,' Luke replied to Yves' comment.

Less than two weeks later, Pershing did move, offering troops for the emergency. On the 19th, they had intelligence reports from prisoners and deserters that the offensive would begin on 21st March – a delightful spring present, as Luke described it when he told them. But all the advance knowledge in the world wouldn't have been able to influence the outcome of this offensive. Its momentum was now carrying all before it, as the Germans swept forward, not in the south as the British and French had hoped, but in the St Quentin area – where George's squadron was stationed.

Even at this grim time there were treats. One of them should have been this evening, the 23rd, as Simon, Tilly and Penelope had invited Yves and herself to dinner in Norland Square. Even Field Marshal Haig had 'treats'. On the very day of the outbreak of the German offensive, his first son had been born. Caroline's treat was doomed, however. She had noticed that Yves was avoiding her eye during the afternoon and instantly divined the reason. 'You can't come this evening, can you?'

'I am sorry, Caroline.'

'Oh, *Yves!*' She couldn't help the cry of dismay. 'Everyone must have some time off.'

'Not tonight,' he replied quietly. 'We have

just heard the British are retreating to the Somme, and that the Germans are shelling Paris. Many people have been killed there.'

'*Paris?* But that's miles away.'

'Long-range guns.'

'Even so—' Caroline broke off. Surely, oh surely all the fighting so far could not have been in vain. Could the Germans take Paris, and win the war so easily? All the discipline in the world could not prevent that sick fear churning in her stomach.

Irrationally, disappointment over the evening predominated by the time evening came, and ate at her all the way to Bayswater on the Central London Railway. It was a wearisome journey by underground, whereas Yves could easily have commandeered a car. He didn't even suggest she took a cab. Caroline felt aggrieved, though she knew she was being ridiculous. The loss of his company for one evening was a small price to pay besides that being paid by most people in the country. She fumed at the slowness of the train, irritably riffling through the pages of *The Lady* early spring fashion number. She stared savagely at an advertisement for a holeproof corset (guaranteed if the supports gave way or a hole in the fabric developed). She didn't believe it, and did it matter in the great scheme of things anyway?

When the train ground to what seemed a permanent halt at Queen's Road, she leapt out and decided to walk the rest of the way. By the time she arrived at Simon's house, she was windswept but better-humoured. She was put in even better humour by the unexpected guest.

'Surprise!' Isabel, by now considerably enlarged round the waist, came to greet her just as George had done at Christmas.

'Why didn't you warn me?' Caroline was half-laughing, half-crying.

'You'd have told me not to come, just like Mother, Father, Uncle Tom Cobley and all. But here I am, and no Zeps, white traders or American soldiers have got me yet, despite Grandmother's darkest forebodings.'

The evening was a pleasant one and at the end of it Simon, Tilly and Penelope tactfully withdrew so that she could talk to Isabel alone. 'How are things in Ashden?' Caroline asked brightly, meaning how are things at the Rectory.

Isabel of course didn't realise that. 'The William Pear had another go at shutting down the cinema, but the parish council made it clear it was a weapon with which to fight the war and that we'd splash it all over the newspapers if he closed it. He shut up like a goldfish, silly little man.'

Isabel much disliked her parent-in-law, who now lived in East Grinstead, but, much amused, Caroline reflected that she would not have talked of William in such terms several years ago.

'They're beginning to take an interest in Swinford-Browne junior, more's the pity,' Isabel continued gloomily. 'I suppose Robert *had* to tell them, just in case–' She stopped, but it was obvious what Isabel was thinking.

Observation balloons over the Western Front had probably the most dangerous job in the RFC, and if Robert were shot down in flames, the Swinford-Brownes would descend in force on Isabel – not for her own sake, but to commandeer their grandchild. It was not a pleasant thought and Caroline decided it was time to change the subject.

'Tell me about home,' she commanded.

Isabel grimaced. 'You wouldn't believe the stuff Mrs Dibble is trying to pour down my throat to "do me good", in between admonitions that no lady should work while she's expecting, especially the Rector's daughter. I asked her who was going to run the cinema with no young gentlemen to do it, and she couldn't answer that one. Perhaps she should consult Fred.'

'*What* did you say?' Caroline was startled.

Isabel went red. 'I'm sorry, that just slipped out. There's rather a barney on at home.'

'Over me?'

'Not this time. Over Mrs Dibble. You've been temporarily replaced as the black sheep. Did you know that according to Father, there actually were some human black sheep? It was a tribe who got vanquished by the white sheep in ancient times out East somewhere–'

'Isabel! *Tell* me!'

Her sister giggled. 'All right. I shouldn't have said anything, though. Poor old Mrs Dibble has been reading *Raymond* and now believes Fred's his best friend up above.'

'Oh.' Caroline understood immediately what the fuss was about. Everyone knew about *Raymond*.

'Father found out – not through me, honestly,' Isabel explained. 'Mrs Dibble mentioned it to him herself. He raised the roof about it.'

'Oh *really*.' Caroline was infuriated. Father might believe he could control his children's

155

every thought, but he shouldn't try to do the same for Mrs Dibble. She was free to believe what she liked. She had always had a double-sided religion in fact. For Sussex born and bred Mrs Dibble, the land of superstition and fairies existed side by side with God's word, and in Caroline's opinion, *Raymond* was only an extension of this dual belief.

'It's developing into a battle royal,' Isabel was in her stride now. 'Mrs Coombs, who lent the book to Mrs Dibble, has been going round the village raising support to hire a charabanc to visit a medium in Tunbridge Wells. About twenty bereaved parents went off there ten days ago, leaving Father tearing his hair out.'

'But if it gives them comfort and does no harm, is it any concern of his?'

'Apparently the Church's official view-point is completely opposed to it, particularly because of the charlatans around. It does seem rather daft, doesn't it? I mean, if Raymond really is up there communicating through Mrs Leonard's control with earth, why doesn't he give us some important information like what the German plans are rather than nattering on about the family parrot and the heavenly mansion being made of bricks. Not that the parrot was made of bricks, of course.'

Caroline laughed. 'If Sir Oliver Lodge believes it though, and not just because of his son, shouldn't we take it seriously? Just as people took those two ladies who claimed to have walked back into the court of Marie Antoinette at Le Petit Trianon seriously when they turned out to be the head and vice-principal of an Oxford college?'

'Don't you start. Father thinks it's the devil at work, to seduce people from the true Church.'

'The war's done that already. It drives away as many as it comforts.'

'Father believes that instead of strengthening faith in the Lord, this "other side" nonsense is weakening it. I agree poor old Mrs Dibble has cause enough to try anything. After Fred's death she needed some convincing that there was a God at all, and there are many like her.'

'So what is happening at home?'

'Father and Mrs Dibble went at it hammer and tongs and even Mother couldn't get a word in edgeways. She was terrified Mrs Dibble was going to give in her notice, she was so upset. It was Agnes broke it up in the end.'

'Agnes? What on earth could it have to do with her?'

'She's a sensible girl, as you know. She heard all the shouting and guessed what it was about, since she knew about Mrs Dibble's sudden interest in spiritualism. She decided she should go in to the fray as umpire.'

'Father allowed her to?' Caroline was highly amused.

'He told me afterwards he was so astounded at the parlour maid coming in to help him sort things out that he couldn't think of any arguments against what she said.'

'And what was that?' Perhaps she should ask Agnes to come and sort out her own problems with the Rectory.

'That spiritualism was providing a lot of comfort in time of bereavement to a lot of people, regardless of whether the mediums were charlatans or not. That the Rector knew how sensible Mrs Dibble was, and when she got over the shock of Fred's death – which was only eight months ago – she'd come to revalue spiritualism for herself. Wasn't that better, Agnes argued, than telling her it was the work of the devil now? All Father could think of to say when he got his breath back was that the end can never justify the means.'

'And what did Agnes reply to that?'

'She asked who is to decide what are the means and what the end. Suppose, she argued, Mrs Dibble's brush with spiritualism was part of God's plan for the Rector to realise he was failing to communicate with some of the bereaved. If conventional ways wouldn't help, maybe God had provided him with this new means. There are many lanes into Ashden, Agnes proclaimed, besides the main road, and God is a village centre too.'

'Did the pit of hell open up for her?' Caroline asked breathlessly.

'No. Father just said quite nicely, not nastily: "Perhaps you should preach my sermon, Agnes." And, do you know what, Caroline?'

'She did?'

'No, but he preached last Sunday about the need for re-gritting and gravelling in the stormy weather, frost and snow. I told Felicia about it, and she asked me to steal his copy so that she could read it. She was strongly on Mrs D's side. If Mrs Dibble could have the vote this year, she argued, she could also decide her own path to God, whether His mansion was built of bricks, clouds or empty gin bottles.'

'Poor Father. He must be so grateful for you, Isabel. You're the only one of us who isn't kicking over the traces.'

'Do you think so?' Isabel looked hopeful. 'Odd, isn't it? You were all so good and I was the wayward one until I got married. Now it's the other way around. Phoebe wants to marry a divorced man, you're living with – sorry, *loving*, a married man, Felicia is turning her face to the wall away from the church, and, whenever he can, George is clasped in the arms of buxom Kate.'

'*What?*' Caroline stared at her aghast. Kate Burrows, a cheerful Yorkshire lass, had been foisted on them by the Ministry of Agriculture and had departed whence she came after Grandmother discovered her and George in compromising circumstances.

'I'm sure that's where he goes when he comes home on leave. That's why he's so rarely at the Rectory. It's not all cartoon business.' Isabel began to giggle.

Six

Caroline opened the envelope with great curiosity. It was a rare event to see a letter from Phoebe, and even on her birthday last year all she had received was a postcard of Charlie Chaplin with a scrawled 'Wish I was there!' upon it. No doubt she did, Caroline realised with hindsight. Last July Phoebe must have been in the initial stages of her romance with Billy Jones and thus all too eager to be back in London with him, rather than on the Western Front. Billy couldn't be touring for the troops in France all the time. Not that Phoebe didn't enjoy her work, or so Caroline had gathered from her last conversation with her; she seemed to have found her niche in driving. Thankfully, Phoebe was based away from the Front; she met interesting people and was doing a worthwhile job – away from the Rectory, where, she had once confessed to Caroline, she felt the odd one out. Why, oh why, did she have to fall for a middle-aged divorced man? Caroline took the letter out hopefully;

perhaps Phoebe was pouring her heart out in it because she and Billy had separated.

They hadn't. Caroline's cry of dismay made Yves look up anxiously. As usual he was deep in *The Times,* which he scoured every morning for any item of news about Belgium or the Belgian army that might not have reached him through intelligence channels. A week ago, on 30th March, the eve of Easter Day, the Germans had shelled Adinkerke, where King Albert's home was within their range.

'You have received bad news?'

'Yes – no – oh, Yves, read it for yourself. *Look* what she's planning to do now.'

He picked up the letter, read it, and handed it back to her. 'So Phoebe plans to marry. This is not new. You expected it would happen.'

'Yes, but not *now.* And not *there.* And *not* in a registry office. And *not* without Father's consent. She's still under twenty-one, and she writes that I am the only person she's telling.'

Yves re-read the letter. 'You're right, Caroline. It is serious that she is choosing to marry in France for that very reason. I do not know the French regulations on age.'

'Is it even legal to have a civil wedding in

France?' Caroline moaned. 'And only Phoebe would choose to go to Paris to be married when hundreds of thousands of its citizens are getting out as fast as they can.'

The two week bombardment of Paris by the huge new long-range guns was causing panic, as the civilian death rate was high.

'She wrote this letter on 1st April. Is it a *poisson d'avril*, an April fool?' Yves asked.

'No,' Caroline replied hollowly. 'I know Phoebe all too well. She intends to marry in Paris in two weeks' time, and that's that. You'd have more hope of changing the Kaiser's mind than Phoebe's.'

'Then you must try to persuade her to come to London instead, *and* get your Father's consent. She will, after all, want her marriage to be legal.'

'No, I'll advise her to wait.'

Yves hesitated. 'Has it occurred to you that may not be possible?'

'Phoebe will just have–' Belatedly Caroline realised what he meant. 'Oh. I don't think so.' She remembered Phoebe denied they were lovers at Christmas. A lot could happen in three months, however.

'Even your father would not hold back his consent in those circumstances.'

Perhaps he thought that might comfort

her. If so, Yves was wrong. It would be a nightmare for Father. First she, now Phoebe, would in his view have defied the moral precepts that had guided them all their lives.

'Phoebe will just ignore me, whatever I suggest,' she answered miserably.

'Billy Jones won't. And he's in London.' Yves glanced at her and read her expression correctly. 'I will go to see him. It will be easier.'

She could have sobbed with relief. 'I suppose I should be happy for Phoebe, but I keep thinking of everything that could go wrong – and the upset.'

Yves glanced at her. 'There is even more serious news in the newspaper, *cara*. Can you bear to hear it?'

She braced herself. 'The Germans have taken Amiens after all?' If Amiens fell, the way to the Channel ports lay open, but yesterday, on 4th April, their headlong onslaught had been halted at last.

'No, my love, the English sausage is under threat.'

'*What?*'

He laughed at the incredulous expression on her face. 'Your Government Food Controller wishes to bring the content of

164

sausages under his control, as he has tea.'

'He can't do that.' Caroline was immediately indignant. 'You're right. It is serious.' Every butcher, every cook had his or her own recipe for sausages. 'How can he control it?'

'There are plans for pork mince to be distributed all over the country by one manufacturer who will be closely under the Ministry's eye.'

'Once the country loses the freedom of its sausages,' Caroline proclaimed, 'there may be revolution, as in Russia.'

'I believe you, Caroline. This may be a Bolshevik plot. Or perhaps the Unseen Hand has penetrated the Ministry of Food.'

She caught Yves' eye, ran round the table and into his waiting arms. 'Into battle, *mon capitaine*. Let us to work to defend the noble sausage from rape and dishonour.'

Margaret read the news with great disquiet. If it wasn't one thing it was another. No sooner had the enemy met his just desserts at Amiens, where the British army stood firm, than the Government slipped this through. Meat rationing was one thing, laying Government hands on the sausage was quite another. What would they do

165

about home-produced sausages? Every decent housewife could make their own sausages, and what else had the Good Lord sent us sage to grow in the garden for? Despite her talk at the cinema on this coupon system, Wally Bertram complained he had a queue a mile long while he worked out how to clip the blessed coupons. She'd told him if he could be bothered to come to her talks, he'd find out. He pointed out someone had to be in the shop, but that was no excuse, for he opened and shut when he felt like it, and Mrs Bertram was there often enough when he fancied a lie-in. Being a churchwarden, he reckoned he was too high and mighty to be bothered with coupons. He was always in the right, just like – this traitorous thought slipped unchecked through her mind – the Rector.

Mind you, the Rector hadn't said anything more to upset her when she returned from Tunbridge Wells. He knew where she'd been all right, but it was her afternoon off and she'd do what she liked. If that was going to a medium to have a chat with Fred, it was her decision. The Rector just asked her whether it had helped. She'd said yes, because she couldn't very well say anything else. On the whole, though, she wasn't sure it wasn't more upsetting than comforting. Perhaps Percy had been wise not to come.

She used to think messages from the other side came to you through the table rocking, but it wasn't always like that with Raymond's medium, nor with Mrs Orvino in Tunbridge Wells. They'd all sat there quietly waiting and hoping, as she went into a trance. That meant she was being taken over by her control, and so she had begun speaking in a very gruff voice. It turned out her control was called Pythagoras. One by one Mr Pythagoras contacted all their loved ones, and passed over their messages. After Mrs Hubble had heard from young Timothy, and poor Mrs Sharpe had heard from Joey who'd gone down with his ship when the *Tuscania* was sunk by one of those sneaky German submarines in February, Margaret began to get cold feet, for soon it would be her turn, and there was no doubt it was scary. She had reminded herself that the Rector had declared that Fred was up there in heaven, and that was all she needed to know really, for it stood to reason that one could not be unhappy in heaven. Why bother with dragging Fred back? Then Mr Pythagoras had said in his funny deep voice: 'There's somebody here who's very cheerful with a big grin. An F, is it? Or A?'

Margaret had gone very cold. 'Alfred,' she croaked. 'My Fred.'

'He's saying something. He wants you to know he hasn't broken a single egg since he reached the other side.'

Well, that had almost finished her. She was in tears right away. It was Fred all right, making a joke about the way he used to break some of Nanny Oates' eggs when he carried them into Tunbridge Wells to sell. There was no way the medium could have known about that, was there? It proved it was Fred up there. Even so, she wasn't sure, now she'd been reassured, that she'd want to go through it again. Mrs Orvino had said they'd try the table next time, or even writing under the influence, which might not be so scary.

She had to admit the level of messages from above hadn't reached that of *Raymond*. Raymond had explained to Sir Oliver about the spheres and how those very fond of someone on earth never went too far away in the heavenly system but remained near so that they could greet you when you yourself passed over. Now, that was a lovely thought: Fred would be there grinning his silly old head off as soon as she got up to heaven.

Unfortunately everything had gone clean out of her head when she had realised Fred was actually there. She should have asked a thousand things that had since come to her, but all she had found herself blurting out was:

'Are you eating well, Fred? Keeping your strength up?'

No one in the room or even Mr Pythagoras seemed to think this was silly, so Margaret took heart, and presently the answer came back: 'Yes, but I miss your Sussex pudding, mum.'

That did it. Margaret was jelly for the rest of the evening. Fred was there even though she couldn't hug or scold him. Perhaps she'd come again, because he'd miss her if she didn't, her having made contact once. The others had been back twice already, but Margaret had two living children to think of too. Maybe she'd pop back for a word with Fred when there was good news to impart. Or would he know it already? Her lip quivered. It was hard to work out what was what up there.

On the way home she remembered what Lizzie had said about some German woman feeding Fred, and suddenly made her mind up. Unpatriotic or not, if Rector and Mrs

Lilley didn't mind – and how could they? – she'd take action. After all, she didn't want to miss her chance of meeting Fred again by being consigned to hell for passing by on the other side, like a 'Bad Samaritan'.

Next morning, she packed a basket, put on her hat and coat and boots, and set off in the bitter cold for Lake's Farm. It might be April, but that poet who wrote about blackbirds singing couldn't have had April 1918 in mind. It was colder than most Januarys, and Percy was fussing about the effects of frost on his vegetables. It was his own fault; she'd warned everyone it was a blackthorn winter, and she'd been right.

'Whatever are you doing here, ma?' Lizzie straightened up with amazement. She was looking weary and no wonder, her mother thought. It was no life for a girl digging fields in this weather, and her with a baby to look after and a convalescing husband too. Well, almost a husband. Frank was now pottering about the cottage garden, in which, with the Lakes' permission, Lizzie grew her own produce.

'I've come with some oatmeal scones for you and Frank, and–' Margaret took a deep breath and plunged – 'for that Jockey or whatever his name is.'

Lizzie grinned. 'Thanks, ma.'

'What's more, I've asked Mrs Lilley if we can offer him the odd meal with us in the servants' hall, and she's no objection. She knows one or two others, too. I wouldn't want any of them to starve.'

'You won't be popular in the village, ma. "Let 'em starve" is most people's attitude, "because we're half starving ourselves, thanks to them".'

'Then most people need educating. You leave the village to me, my girl, and get on with your digging. And you watch you don't overdo it. You're looking peaky.'

'It's not the hoeing, ma. We've had bad news. Now conscription for men up to fifty is probably coming in, Frank may have to go back.'

'Back there out East?' Margaret was aghast. 'Haven't the troops out there got some nasty germ? Influenza of some sort? They can't do that to Frank. It'll kill him.'

'We hope he'll get home duties, but you never know. He's only just forty.'

Margaret had read about this in the papers, but hadn't thought about its affecting Frank. A lot depended on when your birthday was. There was a couple of twins in the village. One born at five minutes to midnight, the other five minutes past, fifty years before the bill became law. So one brother would escape conscription because he was fifty-one, and off the other would go, probably to his death. And him with a grandchild the age of Baby Frank. There was no justice anywhere.

'Did Billy see sense?'

Caroline had stayed up waiting eagerly for Yves to return. He was very late. He had gone out to dine with Billy after his show finished at the Theatre Royal, east Stratford, in London. From there Billy had insisted on taking him to Chinatown. Limehouse, he had told Yves gloomily, was not the place it was; the war had seen to that. Dora, the Defence of the Realm Act, had banished the more esoteric and dubious amusements carried on in alleyways behind closed doors; the Food Controller had laid his bland hand on its colourful food, and though dockland was packed with seafaring humanity of every colour and race, the war had robbed them of zest and consigned them to destitution. Nevertheless Billy had managed to find a pale imitation of the old Limehouse in a back alley, which provided them with chow-chow, noodles and a fight with flying crockery, overturned tables, and ripped clothes. Billy had put an end to it by singing one of his famous songs so that he could then get on with his awabi and *ersatz* suey-sen tea.

'Never mind the food, what about Phoebe?' Caroline demanded, patience at an end.

'Good and bad news. He can easily persuade her to change to London by telling her he is committed to theatre perform-ances here.'

'And the bad?' Caroline waited, heart in mouth.

'Phoebe wasn't telling you the entire truth. Billy had insisted on seeing your father, who did not take the news well. In fact, he refused point-blank to give his consent. Billy mentioned a look of Henry Irving. Does that make sense?'

'It does.' Father had nursed a secret desire to be an actor, and unaware of what he was doing would often fall into dramatic poses in dramatic situations. If he was playing Henry Irving, Yves was right. It was bad news indeed. There would be no changing his mind. 'What happened?'

Yves took her hand. 'The wedding will go ahead, *cara*. It is as we suspected. Billy has told your father that Phoebe is to have a baby in November. He has therefore given his consent, but refused to bless the marriage or to be present. Your mother supports him, and your parents both informed Billy what they thought of him.'

'Poor Billy,' Caroline said soberly. 'I can imagine he ended up feeling like a Chinese noodle himself.'

'On the contrary. He was upset and annoyed on Phoebe's account, but as for himself, he told me that he might look a skinny runt, but he had a back as broad as the fat lady at the circus.'

Caroline tried to laugh, but failed dismally. 'What a beginning for a marriage. And what's Phoebe going to do? She can't go on working. And what about Father? And—'

'Cara.' Yves put his arm round her and pulled her to him. 'You once took a decision that raised even more questions over the future. Let us sort ours out, leave Billy and Phoebe to their own.'

'But Phoebe's so young.'

'Not any longer. War is a predator of youth.'

Georgette? Brocade? Surely for a wedding

even in a registry office one need not adhere too closely to the austerity of war, but on the other hand a formal white wedding gown for Phoebe and bridesmaid's dress for herself would look out of place, not to mention inappropriate, even if white and cream had started coming back into fashion after a year or two in abeyance at the beginning of the war. Phoebe had telephoned to say she didn't care what she wore and she'd leave it to Caroline to buy a dress for her. The wedding had been arranged for Wednesday the 17th, and Caroline had promptly panicked at this responsibility. She had telephoned to Isabel, the family's fashion consultant – or rather, she used to be. Isabel turned up trumps and insisted on coming up to superintend the purchase herself. 'After all,' Isabel had pointed out, 'you have no dress sense at all, so it's the least I can do for Phoebe.' With only two days to go before the day, there was no time for failure, and Caroline had taken leave so that the clock would not hound her.

It was not to be. Just as Caroline was about to leave to meet Isabel at Victoria, the telephone rang. It was Isabel.

'I won't be coming on the shopping trip. I'm sorry, Caroline.'

'Nothing's wrong with the baby, is it?' Caroline was alarmed at Isabel's strained voice.

A pause, then a muffled: 'No. It's Robert.'

'Oh, *Isabel.*' Tragedy struck out of the blue. You knew the odds were on its coming sooner or later, but nevertheless the shock of the telegram's arrival was undiminished. How could Isabel be so unlucky? Why now, just as she had found happiness again with Robert, and was carrying his baby? 'Is he–?' Caroline couldn't frame the word.

'No. He's missing, and you know what that means. The balloon was apparently shot down over enemy lines. He was carrying one of these parachute things, but the Germans shoot at them anyway.'

Till recently, George had told her, the Royal Flying Corps (now a new service called the Royal Air Force) had refused to provide parachutes for they were thought bad for morale. In fact, George said, the numbers of deaths on the Western Front had meant the opposite was true. But parachutes or not, that didn't mean Robert was safe, for apart from the danger of enemy planes shooting at him, often these parachutes failed to work.

'I'll come down,' Caroline said immediately, and unthinkingly.

'Don't,' Isabel replied. 'It would be hard on you, and what can you do? Besides, unless you want to change your mind about Yves and the Rectory, where would you go? I know you're thinking of me and that's enough. Besides, I don't know Robert's dead for sure,' she added brightly and unconvincingly. 'And there's lots of work to do, now that Lord Beaverbrook has formally launched the first fleet of ten cine-motor cars with his blessing. East Grinstead Council has asked my advice on the best films to show. Imagine, fifteen hundred to two thousand people can watch at once. It's a great—' Isabel's voice wobbled, then gave way, and she burst into tears. How useless telephones were when you wanted to be *with* someone, Caroline fumed, not at the end of a wire miles away.

Hearing about Robert cast a pall over the whole day. How Caroline remembered the dreary days of waiting and waiting for news from the war front. She had to force herself to don hat and coat, and make her way to Oxford Street. Perhaps it was as well she was on her own, she told herself unconvincingly, because to Isabel shopping began and ended in Bond Street, even though they still lived on Robert's salary and the pittance William Swinford-Browne paid her to run the cinema.

It proved an easier task than she'd feared, even though she marched the length of Oxford Street before she found something she thought would please Phoebe in Marshall and Snelgrove – an Empire line, lilac satin and georgette calf-length gown, and, by coincidence, an exact colour-matching hat. Caroline wondered how Mrs Hazel was faring nowadays. Once the village dressmaker would automatically have made all such dresses; now Ashden's social life no longer demanded new frocks even if the materials had been available.

For herself, Caroline chose a pale blue brocade and lace gown, also calf-length, but her satisfaction was the less without Isabel to share it. Ellen, Yves and Luke would have to be her audience. It was only on the bus she remembered she needed a hat. There would have to be yet another expedition.

She decided she would go to the office for the luxury of walking home with Yves, and to see what had been happening today, and was disappointed not to find him there.

'Where's Yves? He said he'd be here.'

'Gone.' Luke was looking harassed.

'You've missed a whole lot of signals from GHQ.'

'Gone where?' she asked blankly.

'To Queen Anne's Gate to pack, and he leaves at six. The balloon's about to go up on the Belgian Front. We've been driven off the Passchendaele Ridge, the Germans have bagged Merville and Bailleul, and good old Foch wants King Albert to release two of his precious divisions to the British. You can see him agreeing to that, can't you?'

'Then why is Yves going now?'

'Because having started fighting on the Lys, they won't stop. It's going to intensify and Yves has to be there. The Belgian army will be under pressure,' Luke explained patiently. 'What's wrong, Caroline?'

'Nothing,' she muttered. How could she say, he'll miss Wednesday's wedding, and he's a witness.

Luke looked at her thoughtfully. 'Seen the new bedroom farce at the Apollo, *Be Careful, Baby?*'

'No,' she retorted through gritted teeth. By the time she had reached home, she had forgotten Luke's warning in a swell of self-pity, made worse by Isabel's bad news. The one bright spot on her horizon had been Phoebe's wedding, and now Yves would not be at her side. She rushed up the stairs, threw her shopping boxes on the sofa, and went to find Yves. It was stupid, she knew, but she could not help herself – or keep the slight whine out of her voice, as she said, 'Luke tells me you're going to Belgium.'

'*Cara*, I have to.' He came across immediately to embrace her.

'Is there no hope you'll be here for the wedding?'

'Almost none,' he replied gently. 'The King has signalled for me to join him, and even had he not, I would believe my place to be at his side. This could be a long campaign.'

'What about *my* side?' The words were out before she could hold them back.

Yves did not reply, turning his back on her to complete his packing.

'Say something,' she shouted at his stiff back.

He swung round. 'Caroline, just like the newest conscript I *have* to go.'

'But you will return?' She began to panic.

He misunderstood. 'I have told you, there is little chance.'

Desperately she sought reassurance. 'But sometime you will?'

'What do you mean?' He stared at her blankly.

'You won't decide your place is already at your wife's side?' she blurted out. 'You promised *me*,' she added childishly, when he said nothing. 'To the end of the war.'

'I did, but now I doubt if it was wise. Perhaps your father knew best.'

'No,' she cried in anguish. 'I *chose*. You chose.'

Yves made a visible effort to speak calmly. '*Cara*, this is not the time, nor the place for us to quarrel or to discuss this. I will return when I can and that is all I can say.'

She watched him finishing his packing, wanting to put matters right, to admit she'd been in the wrong, but she couldn't do it. She couldn't even believe that she was. She wanted to yell at him: if you feel so lukewarm, don't bother to come back. Go back to *her*. She managed to restrain herself, but no other words replaced them. He departed without saying anything more, after one kiss on her unresponsive mouth, and even that he hesitated before bestowing on her. His lips were as cold as ice.

When he had gone, she found herself numb with terror, unable even to cry, and in the following days she threw herself into work, seizing on GHQ situation reports as avidly as if by doing so she was helping Yves.

How could she be so sensible where other people's relationships were concerned and so silly over her own?

'What's wrong with you?' Luke finally asked. 'I may not be Yves, but there's no need to snap my head off every two minutes.'

She apologised and instead exploded her frustration to Ellen at lunchtime. Only to a woman could she explain with any hope of understanding what a mess she had made of the last few weeks. Or so she had fondly thought.

Typically, Ellen dismissed her problem over Yves as of no account. She had no romantic problems of her own, having just become engaged to a soldier on Defence of London duties, and couldn't comprehend others' dilemmas. 'He'll be back,' she informed Caroline matter-of-factly. 'Who's going to be the other witness, if Yves isn't back?'

'I don't know. I hadn't thought about that, but I suppose I could ask. Phoebe's only got a 48-hour pass, and then has to go back for another three weeks before she can leave permanently because of the baby.'

'Why don't you ask Isabel?'

'Surely that's the last thing Isabel would

want to do with her own husband still missing.'

'You underestimate her, Caroline.'

'Do I?' Caroline considered this. Perhaps sometimes she did. 'All right, I'll ask her.'

By the time Caroline had left work that evening, she was feeling almost cheerful again. When she got home, Isabel would already be installed, and Ellen fussing over her like another Mrs Dibble. She was amazed to find when she arrived that Isabel was in no need of fussing at all. She was bright-faced, happy and laughing.

'Caroline,' she shrieked, leaping up to greet her, 'Robert's *safe*.'

'Isabel, that's wonderful news. Was he injured?'

'I don't know. He's a prisoner of war in Germany, that's why we didn't hear at once. Isn't it marvellous that he's not dead?'

'Yes.' Being a prisoner of war was bad enough, but infinitely preferable to Isabel losing him altogether.

'Now I shall really enjoy the wedding,' Isabel continued, 'and I'll never be unhappy again. I even felt young Master or Miss Swinford-Browne inside me give a kick of pleasure on the way up to this flat. If I ever find myself getting miserable again, I'll just remember this glorious moment.'

'Come and inspect the dresses.' Caroline dragged her into her bedroom where Isabel proceeded to tell her exactly what was wrong with her choice, though ending up with a gracious: 'I suppose they could have been worse.'

'Please, God,' Caroline prayed that night, 'let some of Isabel's good fortune rub off on Phoebe and Billy. And if there's any left over–' though she hardly dared ask – 'on Yves and on me.' For the first time since Christmas, she felt that the cloud of bitterness that had blurred her faith was lifting just a little.

The unseasonably bitter cold month of April turned up trumps, thank goodness, and produced a sunny, if still chilly, day for Phoebe's wedding. Perversely, Caroline woke up that morning not thinking of Phoebe's happiness or Isabel's good news, but of Father and Mother, and how sad it was that they would be missing the wedding. Felicia had declared her intention of getting up to London by hook or by crook, even though she was now working at Ashden Manor, and with George away, that meant her parents would be at home alone.

Caroline's heart ached for them. Their hearts were so warm, and their standards so rigid. She decided then to put all thoughts of them out of her mind. It was Phoebe's day, and Phoebe, as had she, had made her own decision. Caroline had to come not only to like Billy but to understand what Phoebe saw in him. At the Marylebone registry office, he looked as proud and pleased as punch – and about as handsome, his future sister-in-law thought irreverently. Even Isabel reluctantly conceded that the lilac dress suited Phoebe, although perhaps her happiness would have shone out over a dress made of dish rags. The Rectory ugly duckling had become a swan at last.

Phoebe's wedding day was a memorable one for other reasons. Luke had worked late into the night after the wedding, and unable to sleep with excitement, Caroline got up to make him and herself cocoa.

He flung himself down on the sofa. 'It's begun,' he told her. 'The Germans attacked in force on the railway line from Ypres to Thourout, and over-ran the Belgian front line.'

Caroline felt dizzy with shock. It was too

much, coming after today's happiness.

'Yves?' she asked stupidly.

'No word yet, but the news gets better. The artillery and the reserves – those that Foch wanted to pinch – recaptured the entire lost ground and took six hundred prisoners.'

She clapped her hands in delight. 'So it's over?'

'Far from it. This is only the beginning of Armageddon.'

Three days later came the next major attack on the Belgian front. Once again the enemy gained ground, and once again they were driven back in a counter-attack into which, so reports said, the Belgians went singing, and 'fought like men possessed', so determined were they to recapture their homeland.

And at last they heard from Yves. Just her luck – Caroline was out of the office when the precious telephone call came through. All Luke could talk about when she returned was how successful the British attack on Zeebrugge had been, and how it was now known that the Belgian army had saved the British in the Ypres salient by foiling a German plan to encircle them.

'Did he mention me?' Caroline asked

hopefully, when Luke at last shut up.

'He sent you his love.'

'But no word of when he'll be back?'

'No.'

Seven

'Can't call this place my own, nowadays,' Margaret grumbled. 'I feel that Food Controller breathing down my neck all the time. And to think it's May Day too. Once upon a time the lasses would be out in the fields dabbling in the dew and hoping for a sweetheart. Now they're dressed up in big boots and uniforms pretending to be soldiers.'

'Times are changing,' Percy remarked without originality. It was his – and most other folks' – response to everything.

'Then not for the better. I can't keep up and that's a fact.'

'Yes, you do,' Percy replied sturdily. 'You keep up marvellously, Daisy.'

It was a sign of approval when Percy called her Daisy. Margaret was gratified, but not going to show it.

'Maybe I do, but what good is one and eight pence a head of beef a week?'

'At least you know where you are.' They had had this conversation over and over again, and both knew what they were really grumbling about was this miserable spring weather and the renewed prospect of war going on for ever. The Germans might have been stopped before Amiens but no one kidded themselves they'd leave it at that.

'And there's Oscar,' Percy added in his usual triumphant finale.

Always Oscar. The whole of England was full of Oscars, all waiting their turn. Once you could tell the time by Farmer Sharpe's roosters crowing so loud they drowned the birds. Now they could hear the birds all too clearly. Someone had told her that over in France they actually ate poor little song thrushes. How could they do it? In the midst of war, to hear the song thrush sing was a sign that somewhere out there was something called hope. She remembered one song thrush whose wing Fred had healed; he had made a lovely carving of it in wood. It didn't sing of course, but then she didn't either.

It was gloomy in the Rectory for all Mrs Lilley tried to keep smiling, and that was hard enough when you couldn't even go to your own daughter's wedding. Although Mrs Lilley had said it was the principle that counted, Margaret could tell how much she wished she were there. She'd heard her telephone Miss Phoebe in London the night before the wedding, when Rector was at evensong.

Margaret hadn't been able to believe her ears when Mrs Isabel had told her Miss Phoebe was going to be married. It didn't seem two shakes since she was climbing the apple trees in the orchard, and the harum-scarum attitude she took to clothes and cooking didn't bode well for her being in charge of her own house. She couldn't run a game of snakes and ladders. Still, everyone grew up and in wartime they did it twice as fast.

'Tell you what, Daisy. Let's go to the pictures tonight, after you've dished up supper. It will cheer you up.'

'What's on?' Margaret asked cautiously. She didn't want to find herself watching *The Battle of the Ancre*. The one on the Somme had been enough for her.

'*The Prisoner of Zenda*, and one of them Pearl White adventures, *The Perils of Pauline*.'

Margaret deliberated. At first she'd thought *The Prisoner of Zenda* was a war film, until she remembered there was a romantic book she'd read once of that

190

name. She could do with a bit of romance. 'All right then. Mrs Isabel would like it if we went. She was saying that only this morning. Now the wedding's over she's down in the dumps again.'

As soon as Mrs Isabel had got home from the wedding two weeks ago, she had come straight into the kitchen to tell her about it. Margaret had been torn between being appalled at Mrs Isabel going to London in her condition, and secret pleasure that she was the first to hear about it, even if she couldn't be providing the wedding breakfast as she would if it were a proper wedding.

'Does Rector know you went?'

'Officially no, but Mother did – and I'm sure she'll tell him. It was such a lovely day.'

Mrs Isabel needed a lovely day or two in Margaret's opinion. She was doing too much, and despite her relief at finding out Mr Robert was alive, knowing he was a prisoner of war must make her anxious. There was no knowing if he was getting enough – or anything – to eat, and it made Margaret feel all the better that she had taken the initiative about feeding Joachim. She had to admit he and his chums were well behaved for Germans, and it turned out they knew all about rectories and what was expected in them. She wondered what life was like in Germany, and if it was as hard as it was here nowadays. She couldn't believe it was, because they had occupied all those other countries, and pinched all their food. If they *were* short, however, their POWs would be suffering just like Joachim.

'Phoebe looked beautiful,' Mrs Isabel said. 'Caroline did well in choosing the dress, even though I wasn't there. I was afraid Phoebe would pick some awful khaki or grey thing just because they're fashionable, but lilac suited her. I took some photographs so I'll show you them when they're developed.'

'What happens in those registry office weddings?'

'They had a similar service.'

Margaret sniffed. 'Without God? He wasn't a witness, was He?'

'I think He was there,' Isabel replied seriously. 'If you could have seen how happy Phoebe and Billy were, you'd think so too. I remembered my own wedding. When Robert comes home...' she managed to laugh, 'whenever that will be, I won't be a young bride any more. I'll be a middle-aged matronly mother.'

'Not you, Mrs Isabel,' Margaret said

comfortingly. 'You'll stay the same whatever age you are. Some folks start out life old, and some stay young. You're one of the latter.'

'Oh, Mrs Dibble, what a comfort you are. I could kiss you for saying that. In fact, I think I will.' She jumped up, planted a kiss on Margaret's suddenly pink cheek, and sat down again. 'Anyway, after the wedding, we went to the Carlton Hotel and had a really nice afternoon. There were only about twenty or so of us. Patricia Swinford-Browne was there, which was nice. You should see her now. She makes a terrifying policewoman. I don't think any man would dare marry her, she's so forceful. Billy didn't want the London stage folk present, so there was just his family. He sang love-songs to Phoebe, and then at the end Phoebe said she wanted to sing a song to him.'

'But Miss Phoebe has a voice like a corncrake.'

'It didn't matter, she sang "I'll walk beside you", in a sort of half-speaking, half-singing voice, and Billy nearly cried with happiness. I do like him, Mrs Dibble, and I'm sure Father and Mother would if only things were different.'

'If all the if-onlys in the world came true—'

Margaret began.

'I know,' Isabel finished for her, 'Oscar would be flying.'

'Elizabeth?' Laurence came into the glory-hole unexpectedly to find his wife in tears. 'What's the matter?'

'Nothing, Laurence.' She blew her nose and sat up straight. 'It's only Isabel's photographs of the wedding.'

'Ah.' Laurence looked at them lying on Elizabeth's littered table, slowly his hand stretched out to pick them up, and his heart wrenched as he saw his daughter clutching Billy's arm, smiling up at him.

'She looks lovely, doesn't she?'

'Yes.' Laurence put the photograph down and pulled up a chair to Elizabeth's side, a difficult manoeuvre in the glory-hole. He took her hands in his. 'What else could I do?' he asked quietly.

'What else could *we* do? Were we wrong not to go?'

'On balance no, but balancing is hard. I couldn't withhold my consent, when there is the coming child to consider, but to have attended when I've upheld the indissolubility of marriage all my life would have been hypocritical.'

'And for me too. And yet... *Why* are these decisions so difficult?'

'I suppose because God did not promise us an easy path out of Eden.'

'What shall we do now, though? Surely this doesn't mean we'll never see them again? That's too cruel, and you liked Mr Jones.'

'*Like?*' Laurence fired up. 'How can I *like* a man who seduces an under-age girl?'

'She loves him. As Caroline loves Captain Rosier.'

'That is not enough, and you agreed with me.'

'And suppose I've changed my mind? Suppose it is enough for me? Answer me, Laurence,' Elizabeth said sharply, when he did not speak. 'War is cruel enough. Do we have to make it worse?'

'We cannot sanction unions unblessed by God under the Rectory roof.'

'Under their roof, then? Can we not at least visit them?'

Laurence did not reply immediately, and when he did his voice was drained. 'I don't know, and if God does, then He hasn't yet shown me the answer.'

'You are hard, Laurence.'

He raised his face full of agony to her. 'Do

you think this is easy for me?'

'You really must do something about your clothes, Felicia.' When her sister did not reply, Isabel added, 'I'm not just being big-sisterish, I *mean* it. Agnes can help.' Then it dawned on her that Felicia was looking very peaky again. 'Are you sickening for something?' she demanded.

'I'm just tired.' Felicia sat in the chair by her bedroom window, while Isabel continued to rummage through her wardrobe, as self-appointed fashion expert of the household. 'Nearly all of these could go straight to Mother's glory-hole for needy causes.'

'*I'm* a needy cause,' Felicia answered, with a glimmer of humour.

Isabel took her seriously. 'I can help you. After all, you can afford it with your wages. Why don't we go on a shopping expedition to Tunbridge Wells?' She grimaced, picking up an ancient dinner gown with distaste. 'I remember this from before the war.'

'Myrtle shortened it for me.'

'I suppose you didn't have the nerve to ask Agnes.' Isabel inspected the hem. 'She'd have consigned it to the rag-bag straight away. Shall we go to the Wells?'

'No.'

'Why not?' Isabel asked indignantly.

'Partly because you are having a baby and partly because I might as well get them in London.'

'*London?*' Slowly it began to dawn on Isabel that something really was wrong.

'I've been asked to leave Ashden Manor,' Felicia continued.

Isabel stared at her in disbelief. 'But they are so proud to have you.'

'The matron isn't. It's my fault, I suppose. Daniel warned me it would happen, if I wasn't diplomatic. I've become so used to doing things my way, and though I tried to adapt I can't have succeeded. Matron and I didn't see eye to eye.'

'Surely it will blow over.'

'*It* may, but I won't. I've decided what I'm going to do. If I stay here I shall feel honour-bound to help Mother with the agricultural rotas, not my forte at all. So I'm going to London to join Tilly at Red Cross HQ until I'm completely fit and then I'll go back to the Front.'

'What?' Isabel burst into tears. 'Oh, but you can't. I'll be all on my own here again and with the baby coming.'

'You'll be fully occupied, Bella, and you'll

have Mother to help,' Felicia said quietly.

'No one calls me Bella but you,' Isabel sobbed. 'I don't want to lose you now. Couldn't you take over the cinema while I'm having the baby? You'd be much better than Beatrice Ryde.'

Felicia grinned. 'No, darling, but thank you for your confidence in me. Anyway, you're not losing me, I'm just going to work away from the Rectory again. Trains aren't being abolished. I can come to visit you. And when the war ends–'

'What will you do then?' Isabel interrupted crossly. 'Assuming the Kaiser isn't giving you your orders by then – sorry, defeatist talk. All the same, this is *May*, and we should be out making merry. Instead it's the gloomiest month I can remember. The grass is green, the crops are growing, but on and on goes this beastly war.' Isabel suddenly realised that Felicia had not yet answered her question.

'Oh, of course, you'll get married,' she continued. 'Will it be Daniel or Luke? Do tell.'

Felicia burst out laughing. 'Even if I had plans to marry either of them, which I don't, it still wouldn't answer your question. Marriage isn't the automatic alternative to giving up nursing.'

'But if you went on nursing, you'd just have a series of matrons each more formidable than the last.'

'Eventually I'd become a matron myself, you see. That's a temptation.'

'You're joking,' Isabel said suspiciously.

'Perhaps.'

'When are you leaving?'

'I'll stay here till Whitsun on 19th May. And don't worry. I can always come down to deliver the baby if Mrs Hay isn't about.'

Isabel laughed. 'Now I know you're joking. That's something you *can't* have had experience of on the front line.'

'You are wrong,' Felicia replied with dignity. 'There is a pair of twins called Felix and Félicie in a small French village who owe their existence to me.'

'Was Luke or Daniel the father?'

'Very amusing. I *delivered* them.'

A party would take her mind off the gloom everywhere. Margaret was pleased. Besides her, it would cheer the Rectory up. Easter had passed in a gloomy state, despite a bit of lamb on the table, but it didn't seem the same. Easter had been on the early side this year, and thanks to the cold weather, there

199

weren't even enough primroses around for the primrose pie, and they'd had to make do with Sussex pudding. But Whitsun would be a different matter. As luck would have it, Miss Felicia had to be on duty even on her last day at Ashden Manor, and wouldn't be home until seven o'clock, leaving precious little time for a family party, but nevertheless there would be a nice little gathering. Mrs Isabel, Mr Daniel, Lady Hunney, Lady Buckford, and the Rector's brother and his wife who would be staying for the weekend, and there was talk of Master George being home on leave.

Nanny Oates would be hobbling over from her cottage, of that Margaret was quite sure. Catch Nanny missing out on her exalted place at the table. She and Nanny Oates had never got on, though they tolerated each other now.

Margaret had to admit she was a game old bird; she'd recovered from her stroke and had taken up selling her eggs again for the war effort. That wasn't bad for an old lady in her eighties. She'd even volunteered to donate Queen Berengaria for the party – her chickens were all named after queens of England – and Rector had accepted gratefully. Margaret kept to herself her suspicion that Berengaria's laying days were over, and that was why Nanny was ready to sacrifice her. Lady Hunney was donating a nice fattened capon, and two bottles of wine from the cellar. Her ladyship liked Miss Felicia which was more than she did poor Miss Caroline, and Margaret often speculated as to whether she thought Miss Felicia (now she was famous) would make Mr Daniel a nice wife. Miss Felicia didn't seem in no hurry to wed, though. Yes, a party was to be looked forward to, even though no party could be complete without Miss Caroline.

In Ashden the fields would be green, the hedgerows full of bluebells, the orchard gleaming pink with apple blossom. Even the Kaiser couldn't stop that. London had its trees and flowers too, even with war restrictions, but it was not like Ashden where flowers grew to their own rules, not to ordered precision. May was a time for lovers to wander in the twilight with birds singing their spring songs, but where was hers? Caroline had not spoken to Yves, and indeed nor had Luke, and considering the pressure on the London-La Panne line it was hardly surprising. She had received several brief notes from Yves, however – much to her relief. They were, she knew, more than she deserved.

Work and more work stared her in the face daily. Luke was often away, and the daily train-watching reports from La Dame Blanche grew longer – a probable sign of the expected next push forward by the Germans.

'I wonder if Ludendorff is playing a game with us,' Luke complained, pushing a report over to her. 'Look at this. Two divisions going not to Ypres but to Laon in the French sector.'

'Do you think it's to deceive us?'

'That's what the French believe.' Luke sighed. 'They always do. We receive intelligence, we share it with them, and they won't believe it because it doesn't come from *their* intelligence service.'

'Yet it seems odd. They pushed so far ahead further north that surely they would try there again, not on the eastern French sector.'

'No,' Luke replied. 'I think it all too likely after Amiens that they're going for the River Marne in the east where they were so nearly successful in 1914.'

'To take Paris?'

'It's the key to France. Why not one more go?'

'The American situation is a factor.' Last month Haig had issued his special order of the day urging the troops to fight to the end 'with our backs to the wall'. Conscription had been extended to Ireland, and the age increased to fifty. Such was the shortage of men on the front and the dire emergency facing them that even Pershing had relented and offered some more of his precious troops to the Allied command.

'Fortunately Pershing's long-term intentions are as much of a mystery to Ludendorff as they are to us.' Luke changed the subject. 'What are you going to do for Whitsun?'

Caroline's stomach lurched. Isabel had let the cat out of the bag about the party. 'There's still a week to go to the 19th. I'm hoping Yves will be back.' At least she could celebrate it somehow.

'You're not going to the Rectory?'

'How can I?' Caroline asked wretchedly. 'Whether Yves is here or not makes no difference really. The position is the same.' A thought struck her. 'Are you going?'

'No. Daniel's going. There'll be plenty of chances for me to see her when she comes up to London, so I'm doing the gentlemanly thing and giving him a clear field.'

'I don't think Daniel would recognise a clear field, he seems determined to muddy it for himself.'

'I can't say I object to that.'

'No.' How complicated life was. Caroline decided she should shut her mind to the Rectory party and try to enjoy Whitsun in London. After all, Tilly and Penelope were in London. Ellen too might be at a loose end. And Luke would be here. She began to cheer up, although she returned home tired after a solid day of reports that produced nothing of excitement but merely contributed to the confused picture of where German reinforcements were building up. All in all, Luke was right. The French lines in the east were the destination of most of the reinforcements, who were new recruits from Germany. Any vestige of rising spirits was promptly dampened by Ellen's cheerful announcement: 'I'm going to see my folks at Whitsun. You can take over the cooking.'

'A woman's place,' Caroline muttered savagely. Now she'd have to battle with queues at the Maypole Dairy and the ever-running campaign of attrition at the butcher's. Rationing worked well, but you still had to queue and battle for the best. Ah well, perhaps London would be at least slightly in holiday mood. The lights had not dimmed for over two months now in London – this was another form of air raid warning to take cover in the underground railway tunnels or house cellars.

'Telephone call for you,' Ellen sang out.

Caroline ran into their living-room. 'Probably a wrong number,' she said gloomily.

But it wasn't. It was the first time she had heard her mother's voice since her visit to Ashden Hospital, three months ago. 'Caroline,' was all she said; her voice hesitant but warm.

Tears pricked at her eyes. Say something, she told herself. *Anything.* But she seemed frozen, and managed only a croak of 'Mother'.

'Caroline, do come to the party on Sunday evening. George is coming home on leave. We thought if you came down with Phoebe – that's if Billy and Yves don't mind not coming–' Her mother's voice dropped as if even she realised how impossible was her request.

'Mother, I can't,' Caroline stammered. 'I'll ask Phoebe, but I don't imagine she would come either under that condition.' She found herself choking. 'I'm sorry.'

A sigh, a 'We love you, Caroline,' and the telephone receiver was hung up.

Caroline promptly burst into tears. How could she go? She couldn't, and that was that.

'Bad news?' Ellen asked worriedly.

'No. The old problem again.'

'Families! Come on, let's go out on the town.'

At twelve o'clock that Friday night, Caroline's bedroom door opened. Always a light sleeper she turned over. 'Ellen?' she asked sleepily, then sensing it was a man, sat bolt upright. 'Luke, what's wrong?'

'Not Luke,' said a familiar voice.

'Yves!' she screamed, throwing aside the bedclothes and scrambling out. His arms enfolded her and swung her round. She could feel the buttons on his uniform pressing through her thin nightdress. He was really back and it was *all right*. 'Oh, it's going to be a wonderful Whitsun,' she cried.

Margaret carefully turned the jelly out of the pineapple mould. Miss Felicia always liked jelly, and jelly she should have, even if pineapples were a thing of the past. Even

Lady Buckford seemed in good form this evening, perhaps because his lordship, her eldest son, was here with his wife. There was another son too, Margaret had gathered, though Gerald was never spoken of, for to Lady Buckford he was even more of a black sheep than the Rector. He'd gone to America, and no one heard from him now. Families were funny things. Lady Buckford was even making the odd joke this evening, even if her idea of a joke was rarely shared by anyone else. Nanny wasn't pleased to see Lady Buckford, for they'd crossed too many swords in their time when she was Rector's nanny, but just for tonight it seemed they'd buried the hatchet. At the session in Tunbridge Wells yesterday, Fred had assured her they would have a lovely party this evening, and if Fred said so, who was she to disbelieve him?

Miss Felicia looked nice in her old blue; it had always suited her, and now it was shorter it was almost unrecognisable, especially since she'd had her hair cut. Margaret didn't approve of all this modern styling, and Miss Felicia's lovely long hair was a real loss. Still, she understood it was necessary, what with her work on the Front – no time for rosemary shampoos there. It was nice to see everyone dressed properly for dinner tonight. Mostly the family ate at separate times now and didn't bother to dress. She'd almost forgotten what a handsome figure the Rector cut in his dinner suit, and Mrs Lilley had gone to some trouble with her red velvet. Even Lady Buckford had put her tiara on and pearl choker. After all, Miss Felicia was a somebody, and Mrs Isabel had persuaded her to put on her Order of Prince Leopold, which she and Miss Tilly had been awarded by King Albert of Belgium. Mr Daniel was looking handsome too, bless him, and when she carried in the roast he was joking away with Miss Felicia in a way she hadn't seen for many a year. Lady Hunney and Lady Buckford were engaged in telling stories of the Rector and Daniel as children, and the Rector and his brother were deep in conversation. When she returned to clear the dishes and take in the pudding, Mrs Isabel was animatedly telling Master George about the success of the cine-motor campaign, and his cartoon film in particular.

'Half a million people have seen them now,' Isabel was crowing.

'I wish I had a penny from each of them,'

George grumbled. 'Not one did I get.'

'Scrooge,' declared his sister, and quite right too, in Margaret's view. 'Don't you love your country?'

'Not half as much as Mrs Dibble's puddings.' George attacked the jelly eagerly.

'That's Miss Felicia's,' Margaret said, shocked, before she remembered her place.

'Let Scrooge have it,' Felicia said.

'Now I can tell a tale or two about Rector and jelly,' Nanny Oates chipped in.

Margaret gave a mental sniff and retired from the room. She had better things to do than listen to Nanny rabbiting on for hours.

'All going well in there?' Percy looked up from his evening paper when she reached the kitchen.

Margaret sighed, suddenly she felt very weary. 'Yes. It's not going to be the same, is it, without Miss Felicia? Having Master George home makes you realise how much you miss him.' She yawned. 'You know, Percy, for once I'm going to let Agnes and Myrtle do the washing up, and go to bed after I've taken in the coffee.'

Myrtle could manage the dishes, even if Agnes was tucked up in bed. She only had a month or so to go now, before the little one was due, otherwise Margaret wouldn't be called upon to do so much of the waiting. The time was getting on anyway. It was gone ten-thirty, and past her usual bedtime. Tomorrow might be a bank holiday, but food still had to be thought of.

'Good idea, Margaret. You mind yourself. You're not as young as you were.'

Margaret saw red. 'Oh yes, I am, Percy Dibble,' she snapped right back. She pursed her lips. She'd donated her final bottle of last year's plums for that jelly, and no one was going to bear out the remains but her. She forgot about bed, and half an hour later she was still up. After all, there was only one more job to do.

'Just in time, Mrs Dibble,' Isabel called, as she took in the coffee – if you could call it that now. 'You can join in the loyal toast.'

Everyone looked flushed and happy, and Margaret didn't want to spoil the fun. 'I don't mind giving King George V a toast, Mrs Isabel. Nothing alcoholic, mind.'

'Of course not.' The Rector sounded shocked, but she could see he was grinning. All right, so he thought her temperance was funny, but say what you like, it was God who made water, sugar, and the grape, and only man who worked out how to make alcohol from them.

'It isn't the King, Mrs Dibble.'

'Who then?'

Mrs Isabel stood up. 'On this lovely evening,' she said, 'there can be only one toast: *Absent hearts!*' She looked round the table. 'Robert in Germany, Caroline and Phoebe in London, and dear ones no longer with us: Fred Dibble and Reggie Hunney.'

Margaret through a sort of blur could see Mrs Lilley trying to hold back tears and failing. The Rector rose to the occasion though. 'Absent hearts,' he repeated quietly, 'but always present in ours.'

Margaret carefully did up her hair in its rags, for all her tiredness. After all, one had to face one's Maker in a proper way on Monday morning no matter what a mess you felt the night before. She smeared on her hand cream (her mother's recipe of lemon, glycerine and eau-de-cologne), said her prayers, asked after Fred, who'd been right about its being a lovely party, sought forgiveness for tonight's nasty thoughts about Nanny Oates, and climbed gratefully into bed. There was no point waiting for Percy since he had to lock up after everyone had gone.

Margaret fell asleep, still planning tomorrow's apple pudding from her bottled apples, and the bit of suet she'd forced out of that miserly Wally Bertram. Suddenly the pudding exploded all round her, the ground was rocking, and she seemed trapped in bits of apple and crust. She realised she must be awake again. Or was she? Everything was spinning round her, it was cold with a wind blowing, and her hand was red with blood. No, it couldn't be blood, surely. There was broken glass on the bed though, and a stifling acrid smell. This must be a nightmare, for there was a dead silence like the end of the world had come; it lasted forever, it lasted no time at all, and then came the screams.

The whole of 'out there' seemed to be screaming. She licked the blood off her hand, and found it was real, and therefore *the screams were too.*

Margaret's brain cleared and she went straight into action. There was no sign of Percy, no light in their quarters, and she couldn't stop to find him. The screams were outside, no, inside; even from here she could hear pounding feet in the Rectory as she rushed through, not even stopping for a dressing gown, just her slippers, into the kitchen. There was broken crockery all over the floor, but one lamp was still lit. In its dull glow she could see Myrtle crouched down, her arms round her head, moaning. Where was Percy? Fear hammered at her in this alien place. And then she saw him, in the doorway, just lying there groaning.

'Get up, Percy,' she croaked, as she ran into the Rectory hall.

The front door was wide open, the wind and dirt blowing in, and through it she could hear the screaming. Outside, in the garden, was it? Or further, on Bankside? She could see Miss Felicia running down the drive and the Rector after her. Mrs Lilley, rushing downstairs in her dressing gown, fell into Margaret's arms at the bottom.

'Isabel, George,' she was babbling. 'They took Nanny home.'

Margaret tried to make sense of this. Something had happened. She'd no proper shoes on, she'd no torch. If she was to do any good out there – whatever it was – she needed both. She ran back to the kitchen to find her old snow shoes, and found a dazed Percy was clambering to his feet.

'The barometer,' he said jerkily. It was lying in the hall, she'd noticed, and must have fallen on his head. Percy would be no use. It was up to her. Margaret threw one of the Rector's coats over her dressing gown and ran after the Rector. There was no sign of Mrs Lilley.

Once outside, she saw the whole of Bankside seemed to be aglow, but it was a different shape somehow, and figures were silhouetted against the reddish light. Still, the screams. She could hear Joe Ifield's voice yelling to make way for the ambulance. Ambulance? What had happened? Someone caught in the fire? She could now see that half of Bankside seemed to have disappeared, but then she stopped thinking at all, as she plunged through the crowd to add her authority to Joe's and the Rector's, wherever he was. Order was needed here, and there she could help, as stretchers were lifted into the ambulance, and the crashing of wood gave place to moans. The ambulance was moving off, and out of the blackness the Rector was running in her direction, following the vehicle. His face streamed with blood, covered with dust, he staggered into her, so hard she had to put her arms round him to support them both.

'Isabel,' he moaned.

'Hurt?' Margaret asked sharply. Miss Felicia could help, wherever she was, and maybe she could give a hand too.

The Rector's reply was a howl of grief, but the words were quite distinct.

'She's dead.'

Eight

Not tonight of all nights. It was Whitsun and tomorrow was a holiday – or was it already today? Whatever time was it? The telephone bell was ringing and ringing insistently.

'If that's C,' Caroline hissed to Yves, 'tell him the operator has the wrong number.' A call in the middle of the night could only mean a top-level call from the SSB; she supposed she had no right to grumble because it was only due to the need for Yves and Luke to be reached at all times from all places that the stingy secret service had provided them with a telephone at all at Queen Anne's Gate. Caroline glanced sleepily at the clock; half past one, and they had not long been in bed, thanks to the air raid.

'I'll go.' Yves was already up and disappearing through the door. Caroline comforted herself that the call could not be for her, for C would hardly be calling the office clerk. Unless – sudden fear made her sit bolt upright in bed, for the night brought nightmares to the semi-wakeful as well as the sleeping – it was bad news for one of them. George, it could be about *George*. She battled to remember whether Mother had really told her George was on leave, and sent up a fervent prayer to wish him safe at Ashden. She could hear her heart thumping, as she sat up in bed waiting for Yves to return. If she lay down, the nightmares would intensify.

At last she heard the murmur of voices, so Ellen or Luke must have jumped up too. She realised she was shivering, although the May night was warm. Surely Yves wasn't being recalled to Belgium so soon? Perhaps it was a call from King Albert, or from GHQ to say that Ludendorff's expected new offensive had begun.

'Come back, Yves,' she muttered, thumping the pillow, 'come *back*.' It was too much, after the noise and disruption of the air raid. It had been an attack in force from the sound of it, and so bright was the waxing moon last evening, she supposed they should have expected it. There had been no raids on London for some time now, however, and everyone had relaxed, believing that the Germans were reserving their bomb power for the Western Front. Then just

before eleven thirty, while they were preparing for bed, came the familiar dimming
of the lights, and the sound of the maroons.
Instead of the luxury of her first full night of
reunion with Yves, they had been in the
basement sheltering while the searchlights
flashed over their limited view of the sky.
Although the aircraft approached silently
now, once overhead the noise was formidable. They stayed there for an hour and a
half before they deemed it safe to return to
bed. And now *this*.

Perhaps it was bad news from Simon's
house. Tilly? Penelope? Caroline's imagination ran riot until at last she heard Yves open
their door. She lit the oil lamp at her side,
rather than turn on the electric light, and in
its eerie glow it seemed to her his face
looked very pale. He sat down by her on the
edge of the bed, rather than returning to her
side under the bedclothes, and she waited
with apprehension.

'What is it?' she whispered. It was not just
the effect of the oil lamp, Yves' face was pale
with shock. 'Do you have to leave again?'

'No. *Cara*, it is terrible news from Ashden.'

'George! It's George, isn't it? He wasn't on
leave. He's been shot down, he's dead? I
must go.' She pushed the bedclothes aside

to move, until he gently restrained her.

'No, my love, it is not George. He was on leave, and was injured, but he is alive. It is Isabel–' his voice broke – 'who has died.'

'Isabel?' Caroline stared at him. His words didn't make sense. 'The baby, you mean? She's had a miscarriage?'

There were tears in his eyes. 'No, the baby too. Both dead. A Gotha must have lost his direction home in the battle with our aircraft, and probably had a hung-up bomb. It fell on Ashden.'

Caroline began to shiver violently. This was all part of her nightmare, wasn't it? It couldn't be *true!* Air raids didn't affect villages like Ashden. She doubted if the village had ever seen a Gotha, it was rare enough to see our own aircraft. Isabel dead, Isabel *dead*, she forced her brain to repeat over and over again, but it still wasn't real. Isabel bouncing into her bedroom, crying, 'Caroline, can I borrow Granny Overton's jet? Darling, I simply must have the jet,' Isabel marrying Robert, Isabel so proudly at the cinema, Isabel's 'I'll never be unhappy again'. Those were real. Bright images of life raced through her mind. The word dead, and remembering Robert in his POW camp, not knowing he had lost both wife and baby

– those were for later.

'Felicia?' she asked jerkily. 'Mother? Father? Everyone else in the Rectory?'

'No one else in the Rectory was seriously hurt, and the Rectory suffered only broken glass and damage to the front door when it was blown in. The bomb fell on Bankside. Your sister was not the only victim.'

It still didn't make sense. What could Isabel have been doing out at that time of night? It didn't matter. What mattered was that she was needed at the Rectory.

'I must go immediately.' She swung her legs to the floor, but Yves restrained her.

'We'll both go by the first train. I have checked and there is none till seven o'clock. Luke will remain in the office, and I will return in the evening, so that he may come down if Felicia wishes.'

Details flowed on through her head without registering, taking on a soothing quality, a stick to grasp in a drowning nightmare. Only one was important. 'There is one task for you, beloved,' Yves said. 'Felicia asked if you could tell Phoebe. Felicia was telephoning from Ashden hospital, and is needed there. Then you must rest to gather your strength.'

Rest? The night would be an endless vigil

until they walked to Victoria to return home to the Rectory.

What terrible places railway termini were. Yves had briefly deserted her to buy tickets, and all around were reunions and partings, tears and laughter, servicemen returning from Whitsun leave, preparing to go back to the Front, and brothers, sisters, wives, parents, sweethearts dispersing after having said goodbye to their loved ones. In the middle of it all stood Caroline Lilley with a lump like lead in her stomach. It felt so heavy it was as if she had only to give it the slightest push and off it would roll, so that she would realise it wasn't true after all.

The train crawled interminably to East Grinstead, and then even more slowly through Hartfield towards Ashden. As they stepped down from the train, the lump of lead inside her dissolved and spread all over her, numbing her. Even at the station, the pall of disaster was heavy in the air, reflected in the pallor and silence of those around them. Through the open door of the booking office Caroline could see Station Road, stretching out into the distance. Once it was a joyful path to tread, but not today.

How could the birds still sing? How could

the hedgerows still flower in their spring glory, when such tragedy had hit the village? Not everything looked the same in Station Road, however. There was more motor traffic going in and out of The Towers than she had ever seen before. Lorries, wagons, staff cars, all fully laden. As Caroline and Yves reached The Towers, they stopped to allow one lorry through the gates. Poking over the side was a grandfather clock, one she recognised.

'Nanny Oates too?' Caroline asked Yves, stunned into fresh horror.

'Yes, *cara*.'

'What are they doing with her clock?' she choked.

'Possessions have to be removed to prevent looting and to clear debris from the buildings.'

Looting happened in Belgium, France and other far-off places. But *here* in Ashden? Caroline tried to brace herself for what she realised she must see shortly, but sickness and dread welled up inside her as they drew near, and she held on to Yves' hand so tight she could feel her nails digging into it. It was ten o'clock. Normally on a bank holiday the village would already be bustling with everyone preparing to enjoy the day in his or her own way. This morning it looked deserted, save for Bankside.

The first thing she noticed was that the oak tree on the corner of Station Road seemed to have turned black, its leaves and branches scorched by fire. It too was in mourning for the jagged scar opposite. Between the Norrington Arms and the cinema had been four cottages. Now there was none, and on the green slope down to the pond before them was a large crater. Part of the pub wall had vanished, and Isabel's beloved cinema now had a gaping hole, exposing its innards like a doll's house. The smell of smoke and dust of the debris hung everywhere, as soldiers and village folk cleared rubble and possessions together. Standing apart from them, like a Greek chorus observing the tragedy, was a large and silent group of villagers. Everyone dealt with it in a different way; some hid their eyes, some had theirs glued on the evidence of reality.

The sight of the Rectory, with its glorious muddle of architectural red-brick styles, made Caroline weep anew, so reassuring was it. Perhaps there had been some horrible mistake? Isabel couldn't really be dead, for if the Rectory had so little damage,

Isabel could not have been killed within its walls, and she could have had no reason to be out so late last night.

'I will stay here, Caroline, until you come for me,' Yves said gently, letting her hand drop with a kiss.

Surely his banishment didn't matter now in this family tragedy? Then, she realised, at least to Yves, it still did, and for the first time she thought of how *he* had felt at her father's rejection. Only she saw Yves as a member of the family, not he, nor her parents.

The Rectory door was open, and it was easier than she had thought to take the first step through it. Felicia was coming down the stairs, but it was a Felicia she scarcely recognised. No need to ask if there had been a mistake – there hadn't. This is what Felicia must have looked like when she was first gassed, only now the yellow skin had become a drawn pallor. She embraced her, and there was only need for a few words.

'Mother was at the hospital sitting with George all night, and Dr Parry has given her something to make her sleep.'

'How is he?'

'Not seriously injured. Cuts and bruises – bad ones. He's in Ashden Manor though, with everyone else.' Felicia gave a hard laugh. 'Odd to think yesterday was to have been my last day. I've been there all night, and Mrs Dibble and Agnes are taking it in turns to sit with Mother, in case she wakes up.'

'And Father?'

'In the study. He hasn't moved since he returned from the hospital. He refused to see Dr Parry, just told us to look after Mother and get some rest ourselves. He came out once to go to the bathroom, but then went straight back. He refused breakfast, everything.'

'Is the door locked?'

'I don't know. His face is, though – I saw it when he came out. I suppose he's shutting us out, and blaming himself for allowing Isabel to take Nanny Oates home instead of going himself. I can't think why – George was there, after all. Oh Caroline, I thought I could bear anything after what I'd seen at the Front, but I can't.' Tears began to soak into Caroline's shoulder, and they stood clasped together in the hallway. 'This morning was awful, when I got home at last. Elizabeth Agnes was laughing and shouting, for all Agnes tried to keep her quiet. She's taken her to her grannie's now. Mrs Dibble is trying to run the house as if nothing was wrong, while looking like a ghost. Caroline–?'

'Yes. I'll try.' Caroline picked up the appeal in Felicia's voice and knew exactly what she wanted.

'There are things to be done,' Felicia said hopelessly.

There were always things to be done after a death – registration, funerals – and Caroline would have to bear the brunt of it all. The whole panoply of horror stretched out clearly in front of Caroline, but the most important element was Father, behind that study door, alone and grieving. She knocked tentatively, after Felicia had left to return to the hospital, and when there was no answer, she went in.

This wasn't the father she knew. He was always in control, so tidy, so calm and reassuring. Today he was unshaven, with streaks of dust on his face and stains on his trousers. Worst of all was the agony on his face. His expression hardly changed as he saw her, but he stood up, though with visible effort.

'Caroline,' was all he said.

She put her arms around him, and could feel the emotion in him.

'I am glad you have come,' he managed to

say. 'You are alone?'

'Phoebe will be here in an hour or two.'

'I am glad for that too. And Yves?'

'He is outside. On–' Caroline could not even say the word Bankside, so she compromised with 'in the drive.'

He nodded, as though this were natural enough. 'I'll ask him in,' he said. And that seemed natural enough too.

She followed her father out and watched him cross to where Yves was standing, regardless of curious, sympathetic eyes from the watching crowd. Father put his hand on Yves' shoulder in a curious gesture, since Yves was the taller. It was almost as though he were seeking support. Yves too had come home.

'Me and Agnes will do luncheon, Mrs D,' Myrtle offered solicitously. 'You go and have a rest.'

Margaret made an effort. 'That you will not, Myrtle. Things are coming to–' She stopped, because she just didn't have the strength to fight any more. 'Thank you, Myrtle. I wouldn't mind having a break.'

The thought of sleep was welcome not so much to restore her after last night's sleepless horrors, but just to escape them for a while. How could she sleep, though, with poor Mrs Lilley liable to wake at any time and remember it all over again? Now Miss Caroline was here, and she could look after her parents. But when Miss – how hard it was to think of her as Mrs – Phoebe arrived, would she have remembered her coupon book for meat rations in all the turmoil?

Margaret's tired brain raced through the hundred and one problems that presented themselves until finally, unable to deal with any of them, she laid them aside. Myrtle and Agnes would do luncheon, Agnes would keep an eye on Mrs Lilley, and Percy was busy fixing new windows. Mrs Thorn had opened up the ironmongers specially this morning. Everyone in Ashden was doing his or her bit, but in the midst of such a tragedy that bit wasn't very much.

She made one last stab at normality. 'You'll find the remains of the beef in the larder, Myrtle. Make a nice shepherd's pie, and put the cold veg in it too, so it goes further. And not too much sugar in the stewed apple. Use a piece of bread instead. Oh, and mind what I told you about the gravy. None of your powders.'

'Yes, Mrs D. Oh, Mrs D!' Myrtle's voice rose in alarm, as she saw that Margaret was crying. It was like Fred's death all over again. It hadn't really seemed real that Mrs Isabel was dead, and Mr George in hospital. Nanny Oates was dead too, but she was old, and Mrs Isabel was at least young enough to have a baby. Now the baby was lost as well as Mrs Isabel. Myrtle began to sniff.

'Don't you go crying into the gravy, Myrtle.' With that, Margaret hurried out of the kitchen before she collapsed.

Caroline had left Yves with Father while she went to release Agnes and sit with her mother. She looked so peaceful asleep, away from the day's nightmare, although every so often lines of pain would spread across her face. Caroline knew everything about that face, every laughter line and every crease of anxiety, but this was a pain she could not lift from her, because she shared it.

'She's been asleep two hours,' Agnes had said, 'but I don't think she'll be asleep much longer. She's beginning to get restless.'

After her mother had woken up and if she could be left, Caroline decided she would go to Ashden Manor to see George with Father and Yves. Felicia came back at lunchtime for half an hour, and told her that George was mainly suffering from concussion and shock, as well as the cuts and bruises. Last night he had broken down when he had learned of Isabel's death. There had been six deaths in all; the others were Samuel Thorn, Father's verger, Nat Mutter's son, a soldier roistering about on the green after the Norrington Arms closed and Jenny Hargreaves, daughter to Mrs Hazel the dressmaker, who lived further along on Bankside. Half an hour earlier there would have been far more deaths as people spilled out from the public house onto the green.

'Where–?' The words had stuck in Caroline's throat, but Felicia understood.

'The bodies are in the hospital mortuary.'

'Can I–?'

'No, darling. It's better not to.'

'She should be here, in her home.'

Felicia took her hands. 'Caroline, you know she is.'

'*Know?* Felicia, how can you still say that? Even after what I went through when I was involved in those bomb incidents, I realise that's nothing to the horrors you've seen. How can you be sure there's a loving God? I thought I'd found my faith again, but this – this has put an end to it.'

Felicia thought for a moment. 'I wasn't sure

when I was first at the Front. But as time went by, I realised the strength Tilly and I found to keep going wasn't just our own.'

'I wish I could realise that,' Caroline said bitterly.

'You will. It's not just the major disasters that restore it. It's the small trials. For instance–' Felicia hesitated, 'there's something you can do for me. Edith and William Swinford-Browne are coming over at four this afternoon and as Mother won't be able to face them, one of us has to. There are still eleven people injured in the hospital, so I must go back.'

Felicia watched her expression as Caroline's heart plummeted. 'Isabel was their daughter-in-law, and the baby would have been their grandchild. Please, Caroline.'

Of course Felicia was right. How could they close the doors of the Rectory to anyone at a time like this? The Swinford-Brownes were part of Isabel's family, and must be received as such. With deep gratitude, Caroline remembered Yves was here and could help her.

In the event, she returned with Felicia to Ashden Hospital, leaving Yves and her father to receive Phoebe when she arrived. Their path was doubly a sad one, for many victims of war had walked along it before Isabel and George. At their head was dear Reggie, whom she had loved so much. That love had never been tested as had her love for Yves, and he remained enshrined in her memory as distinct from the present as were her childhood and girlhood.

George was in a room with two convalescent army lieutenants from France, but he was not joining in their conversation. His eyes brightened when he saw Caroline.

'My big sister says I can come home tomorrow,' he managed to laugh.

'This even bigger sister thinks that's good news.' Did she? Could the household cope with a semi-invalid. She dismissed such stupidity. George would recover quicker at home, surrounded by family, and the fact that he was able to maintain a front of cheerfulness would be another element in his getting quickly on his feet again. He didn't maintain it for long.

'It doesn't seem fair,' he said vehemently. 'How *could* it happen here in Ashden? On the Front we expect it, crashes, dog-fights, deaths, accidents, blood and funerals, but here it's different. It shouldn't have happened.'

'I suppose we imagined Ashden would

remain untouched, while we were away,' Caroline replied sadly. 'We need something to come home to, something safe to remember from the old days.'

'Perhaps. I tell you, Caroline, no more skylarking and cartoons for me. We chaps out there thought we were fighting to keep England unaltered. And all we've done is wreck it. I can't imagine Ashden without Bankside, without Nanny Oates' cottage, and without Isabel. Why wasn't it me? I've been close enough to death scores of times, and yet *she* was killed.' He turned away his head so that she would not see him crying.

Caroline put out her hand to stroke his cheek. 'You *have* helped, and so have your cartoons. You mustn't give them up. They mean a lot to people.'

He took no notice. 'She must have taken the full force of the bomb. I can't bear it, Caroline.'

Caroline shuddered. In the two bomb explosions she had seen at close hand, one dropped by a Zeppelin near the Gaiety and one in a Gotha raid on Folkestone last year, she had seen mangled bodies, torn limbs and sightless eyes in plenty, and the thought of Isabel, her baby and poor Nanny Oates like that brought vomit into her throat. Yes, she knew what it was like, and so did George and Felicia for they had both seen it all. Even Phoebe had been close to war. Now Father and Mother had seen it too, and the bonds of the family must surely strengthen, not break apart.

By the time Caroline arrived back at the Rectory, Phoebe and Billy had arrived and so had the Swinford-Brownes. Yves appeared to be holding his own with William and Edith, but Phoebe leapt up to embrace her. 'I can't believe it, Caroline,' she cried. 'Can I see George? Where's Felicia? And how's Mother? She hasn't appeared yet. Oh, Caroline, hold me tight. I never want to lose the Rectory again.'

Caroline tried to calm her down, but Phoebe would not be silenced. 'There was an air raid in France too yesterday. Six Waacs were killed. It could have been me, but I understand that, because it's in the war zone. It's Isabel I don't understand. That poor baby.' She burst out crying.

'Come upstairs, darling, and we'll talk. You can rest until Mother's awake.'

'*Rest?* How do you think I can rest?' Phoebe moaned.

'Whether you can or not, you've a baby to think of.'

Phoebe was showing no signs yet of approaching motherhood, but that made no difference. She must take life more peacefully and this tragedy was not going to help at all.

Caroline returned to William and Edith, and a thankful Yves. The Swinford-Brownes seemed to have aged considerably, whether through time or shock. Edith looked shrunken and grey against her dark gown, and William robbed of his usual cocksure arrogant manner looked almost human. Impulsively, Caroline kissed them both, and Edith promptly burst into tears.

'How's your poor mother?'

'Asleep.' (I hope, thought Caroline. She would not be able to bear Edith's solicitations, however well meant.)

'The funeral arrangements–' William began, almost diffidently for him. 'Phoebe tells us your father is in a bad way, poor fellow. Edith and I would like to hold it in East Grinstead, if it would help.'

Caroline was saved from the terrible predicament, by her father's entry into the room. 'There is no need. I'm most grateful, William, but how,' he stopped, then managed to continue, 'how could my daughter go to Our Lord without my

235

blessing her on her way?'

'Have you the strength, Father?' Caroline asked quietly. 'No one would blame you for not holding it here. And there are five other funerals, as well.'

'With the love and support of my family, and that includes you Edith and William, Billy and Yves, I know I can.'

Margaret came into the kitchen after two hours' blessed sleep to find Agnes looking harassed.

'What am I going to do, Margaret?' she asked. 'Mrs Lilley still isn't here, so I have to make my own mind up. The Rector doesn't reckon Mrs Phoebe and Mr Billy are married. Should I get two rooms ready, or one? Captain Yves has gone back to London, otherwise I'd have the same problem there. Worse, since they're not even half married.'

Yesterday Margaret would have been in no doubt what to do. Today everything had changed. 'One room, Agnes. That's what the Rector would want, and I'm sure it's certainly what Mrs Phoebe will want, poor girl. There's nothing worse than crying alone.'

Her mother had woken briefly, and taken some tea, but she was still so dazed and distressed that Caroline gave her another pill, as Dr Parry had directed. Reality could wait a little longer.

It waited until the next day, by which time her mother was up, though very silent, and by now Felicia was able to take Caroline's place, and Luke had arrived too. Caroline took on the task of going round the village to visit the bereaved, after her father's calls on them, which he had insisted on making. There was an open door now for the Rector, although many had closed it since the war began, preferring to nurse grief away from what they saw as an impotent church. Now the Rector was one of them again, since he too had lost a loved one.

'Poor lamb,' Mrs Farthing observed. 'And your ma too, bless her.'

Poor lamb? Blessing the Rector's wife? Before the war the villagers would have as soon called Lady Hunney a poor lamb as the Rector, so much respect was he held in. He still was, but the respect had changed direction. It was respect for his humanity, not his role at the end of God's telephone line.

Luke explained to them that evening what

had happened, after taking Caroline's advice as to whether her parents were up to it. It had been a full-scale raid on Dover and London, with nearly thirty Gothas getting through to strike at London. They came in from Kent and Essex, but on reaching the London defences some of them had been turned away. As he had thought, one of them seriously lost direction, coming as far west as Tunbridge Wells. The Crowborough defences fired at it, which had driven it further west and in the process its hung-up bomb had fallen. The raid had caused much loss of life in London and Dover too, with nearly fifty people killed.

They listened in silence. Luke's story assumed reality only when Caroline remembered the funerals on Friday.

Normal life was in abeyance until then, but she made an effort to bear work in mind. 'Do you need me at the office before next week?' she asked Luke.

'Strictly speaking yes, but Yves and I have decided we can manage. Ellen is coming in to help out.'

'Good.' The idea of mad-cap Ellen coming in to sort through reports would have appalled Caroline under normal circumstances. Now it was irrelevant.

Isabel was buried on a calm spring day in a joint service for all six of the dead, which began with an address by Father on Bankside with the congregation – the whole of Ashden – packed around him. The debris had been taken away now, and only the missing cottages and the barren earth where the grass had been burnt from it spoke of Sunday's tragedy. They sang one favourite hymn for each victim, and then moved on to St Nicholas'. In this church Isabel had been baptised, confirmed and married. Its solid grey walls had seen tragedy and triumph over the ages, given comfort and doubled rejoicing, and with Yves at her side, Caroline found the service bearable, simple, loving and dignified. Committing Isabel to the earth was far harder in the stark bleakness of the farewell. How could they turn away and leave her there in the churchyard? Help came from a surprising quarter. After the last committal, that of Mrs Hazel's daughter, Len Thorn stepped forward in his corporal's army uniform.

'Shall it be tonight, Rector?'

Father just stared at him, not understanding. 'Shall what be tonight?'

'The tree.' Len reddened, for when Fred

Dibble had died, he had been the ringleader in insisting his name was erased from the long list of those who had sacrificed their lives in this war carved on the bark of the now war-torn oak tree. 'I reckon your daughter, Rector, and the others, they all died for the war. We Tommies are on the Western Front, and this is the Home Front. There's no difference now between the two of them, so those six names should be on the list with the others.'

Father was finding difficulty in speaking, he was so moved, so Len did it for him.

'I'll do the carving, Rector.'

'And I'll help you, Len.' Nat Mutter stepped forward.

Nine

With a sense of shock Margaret realised this was early June and a Saturday. Normally, even last year, this was the day she would have been busy preparing for the tennis party. Before the war this would have meant all five Lilley children and their friends gathering for a one-set knock-out competition, tea, and in the evening a dance on what was grandly called the terrace, though it was so mossy now, it was more like another lawn. As the war wore on, it had been progressively harder to find enough players, but somehow they'd managed. Now there was one less. Last year it had been Mrs Isabel who had organised it all. This year – she could hardly bear thinking about it, in case it started her off crying again. There wasn't even a court to play on now, anyway.

'This will be the end of the old tennis party, Daisy,' Percy had prophetically said to her as she hurriedly washed the dishes after tea last year. 'You mark my words.'

241

Now the court had been ploughed up for vegetables, at Mrs Lilley's reluctant command and much against his will.

'After the war,' Margaret had said stoutly, 'you can lay it again.'

'Who for?' he'd asked.

Percy was right, of course. Even if the boys came marching home from war, who would bring the girls back? Miss Caroline busy with her own life, Master George already carving a name for himself as a cartoonist, Miss Phoebe spreading her wings in France, Miss Felicia a heroine. None of them would see out their days in the Rectory. 'There'll be only Mrs Isabel,' she'd answered Percy.

'And that won't be for long,' Percy had replied, meaning that she would be making her own home again somewhere with Mr Robert, and most probably it wouldn't be in Ashden. His words had come true all right, and for the worst of reasons.

Margaret's view through the kitchen window of the small patch of garden outside became misty. *Her* garden, she called it, for she and Percy grew what they liked in it. But it wasn't really theirs; it belonged to the Rectory. That hadn't appeared to matter over the years, but what had once been invulnerable, now seemed fragile. Life anywhere could change into death at the snap of Fate's finger. Death took whom it pleased and laughed at man's puny efforts to build himself a refuge. It had taken Fred, now it had taken Mrs Isabel, Nanny Oates and others. If the Rector had been taken too, they'd all have had to leave the Rectory and what would poor Mrs Lilley do then? What would Percy and herself do? The workhouse most like, if there were any left after the war. Most of them were makeshift hospitals now. The only ray of light was good old Lloyd George in charge. He would put things right after the war.

After seemed a long way away at the moment. In the midst of Ashden was a huge hole, not only physically, but in its heart. Everyone felt the same, not just the bereaved. Even though most of the debris had been taken away now, what was left seemed worse. A jagged scar gaped where people had walked and laughed and run ever since Ashden had come into being and that was long before the Frenchies had come marching in in 1066. That was quite enough, the Kaiser wasn't going to follow suit. What had happened hadn't lessened the village's determination about that. Although everyone went about their business just the same, there was no heart left in them. And that wasn't just the bomb for other villages were the same. No one had the same interest in village concerns. The old high days and holidays had mostly gone, or there was no one to run events. Instead, everyone concentrated with a sick desperation on the need to stick it out and get this war won. Instead of that day growing nearer, the situation was getting worse. The Germans picked on the French lines for once, when they began their tricks again at the end of May. Since we were all in the same boat now, that was almost as bad as having a go at our Tommies, and anyway, the papers said that Tommies had been fighting with the French.

True, now the Americans had condescended to take a small part it was a help, but from what she could gather most of them were still training at home. The newspaper said that two days ago the Germans were only forty miles from Paris, and the French Government and lots of Parisians were getting ready to run like rabbits. Americans were as good as a dose of Epsom salts, Percy had said approvingly yesterday. Salts went straight through you, Margaret had thought gloomily, and so the

244

Germans would do to those newcomers to battle. Apparently she was wrong for so far the Americans were holding the line at Château Thierry, and as yet the Germans hadn't broken through for their visit to the Eiffel Tower.

Still, they'd seen all this before. Old Asquith had been right to 'wait and see'. It was too soon to wave flags and although no one really believed that the Germans would *win*, the fact remained that food got scarcer and dearer, queues got longer, bills got higher, and the men still marched off. There was hardly an able-bodied man around, now the age was up to fifty. Thank goodness Lizzie's Frank had been invalided out, and no wonder, he was as weak as a kitten.

Babies got born just the same, though. With all the shock of the bomb, Margaret had thought Agnes might have come early, but she hadn't. The baby was still expected later this month, and with Agnes near her time, all the work fell on Margaret and Myrtle. Each day brought new battles on the food front. How to substitute, how to cope. Coupons for meat, bacon, sugar and now fat was the latest one. Pretty soon you'd have to ask the government before you could visit your own privy.

Inside, Caroline felt nothing but a merciful numbness, which allowed her to work, talk, and even laugh. It was merciful because it meant that tearing grief could not fight its way through. She supposed it must be buried deep inside her, but here in London at any rate that's where it remained. She knew Yves and Luke were worried about her, but this surprised her a little, for from their point of view she was coping wonderfully. She couldn't cry in the office, and Ellen, busy with her own affairs and love life, couldn't spend all her time consoling Caroline, nor could Yves be burdened with her grief. She would continue to work through the mundane jobs of everyday life, and ignore what might be going on within her. It was easier to do this in London than at the Rectory where Felicia had remained for the time being to look after Mother. Towards the end of June the situation changed, however.

'Caroline, do you want to visit home on your next day off?' Luke asked casually. 'We could give you the weekend and an extra day.'

Caroline stiffened, aware that she felt safer here than faced with the painful associations of Ashden, but also that Felicia or no Felicia, her parents needed her.

'Can you come with me, Yves?'

'No, my love, for a few hours perhaps, but there is too much going on. As you know.'

She did. Code-breaking had achieved wonderful results earlier this month when a French code-breaker read the German plans to launch a new offensive on the Montdidier-Compiègne line, and as a result, despite many casualties, the French had resisted the German attempt to push forward. It made their job all the more important at the moment, since Ludendorff would surely be planning further assaults in the near future. The longer he left it, the more likelihood there was of increased American presence in the line. Or so he might believe. In fact, there was little chance of that beyond Pershing's earlier grudging promise for limited troops under French control. New troops were shortly scheduled to arrive in France, but he was hanging on to them for his grand army planned for action in 1919. By which time, if the Germans kept on going at their present rate, there'd no longer be a war to fight.

There was something else keeping Yves occupied too. King Albert and Queen

Elisabeth would be paying a visit to England shortly, partly to celebrate King George V and Queen Mary's silver wedding, and partly to rally the Belgian cause in Britain.

'Felicia is still planning to come. to London to work,' Luke added casually, which explained precisely the reason for their 'generosity'.

'She didn't tell *me*.'

'You were out,' Luke replied patiently. 'She's changed her mind about the Red Cross. She met Dr Louisa Garrett Anderson in France, and has accepted her suggestion that she works at the Endell Street hospital – and maybe go to their French hospital later.'

'She's not well enough.'

'She believes she is. If you can persuade her to stay here, you'll have my gratitude. If she goes to France, she'll be tempted to go back to the front line.'

'Mother and Father need her at Ashden.'

'Caroline.' Luke looked at her reproachfully. 'I've never known you so ungiving.'

'It's always *me* doing the giving, that's why,' Caroline muttered savagely, and Luke said no more.

From Felicia's point of view it made sense. Dr Garrett Anderson, the daughter of the famous Elizabeth, had founded the Women's Hospital Corps in 1914, and once the French hospital was established she and Dr Flora Murray founded the hospital in London. All the staff were women, from the lowest to the highest, and Dr Murray was the chief surgeon. For Felicia to join them made great sense, but it left Caroline with a problem.

'Don't you want to visit the Rectory this weekend?' Yves asked her later in the privacy of their bedroom.

'Of course I do.' She busied herself by wrenching off her boots.

'Now tell me the truth,' Yves said, and when she did not reply, added, 'It is quite normal to avoid grief.'

'I'm not avoiding it.' She was filled with indignation.

'Then it is worse than I feared. To avoid pain is natural, but not to want to return to your home, to your parents and the village of which you are part, that I do not understand. Do you only want the good things Ashden can offer, Caroline? Do you only wish to wander down its lanes, to take sanctuary in familiar surroundings and give nothing back to those who have provided it?'

She burst into tears. 'How can you say such terrible things, Yves? Of course I want to help.' A tiny part of her began to wonder if he was right, however. Had she unconsciously been avoiding Ashden?

He muffled her in his arms. 'Then go, *cara*, and take me with you in your heart.'

Now Miss Felicia was leaving as well. It was inevitable, Margaret supposed, since she was only doing what she'd been planning before it had all happened. That time seemed so long ago, though, that Margaret's mind had dismissed it, since the Rectory world had changed since then. Daily life didn't change, though, it simply plodded along the same old tracks.

She'd done her best to help the Rector, though it hadn't been easy. Like Ahab – well, not their old sheepdog, but the old king he was named for, who turned his face to the wall – poor Rector shut himself up in his study all day long, sometimes not even coming out for meals. Mind you, with rations the way they were, they weren't worth coming out for, but you had to keep your strength up somehow, even if it was only wartime soup.

He was so quiet and subdued yesterday

that she had taken the liberty of speaking straight out to him. She knocked on the study door and took no notice of his patient, unresponsive look when she entered.

'Beg your pardon, sir, for intruding, but I brought you *Raymond* to read. Now I know that you don't go along with all it says, but that doesn't stop you reading it, does it?'

He had smiled at least, even took *Raymond* from her. 'A cloistered virtue,' he murmured.

'Beg your pardon, sir?'

'From Milton – how can one conquer evil by shutting oneself away?'

'Evil?' She flushed angrily.

'I'm sorry, Mrs Dibble, I didn't mean your book. I greatly appreciate your thoughtfulness for me, and I will certainly read it.'

Emboldened by this, Margaret had added: 'That Sherlock Holmes man has approved it, so I read.'

'Sir Arthur Conan Doyle? Yes, I believe I read a review of his new book, in which he endorses *Raymond*. However–' The Rector had broken off whatever he intended to say, but as Margaret left the room she saw he was already glancing through *Raymond*. She had been well satisfied, for that was all she asked. She'd be going to Mrs Orvino again soon. It had crossed her mind that if Fred had been so sure they'd have a lovely party at Whitsun, why couldn't he have given some warning about the bomb? She worried about this for some time, and then decided Fred wouldn't have been able to prevent what was going to happen, and hadn't wanted to distress her by hinting at it. Yes, that was it.

With Rector locked away, and Miss Felicia going, they'd be rattling around in the Rectory like dried peas again. Only Mr George was left, and as soon as he was well enough he'd be off back to France. He wasn't his old self either. Mrs Isabel's death had knocked the stuffing out of him quicker than von Richthofen's circus – if there was one any more, for the Red Baron had been killed in the spring.

Poor Mrs Lilley was wandering round the house like a lost soul, saying nothing but, 'Yes, Mrs Dibble, that would be splendid, Mrs Dibble.' What had been a partnership had turned into Margaret running the house, and Mrs Lilley obediently falling into line, and throwing herself – or trying to do so – into her agricultural work. It was natural enough and Margaret had no objection. Mrs Lilley had supported her when Fred died, and now it was time for her to do the same. Even Lady Buckford was keeping her head below the parapet these days. At least, this weekend Miss Caroline would be here for two whole days.

The first thing that Caroline registered was that where her mother's fine dark hair had grown over the last month, it was now iron grey. Even her mother's hug seemed different. Always before it had been to *give*, now it seemed to Caroline that it was she who was giving strength, and what Yves had implied was right. Unconsciously she had been avoiding this change of role. The child in her, instantly frightened at this realisation, was quickly dismissed. Caroline knew she was needed here as never before, and more, that she *wanted* to be here.

She braced herself, gathering her strength. At the moment, with Yves at hand, her presence could help her parents, but for how much longer would that be so? After that, the roles might well be reversed once more. It had to be thought about, though not yet, for she could not fight on all flanks at once.

'Go to your father, darling. I'm so worried about him,' Elizabeth asked quietly.

Caroline found him not in his study, but sitting in the garden, surveying the produce growing on what had once been their tennis court. He was reading, but as she greeted him he rose to his feet in pleasure. He, like Mother, looked years older, and his face was drawn.

'My dear.'

Caroline had the same feeling as with her mother when he embraced her, and blamed herself once again for her hesitation in coming home.

'You're reading that new Conan Doyle book, *The New Revelation*. Why – ah–' Caroline understood immediately – 'Mrs Dibble.'

'How could I not take her seriously? She was kind enough to lend me *Raymond* and I decided to go to Tunbridge Wells to buy this.'

'That doesn't mean you take all that stuff about whisky and sodas in heaven seriously too, does it?' Caroline could not believe it. *Father* of all people?

'No, but now we have our own immense grief, I understand how many might gain comfort from it. After all, Sir Arthur's interest in the subject was kindled by someone within his own household who had lost brothers on the Western Front. I am impressed enough at this outspoken tract to take it seriously, as you put it. And I confess, my love, that late in the evening and at night, when one does not see matters as clearly as during the day, I have wished I *could* believe totally in *Raymond*. After all, I believe in the after-life; it is but a small step to reason that at times it has methods of communicating with us, and if the image that it manifests is akin to earthly matters, such as your whisky and sodas, that may simply be to strengthen that communication by putting things in earthly terms.'

He was looking at her almost with hope, and Caroline was horrified.

'No, Father,' she managed to reply. 'To *believe* in Isabel's happiness in the next life is one thing, for you to dwell so much on it, which is what spiritualism encourages is quite another. Isabel would not want that.'

Caroline realised hopelessly that she had no idea what Isabel would have thought. Isabel had always been here, and there had been no need for such discussions. If only she could talk her worries over with Felicia, but she had already left for London.

George was at dinner, a more sombre brother than she recalled, but it wasn't until late that evening that she had a chance to talk to him privately. She had left her bedroom door open, in the time-honoured Rectory tradition of signifying one was open to visits from her siblings, but George had never participated so much as his sisters. Today the silent invitation had not been taken up, and she had to beard him in his own room.

'I'm worried about Father,' she told him bluntly. 'Do you think he is going to steer the same path as Mrs Dibble?'

George lolled back on the bed. 'He may be a dabbler, but he's not a Dibbler.'

'Be serious.'

'I am. And, even if he is going to take up spiritualism, it's far too early to try to talk him out of it. It's only just a month since Isabel died.'

It seemed a lifetime, it seemed yesterday, but Caroline admitted George might have a point. Common sense seemed to have deserted her recently. 'How much longer are you here for?'

'Another two weeks, the doc says. I shall be off sooner, maybe.'

'For the right reasons, I hope.'

'Does it matter?'

Caroline plunged. 'It matters if you're still

256

blaming yourself for living when Isabel died. Are you?'

'Yes, as a matter of fact.'

'Then you must think instead of what you originally went into the war to do, think of what our parents need – think of–' she broke off, not wanting to trespass too far.

'You?' He misunderstood. 'You have Yves, for the moment at least.'

'I was going to say think of Kate.'

George looked startled, then the glimmer of a smile came to his lips. 'Kate wouldn't understand.'

'From what I remember of her, you might find she does, only she has practical ways of showing it.'

George grinned. 'You mean well, Caroline, but keep out of it. Look after your own love life.'

'Ouch.'

George groaned. 'Sorry.'

There was something else she wanted to discuss with Father while she was here, but it was not until Father had returned from early communion on Sunday that she had the opportunity to do so. Once Sunday breakfast had been a formal occasion, but no longer. The dishes were still kept on hot plates, but whereas they would have been devoured after family prayers at one go, now one was lucky to have a companion. The Rectory clock had run down, and would it ever be rewound? Today, however, both her parents were here.

'Do you think the cinema will be rebuilt, Father?' It seemed important to her that it was, for it had been Isabel's great achievement.

'I doubt if Swinford-Browne will do so, and you know yourself that he's been wanting to close it for a long time. A great pity, in my opinion.'

'You wouldn't have said so once.' Father had been vehemently opposed to the cinema when it was opened in 1914.

'Times change, even for me,' Laurence sighed. 'There is no doubt it has become a popular meeting place for the village, but even apart from business considerations, Swinford-Browne has taken Isabel's death very hard, and I imagine he's all too happy to walk away from the problem.'

'Suppose I talk to him?' Caroline offered. 'Why don't we invite them to lunch today?'

'I couldn't, Caroline,' Elizabeth said immediately. 'Not yet.'

Caroline understood. She remembered the first time the Swinford-Brownes had ever come to lunch, on Easter Sunday 1914. That was the day when Isabel's engagement to Robert had been announced. Caroline had hated the Swinford-Brownes ever since. Now such dislike seemed irrelevant and even misplaced. 'I'll go to the mountain tomorrow morning,' she said resignedly, 'if he'll see me.'

After leaving Ashden, the Swinford-Brownes, having moved to East Grinstead, had chosen a home even ghastlier than The Towers. Caroline began to regret her impulsive gesture to come here once more a-pleading at the Swinford-Brownes' feet.

It was Edith who awaited her in the morning room, and stripped by grief of all the pretensions she usually assumed, she had a dignity that had been lacking in her previous bearing.

'How nice of you to come, Caroline.' She appeared to mean it, and guiltily Caroline was aware that she would never have dreamed of visiting them if it hadn't been for the cinema.

'Has Robert been told?' she asked quietly.

'We didn't know *what* to do, my dear. We thought, if we told him, he might give up hope for himself, yet if we didn't that he'd hate us for not telling him. Patricia took care of it, and consulted the Red Cross. I believe he now knows, for she had a brief letter of acknowledgement.'

Edith's face was forlorn and no wonder. Robert's relations with his parents had been strained to say the least after he decided to volunteer for action. 'I don't suppose we'll have any grandchildren now,' Edith continued. 'I don't see Patricia marrying.'

Nor did Caroline. Patricia Swinford-Browne was strident and bossy, if good-hearted; the women's police force suited her down to the ground, and she could not see Patricia forfeiting power for marriage.

At that moment William Swinford-Browne arrived to join them. His bulky shape, which had led to the Lilley girls nicknaming him the William Pear, had given way to a very shrivelled pear since she had last seen him at the funeral.

'Good of you to visit us, Caroline,' he greeted her gruffly.

Her guilt increased, and she spent a long time talking generally with them before she introduced the subject she had come to discuss. 'What shall you do about the cinema, Mr Swinford-Browne?' They had never progressed beyond this formality. Caroline hadn't the slightest inclination to address him as Uncle William, and neither did she feel warm enough towards him – or had ever been invited – to call him by his Christian name.

'I don't want to go near the place. I'll sell up when the war's over.'

'That may be a long time. Won't you consider rebuilding?'

Edith burst into tears, and William glared at her. 'That's a trifle on the callous side, isn't it?'

'No. I've thought about it a lot,' Caroline said earnestly. 'I know we were against the cinema when you first built it, but now it's a great force for good. People will need it again once the shock wears off.'

'Maybe they will. I won't though. I couldn't bear to look at the place,' William grunted.

'How can you think of people laughing at Charlie Chaplin right where your own sister died?' Edith moaned.

Caroline flushed, then steeled herself. She had never thought this would be easy. 'It's just that Isabel put so much love and enthusiasm into building up the cinema. If it closes, it would look as if her work had come to nothing. By allowing her to run it, you were the making of Isabel, Mr

Swinford-Browne. It gave her much happiness for she felt she was accomplishing something worthwhile. She would have hated to see it all go for nothing.'

'That's one way of looking at it,' William admitted grudgingly. 'It doesn't change my mind though.'

'If it were rebuilt, a memorial to Isabel in the foyer could be a permanent tribute. Otherwise her work would seem to have been pointless.'

'Oh, William. Caroline's right.' Edith rapidly changed sides.

He glared at her too, but deliberated for a moment. At last he said, 'All right, Caroline. Get it fixed up as and when you can. And cheaply. Don't splash my money about. You'll have to find someone local to run it too. Can't offer them much.'

Caroline was well aware of that, for Isabel had frequently complained of the pittance she received. She'd take one problem at a time though. First catch your turtle...

She was pleased with her victory, for it seemed something she had done for Isabel, and hurried home, hoping to talk it over with her mother. She had expected to find her in the glory-hole where she did her agricultural rota work, but there was no sign of her. Defeated, she went back to the kitchen to ask Mrs Dibble where she was.

'Gone over to the Dower House about a Rat and Sparrow Club,' she said.

'A *what?* And why Lady Hunney?' Caroline was incredulous. Mother loathed Maudie as she was not so affectionately known. Her mother's work on the County Executive Committee was increasing all the time, with the campaign to find yet more land to plough more intense than ever before, and the harvest rotas needing constant juggling. Nevertheless, in the old days Maudie would be last on the list to call for help.

'She goes over there quite often to see her ladyship now. She gets on with her better than with her ladyship upstairs.'

Anyone would, Caroline thought, amused. It was odd to think of her mother and Lady Hunney drawn closer together through common bereavement. That tennis party of 1914 seemed so long ago; there had been but little thought of war, save for a tiny cloud on a distant horizon. She and Reggie had become engaged that day and Isabel was planning her wedding. The tennis balls pit-patted in the warm sunshine, she could hear them now echoing in her ears. So long ago, but those happy voices were still clear: Isabel's, Felicia's, George's, Tilly's, her own 'Because I'm going to marry you' followed by Reggie's 'You'll never cry again, Caroline. I promise, I promise.'

Caroline got up quickly from the kitchen table as Agnes came in carrying the tea tray. She looked white with exhaustion. 'Oh, Agnes, let me help you.'

'I'm all right, Miss Caroline.' She let her take the tray from her all the same. 'I've been overdoing it a bit. The baby's due on the 29th, and Jamie's coming home tonight on leave. That's bad timing, isn't it? Oh, Miss Caroline, it doesn't seem right me being here, having a baby, and poor Mrs Lilley losing her grandchild. I offered to go, but she said no, but I do feel awful.'

Late that night, not long after Jamie arrived, his second child decided to arrive a week early. Caroline was awoken by the commotion as Jamie thundered down the stairs for Mrs Dibble, Mrs Dibble telephoned to Mrs Hay, and in due course, with the whole house roused, Mrs Hay sent for Dr Ryde because Agnes was having such a difficult time.

Caroline joined her parents in the kitchen

where Mrs Dibble had ordered Myrtle to make cocoa and tea to see them through the night. Her mother looked as if she were about to cry, and Caroline searched desperately for something to take her mind off Isabel's baby.

'What, Mother, is a Rat and Sparrow Club?' she asked brightly.

It was not the most sensible of questions for two o'clock in the morning, and her mother stared at her blankly.

'Like a cock-fight?' George slouched sleepily in for his mug of cocoa.

It was Percy who answered in the end. 'Club set up to do away with vermin. They arrange shoots.'

'But sparrows aren't vermin.'

'When they eat my crops, they are. I don't plough up tennis courts to feed them.'

'At the Front,' George said quietly, 'a sparrow's chirp is a precious thing.'

Caroline said no more.

They returned to their bedrooms to try to sleep, but renewed commotion towards dawn sent Caroline scuttling up to Agnes's room in her dressing gown to see what was going on.

Jamie, as white as a sheet, was in the doorway of Agnes' bedroom, but he was grinning.

'A boy?'

'It's a girl, and I'm glad, Miss Caroline. That I am. Boys go to war, so my little ones will be safe.'

Safe? There was no guarantee of that, but she said nothing save to congratulate him, and since she was leaving early to return to the office, asked if she might see the baby. She found her mother already in the bedroom. 'Poor Agnes is very weak, Caroline. She's had a bad time. What are you going to call her, Jamie?'

Agnes roused herself. 'Jamie and me – if you've no objection – well, we'd like to call her Isabel. If it's not presumptuous. If it won't upset you.'

'I can't think–' Elizabeth tried again. 'I can't think of anything nicer.' She burst into tears, and Caroline bent over to kiss Agnes' forehead.

Ten

'I don't *want* to march, Caroline, but they say I must,' Felicia said crossly.

Caroline was flying around her bedroom endeavouring to smarten up her WAAC uniform – why did it *have* to be such a drab colour? – and to get ready herself for the afternoon's parade through London of women war workers. Felicia looked almost as wan as she did, thanks to the grey-green uniform and veil that the nurses at Endell Street Hospital wore. Felicia's uniform had been a problem. In terms of formal training, she was an unqualified nurse; in experience, however, she was more than qualified, and Endell Street treated her as such.

'I hate being forced to parade like a trophy,' Felicia continued viciously.

'You can't blame them,' Caroline pointed out. 'There has to be a contingent of nurses from the hospital and with your fame you have to be there clinking your medals.'

'You're used to marching in processions. I'm not.'

'I helped organise one, three years ago,' Caroline pointed out patiently. 'I then marched with it. It poured with rain and my feet hurt. It doesn't make me an expert on processions.'

'Compared with me you are.'

'You're not usually so obstinate.' Caroline struggled not to laugh at this new side of Felicia.

'That's because you haven't seen much of me these last few years.'

'No,' Caroline agreed. It was hard to believe that her sisters had changed for ever. Once, she had supposed that when this war ended it would vanish, along with all its effects on people's lives. It was plain now that would never happen.

'I can't stand it, you know, Caroline,' Felicia said despondently. 'I *hate* being told what to do. I shall *have* to go back to France, at least to the hospital. What I really want is to return to the Front though.'

Caroline groaned. 'The doctors, everyone, even Tilly, have said how stupid that would be.'

'I don't have to take notice of Tilly. I'm *free* there, Caroline. I can achieve good and see myself achieving it. At Endell Street, it's the Manor hospital all over again, rules, regulations, and neat white beds. Excellent, but it's not me.'

Caroline struggled to subdue panic. She had to be careful, or she would just make Felicia more determined than ever, yet all she could think of was that Felicia might be killed, just when she'd thought her safe. George's leaving again was bad enough, but he had no choice. So far he and Felicia had led charmed lives, surviving against the odds. How much longer could that luck hold?

'Think what it would mean to Father and Mother.' Caroline wanted to say, think what it would mean to *me*, but she could not.

'I can't. I have to do what I do best.'

For the first time that she could remember, Caroline's patience with her sister snapped. '*Why?* What makes *you* so privileged, Felicia? We'd all like to do what we do best, for heaven's sake, but this is war, and we can't. We're all tiny spokes in a huge wheel, until it's over. After that, we *might* have the privilege of doing what we like.'

Felicia stared at her in amazement at this outburst. 'Very well, put it this way. I can do *the* best job out there. Save more lives.'

'How can you possibly know that?' Caroline retaliated furiously. 'How can *you*

269

compare what effect you are having on the seriously wounded patients in Endell Street with your work at the Front? You're not God. You don't seem to realise you're famous, Felicia, and the hospital quite rightly want to use the fact to help get these men well. There are other women, fitter than you, working at the front-line hospitals and running advanced dressing posts. *Why* do you want to go back so much? Vanity? Or–' a shot in the dark – 'as an escape?'

Felicia was roused too. 'Escape from what, might I ask?'

'You know very well. From your own problems. What to do when the war ends, Luke or Daniel? We've all got problems, sister dear. Myself and Yves, Mother and Father, all of us. Stop being so selfish, and take Tilly's advice to stay here. *And* mine,' she added for good measure.

Felicia rose to her feet, a red spot of anger on each cheekbone. 'I'll make my own way to Hyde Park.' With that, she marched out of the flat.

Ruefully, Caroline examined her conscience, but to her surprise for once she found it reasonably clear.

Hyde Park was the gathering point for the parade, in which each main category of worker was represented, including VADs, the Women's Legion, the WRNS, the Land Girls, the Forestry girls, munitions workers, and of course the Waacs of which she was one. Looking at the vast hordes milling into order under a mercifully sunny sky, Caroline thought about the 1915 demonstration which she had helped to organise. They had been marching to demand the right to work, and today's parade was proof of its success. She felt humbly proud, and sorry that Felicia did not share her mood. There was no hope of finding her here, and she did not try.

Yves had been occupied during the last few days with preparations – mostly shrouded in deep secrecy – for King Albert's visit to Britain, which would begin on 5th July, in six days' time. Four days after that, he pointed out, His Majesty would be reviewing the fleet in the Firth of Forth, including a visit to an American battleship operating with the British squadron, and before and after that he would be at Buckingham Palace with the King and Queen of England. His liaison officer was, therefore, busy, he replied when yesterday she complained mildly of never seeing him.

'I'm going to see the King too,' she had

told him amicably.

'*You?*' That had shaken him.

'Yes, *me,*' she replied with dignity. 'You don't object, do you?'

He looked at her suspiciously. 'A personal interview?'

'Yes. Myself and a hundred thousand other women packed in the quadrangle of the Palace. Still,' she added, laughing, 'the King is coming to speak to us, and the Queen too if we're lucky.'

'Naturally. Miss Caroline Lilley is a famous young lady, as well as beautiful and indispensable to a humble Belgian soldier.'

Indispensable was an unfortunate word and it hung heavily between them. 'At work, perhaps,' she had answered, to which Yves had no reply.

After the parade finished, Caroline felt elated. She was but one of the hundreds of thousands of tiny spokes that turned the war, and she loved it. She reproved herself for self-righteousness, but it was difficult not to feel that way while the King was praising all they'd achieved. That wasn't his reaction when that poor debutante had pleaded for the vote at his feet four years ago.

That evening she was dining at Simon's

house with Tilly, Penelope and Felicia – or so she had thought. Unfortunately, Felicia had telephoned, she was informed on arrival, that she wasn't free to come. Was there any significance in her choice of words, Caroline wondered somewhat guiltily? Tilly, who was now driving for the FANYs in London, which in effect meant for the Red Cross, told her not to worry about it. Felicia was Felicia, and had a marked objection to being told what to do, as Tilly herself had found. Luckily, Tilly could outflank even Felicia's obstinacy, but Caroline hadn't yet learned the knack. Penelope had followed Tilly into the FANYs with great glee, tired, she had proclaimed, of handing out teacups at canteens and food kitchens.

Simon observed: 'She should be driving for the Germans. It would do more to help the war effort than anything else I can think of.'

'Stop being so *ancient*, Father,' Penelope countered blithely. 'Just because you drive at five miles an hour and would prefer a man walking with a red flag in front of you, you think the rest of the world should stand still with you.'

'She's right, Simon,' Tilly agreed. 'That

273

Daimler of yours is like a greyhound on a lead.'

'I would point out,' Simon replied mildly, 'that we have to conserve what petrol we have.'

'Remember that Austin of yours,' Caroline broke in hastily, 'is still stored at Ashden.'

'I remember it with much affection, especially when I came to Ashden after leaving prison. Has Laurence forgiven me yet for enticing you into the suffragettes and fleeing the nest?'

'Poor Father. Things changed so fast around him, he couldn't keep up. And now–' Caroline involuntarily choked with grief '–*this*.'

Penny put her hand out to cover Caroline's, and she managed to continue: 'I think if Father had seen the procession this afternoon, even he would concede that it had all been worthwhile – though I shouldn't mention your burning churches for a few years yet, Tilly.' She fell silent again since even the effort at lightheartedness seemed wrong while grief raged so strongly.

'How's Frank Eliot?' Penny asked hastily, to change the subject.

'Recovering well.' Caroline grasped her offered straw. 'It's all working out splendidly. In fact – hold on to your tin hat, Tilly, but he's going to run the cinema now that Swinford-Browne has agreed to open it.'

'Dear William,' Tilly observed wryly. He was an old enemy of hers.

'He's not so bad as I thought once. Isabel's death has hit him hard.'

'You mean his putative grandson's death has hit him hard. The heir,' Tilly said scathingly.

'Perhaps,' Caroline answered, somewhat shocked. 'Who can tell?' She reminded herself that Tilly had not seen with her own eyes what war had done to Ashden, and to its people, or she would not speak so. And 'people' included even Swinford-Browne.

'Tilly, shut up,' Penelope interjected.

'Peace, Penny,' her father said. 'I'm still hoping that Tilly will become your step-mother.'

'Perish the thought,' Tilly answered decidedly. 'At least, there would have to be strict rules worked out, and one of them will be that I won't be Aunt Tilly, Mother Tilly, Stepmother Tilly–'

'Lady Matilda?' Penny laughed.

'And especially not Matilda.'

Simon was looking at Tilly as if he

couldn't believe his ears at her answer. 'It takes a lot for a diplomat to become over-excited,' he said carefully, 'but do I take it, Tilly, that you are at last seriously considering my offer?'

Fascinated, Caroline held her breath. Simon was popular at the Rectory, and fingers were crossed that he and Tilly would indeed marry.

'It's always been seriously considered, Simon,' Tilly answered quietly. 'The question is what's best to do—'

'When the war ends,' Simon finished for her. 'You and Felicia both.'

'Perhaps I caught the idea from her,' Tilly said. 'She believes no one can guess while the war is still on what the future holds. In her case, the question might be would she want to bring children into a world in which they could not live freely. In my case—'

'You have dear little me,' Penny said gravely. 'Not to mention James.' Her brother had been in the East throughout the war.

'I had a row with Felicia today about that,' Caroline confessed ruefully. 'I suspect that's why she's not here tonight. She still wants to go back to France, and probably the Front despite your advice, Tilly. She's tired of Endell Street discipline.'

'Ah.' Tilly looked pensive. 'As I said earlier, Felicia can be obstinate.'

'You both can,' Simon pointed out. 'That's why you achieved what you did.'

'Could you talk to her again, Tilly?' Caroline pleaded. 'I've tried all the arguments I can think of: her health, Mother and Father, and the best for the war effort.'

Tilly thought for a moment. 'You could try saying "Slug" to her.'

'What or who is that?' Caroline was suspicious.

'She'll know what it means.'

'Anyway,' Penelope said brightly, changing the subject yet again. Caroline began to suspect that Penelope must get bored with talk of Felicia. 'Frank's going to run the cinema. That's good, but what will happen when the war finishes?'

'What do you mean?' Caroline asked. 'The cinema won't close. There'll be all the more need for it, whatever happens.'

'Frank might leave the village though.'

Caroline suddenly realised what she meant. If Rudolf came back from Germany would Lizzie choose Frank or him? Still, that wasn't the problem. It wasn't Frank Penelope was interested in, but the cinema.

'If he leaves, I could do it myself after the

war. It will give me something to do, and Isabel would have loved the idea. Yes–' she warmed to the idea – 'I could do it.'

'Won't you want to stay in London?'

'Not without...' Yves' name choked in her throat, as she stared miserably at the pudding.

Simon rescued her. 'Take your time to think about it, Caroline. You've moved a long way from the Rectory, and not only physically. There'll be opportunities in London, even by staying on where you work now.'

'No. I *couldn't.*'

'That's probably what Felicia's saying,' Tilly observed.

'I can't think *why* you're my favourite aunt,' Caroline snarled.

Two days later, she met Felicia for dinner at the Trocadero. Felicia was in penitent mood – though only as far as her anger was concerned. 'I still intend to leave,' she told Caroline blithely.

'Aunt Tilly says "Slug".'

Felicia stared at her, suddenly silent.

'She said,' Caroline added, 'you'd know what she meant.'

'Hell and Tommy,' her normally reserved sister swore. 'Tell Tilly I remember a thing or two as well. No, on second thoughts I'll tell her myself.'

Whatever 'Slug' meant, it worked, for Felicia telephoned her the next day to say she'd be remaining at her post in Endell Street.

The first of July and so it was over a year now since Fred had died. True, the Germans hadn't won yet, but nor had we. Time hadn't made it much easier. The loss of poor Mrs Isabel had brought it all back, and now there were two to mourn for. Margaret even mourned for her old enemy Nanny Oates, who'd been as much a part of the Rectory as she and Percy. Nanny Oates had seen Mrs Isabel into this life, and had gone out with her too. It was a weary old world, and no mistake.

It was a weary old war as well. Ludendorff would be sure to have another push soon, so Master George said. 'You push right back, Master George,' she'd replied mechanically. It was all she could manage, for with his leaving to return to France the last spark of life was going, from the family side of the house at least. To compensate – if that's what it was – there was a new baby on the service side of the house, and that was taking any energy she had and more. Agnes had still not recovered all her strength following what had been a difficult birth. The extra work included Elizabeth Agnes, and the demands of the new baby.

Not that Margaret got much of a look-in there. Miss Lewis, Lady Buckford's maid, had taken a fancy to Isabel Mary, but to her astonishment so too had Lady Buckford herself. Margaret had seen her one day attempting a goo-goo-goo for the babe's benefit, but Lady B's mouth was so out of practice at curving that it was more likely to frighten her to death than amuse her.

And there was still poor Mrs Lilley to cope with, a shadow of her old self. Only Miss Caroline had a magic touch with her nowadays, and that was a fat lot of use with her in London most of the time.

'Oh, just make a Mysterious Pudding,' Mrs Lilley had replied when Margaret had asked her if she had any suggestions for dessert. Margaret continued to observe the tradition of consulting her over menus, but since Mrs Lilley would never remember what she said anyway, she might as well do what she'd planned. They'd worked their way through the strawberries and the raspberries weren't ready yet. Summer was easier than winter in the kitchen, and there was no doubt rationing had made things easier in one way. At least you knew where you were – even if this meant having virtually nothing. Margaret thought wistfully of the days when the Rectory ranked next to the Manor for 'little extras'. Not now. The only mysterious thing about this pudding is why anyone should bother to eat it. Steamed eggs and marmalade and butter for midsummer, indeed.

'Yes, Mrs Lilley,' she'd replied, but she had no intention of cooking it. Eggs were too precious to use in puddings, butter wasn't butter any more, and anyway Mrs Lilley looked as though she was forgetting what food was, for weight was falling off her. What a mercy Agnes had had the idea of calling the baby Isabel. She was a brave girl to suggest it, but it turned out just right.

'Morning, Mrs D.' Frank sauntered in through the tradesmen's entrance. He was looking more like his old self now, helped by little Frank beginning to totter around. Family life suited him. Margaret recalled how much she'd taken against him at first, but she had to admit Frank had stood by Lizzie wonderfully. She pushed to the back of her mind the problem of what would happen if Rudolf came marching home.

A German in Ashden wasn't going to be very popular, no matter who he was. She found herself hoping desperately that Rudolf wouldn't come, and then had to battle with her conscience that she'd been witness to Lizzie's promising to love Rudolf till death them did part. Loving wasn't the same as living with someone, but God wasn't interested in the letter, only the spirit of His law.

'I've come to discuss your cookery talks in the cinema, Mrs D.'

'In advance of yourself, aren't you, Frank?' It was only a week or so since Miss Caroline had arranged with old Swinford-Browne for it to be rebuilt. She'd come home jubilant after that success, only to follow it with a stroke of genius. Frank could carry on Isabel's work. He'd jumped at it, now he'd been officially invalided out. 'Till the end of the war, at any rate,' he'd added casually, and they both knew what he meant.

Frank grinned. 'The rebuilding won't take long. Swinford-Browne doesn't let the grass grow under his feet when he sets his mind to it. I should know.'

He should indeed, having managed the

hop gardens on the Swinford-Browne estate before he went off to war. As it was currently occupied by the army, Mrs Lilley's agricultural force, chiefly Land Girls at the moment, had taken over their cultivation and harvest. What would happen after the war was anybody's guess.

'And I don't let grass grow either,' Frank continued. 'You'll still do your talks, Mrs D?'

Here was a pretty kettle of fish. Margaret was still giving the Government-sponsored cookery demonstrations in Tunbridge Wells once a month, and with everything going on here that was quite enough for the present. True, she missed talks to the village, but if she went back, would Mrs Lilley mind? Margaret sighed as she debated the problem. Perhaps she'd have a word with Fred at the next seance in the Wells to see what he thought. In the old days when Fred had been here on earth, it would never have occurred to her to consult him on anything, but she had convinced herself that God must have put things right in his brain by now. For the first time, however, she found herself doubting the wisdom of this. Even if Fred was contactable in the after-life, was it fair to bother him when he was so happy? *If*

Fred were contactable... Margaret thought again about the Mysterious Pudding. All that was certain in this life was pudding mix and vegetables. Life had to go on, and she must make her own decisions, not rely on Fred.

'I'll sleep on it, Frank,' she replied.

'Good. Could you begin the demonstrations next week?'

'*What?* You've a cheek, young man. They won't be finished building by then. There aren't the menfolk.'

'No. But the loss of one wall doesn't mean that the whole building is unusable. The stage is still there.'

'It's going to be on the draughty side, isn't it?'

It was a perfunctory objection, and she thought about it after he'd left. It was summer, so lack of a wall wasn't an insurmountable problem. Myrtle could look after things here for an hour. She could use the old portable stove. She could show them her fricassee of rabbit, cooked in the haybox. She found herself singing loudly: 'God moves in a mysterious way/His wonders to perform...'

The office was becoming unbearable. Luke

was so jubilant that Felicia was remaining in London that he spared little thought for anyone else and she hardly saw Yves at all. With only a day or two left before the King and Queen's visit began, this should not have been surprising, but desolate herself, his absence increased her isolation. 'One would think no royalty had ever visited Britain before,' was all she permitted herself in the way of protest, when he came home in the small hours one morning.

'None has under the organisation of Yves Rosier,' he replied mildly, as his comforting shape materialised in the bed next to her.

'All going well?' she asked sleepily.

There was a large question mark over the visit for although the Belgian Front was quiet at the moment, and the chances of Ludendorff's expected renewed assault affecting the north of the line slim, if all their intelligence was wrong and the blow did fall there, the King would not leave his army.

'I had a word with Ludo who promised he would not attack the Belgian front this time. Now, my love, do you know what tomorrow is?'

'The day before the King arrives,' she retorted crossly.

He hugged her closer. 'More important still. It's Independence Day.'

'For whom?' Not for her, that was for sure.

'The Americans.'

Now that the American troops were gathering in London in huge numbers on their way to France, anything that affected America now affected England. The American presence and success on the Front had provided a much needed boost to morale, so it was said, but here in London, Caroline was aware merely of one more set of uniforms crowding out the London restaurants, theatres and pubs, changing the city out of all recognition from its pre-war days.

'Tomorrow, Caroline,' he rocked her as he cuddled her in his arms, 'Luke and I have an important engagement, for which we have decided we need the assistance of a Waac.'

'What is it?' she asked guardedly.

'A baseball game at the Chelsea Football Ground.'

'Very funny. Now can I get back to sleep please?'

'This is not a joke,' he whispered. 'It will be an important occasion. This will be the first time Independence Day is celebrated in England, and the first time British and the Americans have fought on the same side since they won their freedom.'

'Freedom?' she echoed indignantly, and poked her elbow back into his chest.

'My apologies. The first time since the rebels foolishly and disastrously chose to call themselves a separate nation.'

'That's better.'

'The US Army is playing the US Navy tomorrow. Your king and queen will be there, Queen Alexandra and the princesses, and every dignitary under the sun, including Colonel Yves Rosier, *and* his staff.'

Sandwiched between Yves and Luke the following day, Caroline could hardly hear herself think. They were both entering into the spirit of the occasion and yelling alternately for the Army and the Navy. 'Nobody,' she tried to cry out to them over the uproar, 'shouts like this at a cricket match.'

'No,' Yves agreed. 'So I've noticed.'

She could make little sense of the game itself, although Luke had tried to explain it to her. All she had gathered was that the players made runs, the game seemed rather like rounders, and there were players called pitchers who seemed to be important. Among the spectators, there were, Luke told her, equally important gentlemen called rooters who led the yelling, chanting and songs for the different sides.

'They're doing a good job,' she shouted fervently.

The din was tremendous, as every pair of American lungs seemed to be yelling at full strength, and everyone else at least at half. Nor were the songs ones she had ever heard before. They were more like chants. She tried hard to identify the words of one, and so far as she could make out it ran: 'Strawberry shortcake, huckleberry pie. Victory. Are we in it? Well, I guess. *Navy, Navy, yes, yes, yes.*' That didn't make sense, did it? What on earth were huckleberries? There was only one moment in the entire afternoon when there was absolute quiet, as the Welsh Guards played 'The Star Spangled Banner'.

At the end of the match, won hands down by the Navy (she was told, for she couldn't have worked it out for herself), every single spectator seemed to be surging onto the field. 'Are they going to attack the winners?' she asked.

'Guess so, lady,' Luke replied cheerfully.

Caroline regarded him severely. 'If my father could hear you talking American slang, he'd forbid you entrance into the family.'

He did not comment, and Caroline was annoyed with herself that in her pre-occupation with her own problems, she had once again overlooked those of others. Instead Luke went on to explain the surge onto the field was normal procedure.

'Maybe they'll do it when the war ends,' she commented.

'Maybe we'll *all* do it then.'

George looked over the side of his SE5a at the flat green fields of France, interspersed with areas of mud. Down there were the trenches, miles and miles of them now that the fighting was so fluid. German advances swept over the original British trench lines and counter-attacks pushed them back. He had never understood how the Tommies could bear to be down there packed like sardines, at the mercy of shells and gas and with rats swimming round them. He supposed the answer was that they had no choice and that some of them could *not* bear it. The Army showed short shrift towards deserters. Now there was a new enemy on the front too – the so-called Spanish influenza that had first crept in in April, and had now gathered momentum in a second wave.

Up here the air was clear, he could breathe, it was a straight and equal battle between the enemy and himself. It was possible up here even to forget his guilt at being alive at all, though he was aware that he now behaved more recklessly in the air than once he did. It had resulted in three victories since he'd been back, and yet he was still alive. The green fields below made him think of summer at the Rectory, but now there was a deep and terrible scar etched deep into the image of home. When he was killed, as soon he surely must be, Mother and Father would grieve, but he reasoned they had Caroline, Felicia and Phoebe to look after them – more than many families nowadays. Florence, for whom he was aware he felt a love that had little to do with the feelings he'd once had for Kate Burrows, would grieve too, but she was young and would recover. In time, he'd be a photograph in her memory, not a living person. He began to wish he hadn't teased Caroline by pretending he was still seeing Kate. Why had he wanted to keep Florence all to himself for the moment? Because, he supposed, they probably had so little time, and he had to make Florence a life apart from his job.

He didn't score on this patrol and that vexed him. If he was going to die, he wanted to take a few more of the enemy with him first. He landed the aircraft skilfully, bumping over the rough grass, and then strolled over to join the mechanics. Preoccupied, he did not notice the subdued atmosphere for a while. When he did, he asked: 'What's up?'

'McCudden's gone west, sir.'

'*The* McCudden?' George repeated incredulously. 'You mean he's dead?'

For a moment he was sure he'd got the wrong end of the stick. James McCudden, with his scores of victories, was immortal. It was only in March he'd left 56 Squadron, where George had known him well, and then he'd been awarded the VC in April. A week or two ago he'd returned to France to join 60 Squadron. Now he too had gone. 'How did it happen?' he asked dully.

'Accident, sir. Engine failure, they think. Just after he took off.'

George was angry. How could mere chance take McCudden, just as it had taken Isabel and Nanny Oates? And what right had he, George Lilley, to have contemplated death with such inevitability when death could reach out and pluck whom it wished?

From now on, he vowed, death would have a fight on its hands, and so would the enemy. After the war, which the Allies would surely win now, he would concentrate on his career as a cartoonist, take Florence to the Rectory, marry her if he were lucky enough, and have children of his own. The first daughter would be Isabel, and the first son would be called James.

Any moment now the train would be steaming out of the station, King George and Queen Mary would return to Buckingham Palace, the band stop playing and the guard of honour of the Reserve Battalion of the Scots Guards depart. Yves would cease to be in attendance on King Albert twenty-four hours a day, and life could resume some sort of normality again. Caroline Lilley was merely allowed to join the small crowd permitted within Charing Cross station itself as the very grand Colonel Rosier's WAAC clerk, of course. He had just been promoted by King Albert. It was less than a week since the King and Queen Elisabeth had arrived in two separate seaplanes from Calais to begin their hectic visit. Their method of arrival had been one of the best-kept secrets, as a security measure. Their visit had begun with the celebrations for the silver wedding of King George and Queen Mary on the Saturday, then they had rushed up to Scotland to review the battleship squadron in the Firth of Forth, returning yesterday to sit in on a War Committee session with Lloyd George.

Caroline had not seen Yves since their arrival until he hurried in yesterday evening to sweep her off to a superb evening concert with a Belgian band at the Albert Hall, in honour of the Belgian King and Queen in the royal box. Lord Curzon had given a speech praising King Albert as 'a king among men and a man among kings', which had pleased Yves (and presumably the King) mightily. When the Belgian national anthem was played, she had even detected a tear in Yves' eye, and saw he was beginning to relax at last. It had been vital that everything went well, since wholehearted Belgian support was essential if the Allies were to withstand the German onslaught.

'It's been a successful visit,' she remarked to Yves at breakfast the next morning, 'thanks to you.'

He had shrugged off his own sterling efforts, but was evidently pleased at her approbation, and had asked her to come today to see King George and Queen Mary bid farewell to their guests. He made his way towards her as the dignitaries left.

'Shall we take lunch at the Ritz to celebrate? A little *foie gras* or caviare?'

It was a well-worn joke. A celebration meal anywhere was impossible nowadays, and a game of pretence over the deliciousness of the repast was the easiest way of making the best of things.

It wasn't the Ritz, nor even Gambrinus. Everywhere was packed out and they ended up at a War Kitchen where the cooking vied with Ellen's for monotony.

'What's worrying you, Yves?' He clearly had not completely relaxed after all.

'You are right as always, *cara*. You know me well.'

Did she? Sometimes she thought so, but not often now. She could not read his silences with accuracy, for her own emotions clouded her mind.

'His Majesty had information from Belgian forced workers who had managed to cross the Yser to the Belgian Army,' he continued, 'and it confirms La Dame Blanche's reports. Ludendorff is building up his forces opposite our army and your Second Army to an even greater extent than we thought. Von Arnim now has fourteen divisions, five of them facing the right of our army. His Majesty is convinced this means an imminent new assault on our lines, but I do not agree. Ludendorff must succeed further south before he tackles the north.'

Caroline had nothing to contribute to this but dismay. On and on it went. How could Yves think that the war would be over this year? If Ludendorff broke through to Paris it would indeed be over, but not with an Allied victory. And either way she would be without Yves. Her stomach lurched with love as he smiled at her. How could she live without him, either emotionally or physically? He had awakened her body, so how could she command it to sleep again and expect it to obey?

'Suppose Ludendorff–?'

He laid his hands gently over hers, and she stared down at them, ashamed of her depression. She remembered those hands as they had first come into her life outside the Gaiety Theatre. His hands to her were like Van Gogh's painting of boots, she thought crazily. They revealed Yves' whole life and being.

'There are no ifs, no supposes between us, *cara.*'

'But–'

'Nor buts either.'

'It is hard, Yves.'

'For both of us, *cara*. Does that not make it easier, that we share it?'

She longed to say yes, but she could not, for it was not true.

On the following evening, Yves did not return from the office for dinner as promised, nor had he arrived by midnight. She went to bed, but lay awake wondering what new emergency might have arisen. The darkness lent fuel to her imaginings – had the King been assassinated? Had Yves had to parachute into occupied Belgium?

By the time he arrived, she was wide awake.

'Tell me what's happened,' she insisted.

'Not at two o'clock in the morning,' he pleaded.

'*Tell* me.'

He surrendered. 'There've been serious developments.'

A shiver ran down her despite the warmth of Yves' arms, and she wished she had not asked. In the morning this would be work. At night, far more; it meant the survival of home and all she held dear.

296

'We know Ludendorff will attack the French and American sector near Château Thierry once more on the 15th. Some POWs have spilt the milk.'

'Beans, actually.'

'*Je m'excuse?*'

She giggled, then realised that even in bed this news should be taken seriously. 'Then George will be safe.'

'Von Arnim has brought in the *minenwerfer* and so His Majesty fears that the Champagne assault will be a diversionary one and that the main attack will be on the Belgian and British fronts.'

Eleven

'You're looking happy, Agnes. Little Isabel stay asleep all night, did she? She's a good little girl.'

More than her namesake had been, Margaret remembered. It was true Mrs Isabel had been a year old when she and Percy came to the Rectory, but the din she used to make then suggested poor Mrs Lilley had found her a handful in the early months, and Nanny Oates couldn't have been much help. Belatedly, Margaret remembered her old enemy had met a terrible end, and conscience-stricken, she made a silent prayer of apology. She had the uneasy thought that perhaps the fact that Nanny had already been installed here when the Dibbles arrived might have had something to do with their never seeing eye to eye. Another prayer would be in order tonight. Tragedy brought reconciliations. For the first time in living memory the Mutters and Thorns had not only sworn a truce after one of each family had been killed on Bankside,

298

but resolved never to feud again. The Rector had been delighted, but Percy said once a Mutter, always a Mutter.

'Yes, she did, but that's not the reason I'm happy.' Agnes glowed. 'I've had a letter from Jamie. I was beginning to worry because I'd heard nothing.'

'What's he got to say for himself?'

Jamie was still on the Western Front with the 7th Sussex. Field Marshal Haig had said they had to fight with their backs to the wall, but the way things were going they'd soon have their backs to the seaside.

'He sounds cheerful – like he always does. He doesn't want me to worry, he says. We're going to win the war and that's that.'

'I'll believe it when I see raisins back in the shops,' Margaret said grimly.

Agnes was lost in her usual dream in which she lived in a home of her own with Jamie and the two kiddies. She sighed. A little confidence that the dream would come true was no bad thing, but a little evidence that Jamie was right about the war would be better. Like the troops sang, 'Oh my, I don't want to die, I want to go home'.

'So will I. They've been saying it will be over by Christmas ever since 1914,' she said bitterly.

Margaret had no comfort to give, though she tried. 'Just one more push is all it needs.'

'Aren't you enjoying it?'

London theatre shows were hardly of the high quality of previous years. With the capital packed with every nationality under the sun, all seeking escape in entertainment, this was to be expected. Even so, Felicia's obvious lack of interest in *The Boy*, which was a musical adaptation of a Pinero play, surprised Caroline. It was better than most current offerings.

Felicia shrugged apologetically as Caroline handed her her drink in the Adelphi bar. 'The last play I saw in London was *Chu Chin Chow* two years ago. Remember? All I've seen since are the occasional travelling plays or revues for the forces if I happened to be at the right place at the right time. I even saw Phoebe's beloved Billy once. Odd, isn't it? Phoebe seems to have found happiness at last, and yet of all of us she seemed the least likely to do so.'

'She's getting very bored with staying at home as a lady in waiting.'

Billy had put his foot down, much to Phoebe's annoyance, and forbidden her to continue her driving work either here or abroad. For the sake of the baby she had reluctantly agreed it was sensible.

'She's only been at home a week or two. She told me she was getting bored out of her mind, and certainly she still looks fit enough. You'd hardly know she was pregnant.'

'Bored? What a surprise.' Felicia laughed. 'I'm glad Phoebe hasn't changed completely. Anyway, you're out of date. She's got a new project.'

'Tell me the worst,' Caroline groaned, remembering Phoebe's venture at Ashden. 'What's she doing? Serving lemonade outside Victoria Station?'

'No. She is still driving, but she's come to a compromise with Billy. She's taking convalescent soldiers to wherever Billy's singing in London. There'd be too much competition from the WVS for her to serve teas and lemonade. Not much room for individual effort now,' Felicia added ruefully.

'It's the overall effort that's the vital one.'

'Don't be sanctimonious,' Felicia replied amiably.

'Why not? You are.'

'Am I?' Felicia was taken aback. 'I never used to be.'

'I suppose,' Caroline said thoughtfully, 'it's the war caused that, not just for you and me, but for most women. We began the war with a fight to gain recognition that we had a wider role to play in it than the traditional female one, and now we've proved we can do most things just as well as men, and we're indispensable, smugness is the result. It will be interesting to see what everyone does after the war – retreat into the home nest or spread our fledgling wings further.'

'In our different ways I think the home nest is ruled out for both of us, don't you agree?'

'I don't know.' Caroline felt bruised at another reminder of a future she dared not think about too deeply. Why couldn't everyone just keep *quiet* about it, till it happened?

Felicia must have noticed, for she compensated with surprising openness. 'Luke's asked me to marry him two days after the war's over.'

'Ah. And have you accepted?'

'Ever seen an ostrich?'

Caroline laughed. 'Indeed I have. Our heads will collide in the ground. I'm as bad as you. I just daren't think beyond the end of the war.'

'That may not be good.'

'Look who's talking.'

'I don't know what to do, Caroline. I love Luke in one way, Daniel in quite another. He's *part* of me. Luke wants to marry me, Daniel won't.'

'It seems obvious from that which way you would like to jump. Are you still seeing Daniel?' Felicia never mentioned him, so Caroline could not resist this opportunity to ask.

'I've seen him twice since I've been in London, which at least is more often than when I was at Ashden. I suppose he feels now he's done his bit by bringing me back to England, he can walk out of my life again. I know it can't be easy for him, because he *does* care for me. So much in fact that he wants me to forget all about him, and marry Luke. Whatever I say I can't persuade him that I can live without children and without physical love; he thinks I'm just being noble. He doesn't credit me even now for knowing my own mind.' It was the first time Felicia had confirmed what Caroline and Luke had suspected.

'He probably does, but he's thinking of your best interests.'

'*I* decide that,' said Felicia firmly. 'Not Daniel.'

'He does have a say in it.' Caroline felt torn by the problem, fond as she was of both Luke and Daniel. 'Is Luke coming to Ashden for my birthday party on Sunday?'

'Ah. I'm sorry, Caroline. I forgot to tell you. I can't come. I'm on duty, and though I tackled the Medusa' – her name for her *bête noire* at Endell Street – 'she set the snakes on me.'

Caroline tried to hide her disappointment. This year of all years she had wanted to spend her birthday not only with Yves but with her sisters and parents at the Rectory.

'I can't wait for the war to end,' Felicia continued viciously, 'so I can tell Medusa what I really think of her. Stupid, isn't it? Longing for it to end, and at the same time dreading it, and you must be in the same boat. When does Yves think it will be over, this year or next?'

'This year,' Caroline replied bleakly. 'It looks as if Ludendorff's latest offensive isn't going too well. To turn the tide just needs one more push.' It had indeed been on the Château Thierry front, and thanks to good intelligence and a brilliant deception thought up by the French, the initial attack had not been as successful as the Germans had planned. They were forging ahead now though, and had to be stopped.

Caroline pored over their copy of the Order of Battle compiled by GHQ Intelligence in Montreuil from the information they gathered from all quarters.

'They think now the German attack in Champagne has failed' – the French-American counter-attack had reclaimed the whole of the Château Thierry area – 'that the chances of their continuing as planned to strike in the north are nil. Do you think that's reliable, Luke?'

'It was partly based on the lack of troop trains and other transport reported via us from La Dame Blanche,' Luke replied drily.

Caroline smote her head. 'Of course. I'd forgotten.'

'Waacs aren't supposed to forget. Their job is to remember everything that *we* forget,' Luke proclaimed. 'Incidentally Felicia's invited me to your birthday party.'

'You haven't heard, then. She's on duty that evening.'

'You won't want me then.' He looked cast down, and she hastened to reassure him.

'It will be a family picnic, and of course you must come. It's – it used to be great fun. We've abandoned picnics while the war's been on, but I felt we should all be together, this year of all years!' Memories of past birthdays swamped her mind, Isabel falling over the tree trunk flat on her face into the pond, a young Isabel climbing the tree and crying out: 'Look at me. I'm beautiful and so is the tree', Isabel kissing her crying, 'Oh, I'm glad I have such a lovely sister', Isabel...

She stared down at the Order of Battle but she could no longer see it for the tears in her eyes. She had seen so many horrors in the last few years, and had believed nothing could touch her any more. How could Fate have had one more cruel trick up its sleeve? She knew families must be saying that all over the world, but what help was that?

George almost stumbled into the mess with tiredness. They were in action day and night on offensive patrols and bombing raids, now that the British were attacking on the Flanders front. They were raining bombs down behind the enemy lines, and it was clear that the RAF's contribution to the battle was crucial. The CO had said the clack was that the war wouldn't end till 1919, but that Haig was determined to make it 1918. If there was anything George Lilley could do to help that, he would. He began to plan a cartoon of Ludendorff and the Kaiser cancelling plans to spend Christmas in Buckingham Palace. That way he could divorce himself from the grim reality of his daily life. He had not seen Florence for two weeks now, and he hardly cared, for he was so tired. Soon, they would be together for ever.

Just one more push was all it needed to end this war.

'Jokey's done us proud with them lettuces,' Percy announced, bringing three samples into the kitchen. 'He told me in Germany they grow different sorts.'

'They're all lettuces, aren't they?' Margaret said. 'To think that over there in Germany they're growing the same as us.'

Joachim had been granted special permission to give Percy a hand in the garden after he'd finished his supervised work at Lake's Farm. In theory, he had a soldier detailed to look after him while he did so, but in practice it was usually a Land Girl, and sometimes he even came on his own. Margaret had grown quite fond of him in a way; he was a quiet lad, rather like Joe. She tried not to think about Joe, for the thought of another telegram made her sick with fear.

He was still with the 5th Sussex on dangerous pioneer work, and Muriel said he was up in the north of Italy somewhere. It was a long way away, and the thought of his one day coming marching home again made her so dizzy with happiness she had to dismiss it instantly in case it never happened. Over in Germany some poor woman was probably thinking the same about Jokey.

'After all,' Lizzie had said about Joachim, 'where would he run to? He'd be mown down long before he reached the seaside.'

'Mown down? Only by a steamroller,' Margaret had snorted. 'We don't have no *minenwerfer* in Sussex.'

'There's something Jokey wants to ask you, Margaret,' Percy announced, and Joachim appeared nervously behind Percy.

'What is that, Jokey?'

'There is a shed in your garden. It has carved animals in it. And carving tools.'

Margaret went cold. 'You've been in Fred's shed, Jokey?' she asked grimly. *No one* went in there save her and Percy and the family, though even they seldom trespassed.

'*Nein*,' he said hastily, 'I look through windows. I like animals. I like carving.'

'You do, do you?' Her amazement was almost rude.

'*Ja*. At home I carve animals too.'

'Like I said, that's Fred's shed.' Margaret spoke so sharply that Joachim backed hastily out of the kitchen, and she had to call him back. 'I'll think about it, Jokey.'

His face was so delighted she thought maybe he'd misunderstood her. 'Only *think*, I said,' she added. She was thinking very quickly, however. There were knives in there. The next Tunbridge Wells sitting, however, wasn't for another three weeks, so she couldn't ask Fred's advice. Anyway, couldn't she guess what Fred would say? He'd nod vigorously, grinning in his old way. He liked company. She remembered the way Miss Felicia had sat with him for hours on end while he carved, and helped him look after wounded birds and animals.

'All right. You can go in,' she suddenly shouted aggressively, so Jokey wouldn't think she was soft.

Joachim took it from the tone of her voice that he was being refused, and scuttled hastily to the door once more.

'Wait a minute, young man,' she bawled, and he stopped in his tracks. 'You follow me.' Margaret took the precious key and marched down the garden path towards Fred's shed, with Joachim following nervously behind. Carefully, hands trembling slightly, she unlocked it and threw the door open. There were all Fred's animals and birds, just as if he were still here. And perhaps he was. 'There, see what you can do, Jokey. You'll find some spare wood around.'

She left him to it, for she couldn't have stayed a second longer.

Fred would have approved, wouldn't he? Funnily enough, she didn't seem so concerned as once she would have been. Perhaps it was because with Mrs Isabel's death, creating a little happiness seemed more important. Margaret even found herself wondering if everything *Raymond* said could be relied on. The medium had said some very odd things, and Margaret still wasn't quite sure why Fred couldn't speak to her direct instead of through that Egyptian slave and the medium. The Rector had been very grateful to her for telling him about *Raymond,* but she had a feeling he still didn't approve.

Perhaps with Joachim using the shed she might come to terms with it all. Perhaps it wasn't right to close herself up so much against the world. She should throw open her own doors like this shed, and let a bit of life into herself. See what she could do to cheer the Rectory up. Poor Mrs Lilley was like a ghost, she was so thin now. The Rector was getting greyer by the day and more silent. Now most families had suffered bereavement, people had given up wearing black and often they didn't even wear arm bands. Margaret wondered if people in Germany felt like they did. Odd really. When this war started, she'd only thought of Germany as the place where the Kaiser lived. She thought of it quite differently now she knew people were over there struggling to grow food to eat and battling with grief, just like they were here.

Agnes came slowly into the kitchen, with her beeswax polish and cloth, looking as if even a touch of elbow grease was too much for her.

'Sit down, Agnes. I'll make some tea. You look all washed up.'

'The baby kept me awake last night – it looks as if her good period is over. And I had another letter from Jamie, not so happy as usual. All this to and fro-ing has knocked the stuffing out of the Tommies' morale, and it's made worse by the miners and engineers being on strike here.'

'It doesn't seem right, does it?' Margaret

sympathised there. You never knew who was going on strike next these days. 'There's men out there fighting for their homeland, and there's them exempted from call-up because of their job, then refusing to do it so that the men at the front are short of ammunition.'

'I keep thinking my Jamie might be killed all because of them.' Agnes burst into tears.

This was something Margaret could deal with. She slid a cup of tea in front of the weeping girl. 'Now, Agnes, you're overtired. Anyway, I read that Winston Churchill is going to have them called up if they don't go back to work.'

'And a good job too,' Agnes said fiercely, wiping her eyes, and managing a giggle. 'Suppose you went on strike from your Food Economy classes?'

George circled over base. He was keyed up and exhausted. The RFC – no, RAF – he still found it difficult to think of the force under its new name – was doing its best to slow down the enemy advance. They were still raining down bombs like Mrs Dibble's rock cakes, and though there were Fokkers and Pfalzes around in plenty, especially in the evenings, nothing was going to stop them from raining down thousands more. Today the squadron had bombed Epinoy aerodrome in company with 3 Squadron and two others, and George was carried away with the thrill of success. Their 25-pounders had set not only hangars on fire, but enemy machines. One of them was thanks to the Major who had dived down to within ten feet to hit a Pfalz scout, and the plumes of smoke from workshops had filled George with fierce glee.

He landed his kite back on the bumpy grass, and to stretch his legs decided to stroll over the rough field to its perimeter. By the ditch at the far side, almost hidden by undergrowth, he stumbled across a wooden cross, and sick with horror George realised he was standing on a grave. This land had been fought over many times and there was nothing to indicate whether the occupant of this grave was British, French or German. And did it matter? George wondered wearily. Known unto God, wasn't that the phrase? Just some soldier, who would never laugh again. Who died for what he believed was right. Or maybe he hadn't even believed that. Soldiers fought on for they had no option, whether illusions of patriotism had died or not. The Tommies were still convinced they were fighting for right, however, and that increased their bitterness that strikers back home, so far from supporting them, were ready to starve them of the tools to fight with, for their own selfish reasons.

George swore softly to himself, and promised this unknown soldier that the tide was beginning to turn. Soon it would all be over.

'I,' Caroline proclaimed unsteadily, 'am 26 years old.' To compensate for Felicia's absence on Sunday, they were having a belated sisterly gathering at Monico's. Phoebe had not come to the picnic either in order to avoid wartime train travel.

'Plus three days,' Phoebe added practically.

'Don't be smug. Just because you're having a baby it doesn't mean elder sisters don't have the right to live.' Caroline stopped, appalled at what she had said. Two glasses of indifferent wine and she lost guard of her words so easily.

'It's all right, Caroline,' Felicia said quickly, seeing her ashen face.

'It isn't,' Caroline replied fiercely. 'How *could* I have said that?'

'As easily,' Phoebe said comfortably, 'as I can think of my baby with happiness. As easily as if Isabel were here with us in the flesh as well as in spirit. How's Mother?' she asked, to change the subject.

'She did her best to be birthday-like, but I think she's still in shock,' Caroline replied.

'What comes after the shock?'

'In mother's case,' Felicia said soberly, 'the pain.'

Caroline sighed. 'What can we do?'

'Phoebe's baby will help rouse her.'

'But that's months away,' Phoebe objected. 'She can't go on like this till January–' She looked from one stunned face to another.

'You told us November.' Felicia was the first to speak.

'Yes,' Phoebe said quickly. 'It may be a week or two late though.'

'It's elephants take a couple of years to produce their young, not you,' Caroline said scathingly. 'Just when is your baby going to be born?'

Phoebe toyed with her minuscule chop. 'Actually,' she finally said, 'it's due in mid-January.'

'Mathematics aren't my strong point,' Caroline said crossly, 'but that means your baby started its existence in mid-April?'

'Yes,' Phoebe muttered.

'Which is when you were married.'

'Yes.'

'Do you mean to say—' Caroline was furious – 'that when Billy went down to confess all to Father, there *was* no baby?'

'That's right.'

'Did Billy think there was?'

'No,' Phoebe retorted indignantly, 'that wouldn't have been fair.'

'Fair!' Felicia and Caroline shouted together, and a few curious faces turned to look at them. The level of noise in the restaurant was high fortunately.

'Phoebe,' said Caroline grimly, 'of all the dotty things you've done, this takes the cake.'

'I second that,' Felicia agreed. 'Do you ever think of anyone else? What do you think the effect on Father and Mother will be when they find out, or are you hoping it may escape their notice that your baby is two months late?'

'It was Father's fault,' Phoebe rejoined, looking injured. 'He wouldn't let me get married when I wanted to just because Billy is divorced. He was going to be foul about it whether I married in April or after my birthday in June.'

'But weren't you being a little unfair on Billy?' Felicia asked.

'It did take a lot to talk him round,' Phoebe admitted, 'but even he agreed there'd be an almighty row sooner or later with Father, so why not have it now and we could get married when we wanted to.'

'The deceit!' Caroline was appalled. 'And the hurt, that's why it's not honest.'

'Like you living with Yves as his wife and letting the parents think you were just working with him?'

'That's different,' Caroline cried. 'That was to *save* them hurt.'

'Didn't succeed, did it?' Phoebe answered smugly.

'Phoebe, shut up,' Felicia said swiftly, seeing Caroline on the verge of tears. 'Pick on me if you have to. I'm not so vulnerable. You've behaved dreadfully to us all, and what Caroline said is quite right. What were you going to do if you hadn't got pregnant, incidentally? Invent a miscarriage?'

'I hadn't thought as far as that.'

'That's your trouble, Phoebe. You never do think,' Felicia said sharply.

That set Phoebe off again. 'And you do, I suppose. Very well, what do you think *you'll* do after the war? Return to Ashden?'

'I don't believe I could,' Felicia answered calmly.

'Won't you marry Daniel then?'

Felicia promptly lost the battle. 'I don't know, I don't know. I don't damned well *know*. Is that clear?'

'Yes,' Phoebe said sweetly.

'I've had a letter from home,' Caroline said jubilantly to Yves on 1st August. 'George has been given a bar to his DSO. Isn't that splendid?'

'Good news indeed. Much needed.'

He was right. There still seemed to be stalemate on the Western Front. June had seen yet another big raid on the Belgian clandestine newspaper *La Libre Belgique*, although once more it had resurrected itself. In July the Russian royal family had disappeared and there were many dark rumours over their fate. What worse news could August bring? Caroline wondered.

It brought not bad news, but significantly good.

On 8th August in a major new assault British tanks burst through the German lines at Amiens.

Twelve

Front doors were frightening while you were waiting outside for agonising long minutes before knowing whether the news inside was going to be good or bad. Caroline could hear her heart beating loudly, as she tried to restrain her imagination from fearing the worst. She hadn't seen Phoebe since their quarrel at the end of July, nearly a month, but news that she was having trouble with the baby had brought her rushing over. At long last – or so it seemed – Judith, Phoebe's general maid – opened the door. She had not been trained to deal with emergencies, and spoke by the book in her timidity.

'What name shall I say, Miss?'

Caroline brushed her aside with a kindly, 'You *know* me, Judith. Mrs Jones' sister.'

At the sound of her voice Billy came out from the morning room to greet her. He looked as if he hadn't slept for days – and probably hadn't. He also looked somewhat shamefaced, since he must surely know that

Phoebe had told her the truth.

'How is she?' Caroline asked. 'I came as quickly as I could.' Not more bad news, she could not bear it after all that had happened.

'She's all right, and so will the baby be if she rests.' Billy was crying, but with relief, not grief.

Thank you, God. Caroline made her own silent prayer of gratitude, and now that she knew all was well, Caroline felt the tears pricking at her own eyes. Another night summons, with all its awful recollections of May, had left her expecting the worst, since only the worst ever seemed to happen now. Each telephone call seemed to spell death or disaster, and Mrs Dibble hadn't helped when she announced gloomily – though not in Father's hearing – 'There'll be more bad luck, you'll see. Troubles never come singly.' A little Christian optimism and rather less Sussex superstition might be in order, Caroline felt. The night telephone call had convinced Caroline that Mrs Dibble was right, however, and it took some time for relief to relax the tension in her body.

'Can I see her, Billy?'

'She was dozing, but she may be awake by now.'

Caroline still found it hard to think of Phoebe as the mistress of a house. Marriage had only worked some wonders, however, for the house, run with a cook and a general maid, bore distinct signs of Phoebe's happy-go-lucky approach to the finer details of household management. Not that she could talk. There were many times at Queen Anne's Gate that she silently cried out for the help of Mrs Dibble, since Ellen's household expertise was roughly on a par with Isabel's. This unbidden recollection sent a fervent rush of gratitude through her that Phoebe's baby was safe, and she pushed open the bedroom door quietly.

Phoebe's dark hair was spread out around her, and her eyes were closed. The normally pink-cheeked complexion was pale, and lying unaware of Caroline's presence, she bore little resemblance to the sister she had grown up with. Then she opened her eyes, and Phoebe was back, grinning with pleasure.

'I saved it,' she crowed. 'All by myself. The midwife said I was a born mother. I didn't need Felicia to nurse me.'

'Felicia doesn't get much call for miscarriages,' Caroline managed to joke.

'It wasn't a miscarriage. Although,' Phoebe

admitted, 'it was nearly. I have to stay in bed for at least two weeks. Isn't that awful? I wanted to go on Billy's next tour in France.'

'It will be a chance to catch up on your reading.' Caroline tried to keep a straight face. Phoebe was notorious for her lack of interest in books.

Phoebe's face grew even longer, then brightened. 'I thought I might embroider some cushion covers. Mother could teach me. Is she coming up?'

'I haven't told her yet, darling. I wanted to be able to assure her you were all right.'

'Oh.' Phoebe sighed. 'I suppose it's selfish to expect her to come rushing up when travelling is so difficult nowadays? She could stay here though. Do you think she would? If you could persuade her, I promise I'll confess my dastardly deed to her.'

Caroline looked at Phoebe's wistful face, then thought of her mother's dazed grief over Isabel. 'Do you know, Phoebe, I think it might be just the very thing she needs.'

'Mrs Dibble!'

Margaret looked up in astonishment. Mrs Lilley actually sounded a little like her old self. She hadn't heard that note of excitement in her voice since it had all happened, and here was the mistress hurrying into her kitchen just like she used to.

'Mrs Phoebe isn't well, Mrs Dibble. Caroline thinks it would help if I spent a few days there to ensure she does exactly what the midwife orders. My husband agrees. Do you think you can manage without me for a little while?' Elizabeth asked anxiously.

It was hard for Margaret to keep a straight face. Poor Mrs Lilley was more hindrance than help nowadays; half the time she was unarranging everything that Margaret had just arranged. She had tried to help out with the shopping one day when Lady Buckford had one of her officers' parties in the drawing room, and had managed to use a whole month's sugar allowance. These newfangled ration books took some getting used to, even for those with all their wits about them, and Mrs Lilley was as scatter-brained as dear Mrs Phoebe at present.

'You stay as long as you like, Mrs Lilley. Mrs Phoebe needs you and that's more important than rations and agricultural rotas.'

The minute the last two words were out of her mouth Margaret realised she'd put her foot in it. Mrs Lilley's face was as horror-struck as Pearl White's when she saw the train speeding down the tracks to which she was tied.

'Oh, Mrs Dibble. I hadn't thought of that. What am I going to do? I can't possibly leave. I have my job to think of. And there's the petrol allocations to do, not to mention a Rat and Sparrow Club meeting. Oh, what *shall* I do?'

Margaret scrabbled for an answer, and the Lord provided one. 'Don't you worry about a thing, Mrs Lilley. My Lizzie and her Frank can manage everything between them.'

'But–'

'But's a word we don't use in wartime, Mrs Lilley,' Margaret said briskly. 'Best foot forward, as they say, and your best foot is needed to take you to Mrs Phoebe at the moment.'

And that was that. Mrs Lilley looked at her doubtfully for a moment, and left, relieved and convinced. Which was more than Margaret was. She hoped she hadn't bitten off more than she could chew – or, rather, than Lizzie and Frank could chew. She comforted herself that the cinema couldn't take all his time, and he was well used to agricultural organisation. She decided to put her hat on and go straight away. Luncheon was only rissoles and they

324

wouldn't take long. Frank didn't start at the cinema until the afternoon, and she found him at home looking after Baby Frank. She still thought of him as Baby Frank, for all he was toddling around.

'Do you think you can do it, Frank?'

'I think I can cope,' he answered, so straight-faced she had her suspicions.

'No laughing matter,' she snapped. He was her son-in-law after all, and a bit of respect never did anyone any harm. Belatedly she realised he wasn't her son-in-law at all, although secretly she hoped he would be some day.

She found herself asking straight out: 'How do you manage, Frank? Knowing...' She broke off, appalled, but it was out.

He didn't answer her for a moment, staring out of the window as covetously as the Kaiser must look at the map of England. 'You mean if Rudolf comes back?'

'Yes.' She didn't add that it was more likely to be when, rather than if. He knew that.

'I manage like we all manage in this war. I go on from day to day. Even now that we've pushed the Germans back, nothing's certain. It could end this year, more likely next, and who knows who'll be in the chauffeur's seat after that?'

'No need for talk like that, Frank. Not after this last week.'

Only a week ago, at Amiens, our lads had driven them back seven miles, when they broke through on a fifteen-mile front. The newspapers were treating it as a great victory. That had happened before, of course, so like everyone else, Margaret was waiting to see. Percy said it was the tanks that made the difference. So far it looked good because the Germans hadn't regained the ground, even though Ludendorff seemed to have endless supplies of troops. Children, many of them, so Joe had told Muriel, and even in England they weren't too fussy about whether boys had reached their nineteenth birthday or not.

'Can you come to see Mrs Lilley right away, Frank? I'll look after Baby.'

He hesitated. 'Only for ten minutes. I have another appointment at twelve.'

'It won't take you long to get to the cinema from the Rectory.'

'It's at the Dower House.' Frank looked awkward.

Wonders would never cease. What kind of appointment could Frank have at the Dower House?

Margaret dismissed this puzzle from her mind by turning her attention to potatoes as soon as she was back. The only uncertainty about potatoes was whether they had enough. She might have to ask Percy to dig some more, for you knew where you were if you grew your own. The Government couldn't make up its mind whether it wanted you to eat them or not. They had a pile of leaflets giving you potato recipes you'd learned at your mother's knee, and no sooner had that come through the letter-box than one followed telling you not to eat them because they were scarce. Miss Caroline had told her that in London the polite thing to do when invited to dine at a private house was to arrive not with flowers or chocolates but a bag of potatoes. Quite right too.

On her way through to the garden via the 'servants' hall', she caught sight of *Raymond*. The Rector had returned the book and it was sitting not in her own room but on the communal bookshelf. It was with some surprise that she realised that she had not glanced at it for at least a month, and the amount she had to do nowadays it might be yet another month before she did so again. Would Fred mind? It struck her that he wouldn't, because Fred was not Raymond, and Raymond was not Fred. She struggled with this thought for a time, since for months the two had become intertwined.

If she put *Raymond* away, or passed it on to another grieving person – no, she wouldn't do that. It would be influencing people. The important thing was that Fred would still be there, just as he always had been. In fact, she might see more of him. *See?* It wasn't exactly *seeing,* just the sense that Fred was around, and that even if he wandered off on his own devices, that's what he had always done. He used to lose himself for hours at a time in the garden or in the village. What was so different about heaven?

'Tis only the splendour of light hideth thee.' She sang away with fervour as she put the book away in her own bookcase.

'And if you should happen to run into Raymond up there, Fred,' she added silently, 'thank him for me, would you?'

'Cumming has sent us an intercepted signal to von Falkenhausen in Brussels from Ludendorff. Have a look at it. It's interesting.' Luke tossed it on Caroline's desk.

She glanced at it, then read it with more attention. 'He calls 8th August a black day for the German Army. I agree. *Very* interesing.'

Ludendorff's tendency to gloom was by now well known, and if he foresaw the beginning of the end of the Kaiser's scatty dreams, then the army itself would soon see it, for it would percolate from the High Command down to the lowest ranking soldiers. Quite right too. Luke and Yves knew from La Dame Blanche that the indomitability of *La Libre Belgique,* which was managing to print articles smuggled out from the Vilvorde prison, was a severe thorn in von Falkenhausen's flesh, and more good news was that the French had just launched a successful offensive of their own, having failed to persuade Haig into following up quickly on the Amiens success.

'It won't be long, with this kind of intelligence, before Haig does launch another attack,' Luke declared happily.

Caroline did not reply, and Luke glanced at her. 'Mixed blessing for you, sweetheart,' he added sympathetically.

'And maybe for you.'

'Separate the two, Caroline. Rejoice that the war is creeping slowly towards some kind of conclusion even if it's not an outright victory, and even if we have to wait for next year. We can deal with the results of it later.'

That was easy enough to say, Caroline thought crossly, though she admitted he was probably right. The recent apparent upturn in the Allied fortunes had forced her to face the fact that she was living in a fool's paradise. The paradise element was splendid, but she was careering headlong towards disaster if she ignored its short duration.

Whatever the cautious hopes of the military, the general mood of the people, like Caroline's, however, had not changed. Summer had not brought renewed hope, it had brought ration books, fines for hoarding, and the same old daily struggle; now in late August the thought that winter was coming once again, inexorably bringing even more shortages and hardships, added to the gloom. With no fuel, little coal, less food, and a grey drabness in clothes and entertainment, a hush had fallen over everyday life. Any rejoicing at military success was weighed down with the loss of loved ones, and fear that more might be in store. Caroline would have her own form of bereavement to face, and the fact that it was inevitable did not make it easier.

Yves had seemed distracted these last few days, although even more tender and loving towards her, as if the coming parting had become suddenly more real to him also. He had gently warned her that if the next British offensive was planned for the north, he would have to leave.

'For good?' The thought that parting was nearer than she had reckoned with had made her cry out in horror.

'No, I would return,' he had promised, 'but for how long we cannot know.'

'I'm not sure it's my place to tell you this, Caroline,' Luke was now saying to her, 'but I think I will. Have you noticed anything about Yves recently?'

'He's been preoccupied, worried about the next offensive.'

'It's not that,' Luke said gently. 'He's had news of his wife.'

A sledgehammer hit her in the stomach. The wife was *real;* she was probably looking forward to Yves' return. The monster Caroline had built up in her mind transposed itself into a normal, anxious woman, who was far more difficult for her to handle than a monster.

She licked dry lips. '*What* news?' She tried to dismiss a hope that she didn't want Yves back, that she had found someone else to love, and even a sneaking, debasing hope that she was dead.

'Nothing much. I think that's what has upset him. He may have been hoping for a miracle. Life isn't that obliging,' Luke said wryly. 'He's discovered through La Dame Blanche that she's still in their home, that she fiercely resisted billeting German officers, because she was determined to keep the estate for Yves. She's remained close to Yves' family. He has a nephew apparently of whom he's very fond. Did you know that?'

'No.' Caroline's voice jerked out its pain.

'I'm sorry, Caroline. In my experience it's better to know the truth.'

'Is it?' Just at the moment that seemed hard to believe.

It was difficult to appreciate when you were just one aircraft in the sky, George reflected, just what was being achieved, if anything. One counted the enemy planes the squadron had scored, one did one's best to add to it, but how far this was helping win the war was impossible to tell. The amount of bombs they were dropping must be achieving something, though. And then there were all the daytime offensive patrols. And, by jingo, they *were* offensive! Two days after Amiens, Captain Burden had run into a bunch of enemy aircraft and shot down two of them. Not content with that, he had a go at a second group, and shot down another one. Then in the evening he was up again and brought down two more. Then the other day Captain Halleran had dived between two Hannoveraners, with the happy intended result that they collided with each other in their eagerness to attack him, and crashed.

Sometimes it went like that; on the other hand, sometimes you spent the whole day on patrol and saw nothing, or if you did, you shot down nothing. At the moment, however, it didn't seem to matter *who* shot them down, just that they *were* shot down. There was, he felt, a change in the air, a growing conviction that at long last they were getting there, that the achievements outweighed the waste of absent faces in the mess.

George was happy, for he had had a letter from Florence. She had told him she loved him, that yes, she would marry him. He would have to ask Father, he supposed, since he was still under twenty-one, but nothing could touch him now. He was Hun-proof.

Something was going on. Normally Margaret wasn't that curious as to what went on in the Rectory, knowing it would reach her ears sooner or later, but today she was riveted by the strange events. The first odd thing was that Lady Hunney came a-calling on the Rector, after Rector's Hour. Normally the Rector would have gone to Lady Hunney. The second, even odder occurrence, was that Frank was with Lady Hunney, and moreover the Rector seemed to be expecting them both.

Margaret was agog with curiosity, and walked past the study door as often as she dared. Agnes took them in some coffee and came back to report they seemed to be talking about Bankside. She didn't hear anything about agricultural rotas at all, so that was Margaret's first thought dismissed. So it must be something about the cinema, she decided. Perhaps Frank was saying it should be closed down. Or, more likely, Swinford-Browne was wanting to close it down, and Frank and Lady Hunney were asking the Rector to intervene. The mystery was solved, she decided, and wished them well, for although she had to admit she wasn't in favour of the cinema when it first opened, she had felt she had a proprietorial interest in it since Mrs Isabel died. Besides, the cinema provided a nice evening out for her and Percy, there was no denying that. It wasn't all war propaganda films and heroic tales. There was Charlie Chaplin – not to mention Mary Pickford.

Lady Hunney didn't stay as long as Frank. She left in the old carriage she used nowadays, for it was unpatriotic to use fuel for private motoring. Percy reported that Lady Buckford had joined her, and off they both went all pally and friendly just as if they hadn't been at each other's throats when Lady B first came to the village.

Quite by chance – and it *was* chance – Margaret was in the entrance hall when Frank came out of the study, followed by the Rector. She was horrified to see it looked as if the Rector had been crying, and she looked hastily away.

'I was coming to see you, Mrs Dibble,' Frank said formally. 'Can you spare a moment?'

It seemed silly to call Frank sir, although he was calling on the Rector, so Margaret replied, 'I'll make a nice cup of tea.'

Frank was grinning broadly by the time he reached her kitchen.

'You got your way then?' she asked. 'No shilly-shallying?'

'No. The Rector's delighted.'

'He wasn't that keen on it when it first opened.'

Frank looked blank. 'Keen on what?'

'The cinema.'

He burst out laughing.

'And what's so funny, might I ask?' Margaret asked belligerently, hands on hips.

'You, Ma Dibble. Not often you get fooled as to what's going on.'

She drew herself upright, about to point out that she wasn't Ma Dibble to him, thank you very much, but thought better of it. She was too curious now. 'If it wasn't the cinema you were discussing, what was it?'

'Lady Hunney, instead of rebuilding the cottages on Bankside, is going to give the land to the parish as a memorial to Mrs Isabel. She was here to ask permission to call it "Isabel's Garden".'

Margaret sat down heavily, in even more need of her cup of tea. 'Oh, what a lovely idea of hers.'

Frank patted her shoulder anxiously when she began to sniffle. 'I didn't mean to upset you.'

Margaret blew her nose on the inadequate

handkerchief, one Lizzie had sewn for her when she was a little girl, and now washed and ironed until all the colour had gone over the years.

'It will have to be vegetables, not flowers, until the war's over,' he continued, 'but I thought we might plant one rose now, just to remember her by.'

'You? What have *you* got to do with it?' Margaret asked rather rudely. When he said nothing, she realised exactly what Frank had had to do with it. 'It was your idea, wasn't it?'

'Perhaps, but someone would have thought of it. Lady Hunney herself probably, since she was looking for something to do in the way of a memorial to Isabel.'

'Isabel?' Margaret repeated sharply. Why did Frank call her that quite naturally? It wasn't his place. Then as he went slightly pink, she decided not to enquire further. Whatever was the reason, it was past, and buried with poor Mrs Isabel.

Frank didn't answer her – or so she thought. After he had gone, however, and she thought about what he had said, she decided he had replied after all. All he had murmured to himself as he left was: 'Just one rose for Isabel.'

'Look!' Caroline stopped short.

Yves' long stride had already carried him several yards ahead, and he returned to her side anxiously.

'The leaves are beginning to turn *already*,' she said dismally. 'September has hardly begun, and look, there's even some fallen.' She shivered despite the sun, for it seemed to her symbolic of what lay ahead. Here they were, in St James's Park, still full of late afternoon beauty, despite the hideous scar in its middle, and she was meditating on death and decay.

'Why does it matter?'

'It means autumn is on the way – and General Winter.'

'It was General Winter defeated Napoleon in Russia. Perhaps it will do the same for the Kaiser.' When she did not comment, he continued: 'I'm sorry, *cara*. I realise it is not the war that you see in these dead leaves. It is me. You think of our love in that way?' He took her hand.

'Not you, but your leaving.' Her voice was unsteady.

'That is good, for you must surely know–' He stopped and took her in his arms '–our love will never be a falling leaf. It will be evergreen.'

She could not help herself. 'You know that is not so,' she burst out sadly. 'It will grow less and less as the years go on, and finally shrivel until you and I are just embalmed as photographs, to be framed as part of each other's past. Though I don't suppose your wife–'

He put his finger across her lips. 'No, *cara*, I do *not* know that, and nor can you. I do believe the pain will grow more bearable, but that is all. For you one day it can be laid gently aside as a new love replaces it.'

'You *cannot* really believe that, Yves.' Did he know her so little?

'I believe that life is practical. That where it cannot conquer, it seeks an armistice.'

'So that is the way it will be for you? You will lay me aside and remember only your love for your wife?'

'I do not love her. I respect her, I like her, we are companions, and that is all. But I do not believe you are *listening* to me. When I say my love will never die, I mean only that, with none of the interpretations forced on you by doubts and sadness. This has been a year of happiness I could never have dreamed of, and such love does not die. Like these trees of yours, it is still there despite the outward signs of winter. The trunk and branches do not perish. Only the leaves must renew themselves.'

'Hold me close, Yves. Convince me that what you say is true.'

In uniform and surrounded by other embracing couples, they seemed just two more sweethearts thrown together by war, and about to be swept away from each other, like flotsam and jetsam.

'And now,' he whispered, as his lips left hers, 'I must tell you something that will make you sad, *cara.*'

'You're going *now?*'

'Very soon.'

'The offensive?'

'This month. But I will return. Death will not take me.'

'You mean you'll be *fighting*, not just on liaison work?' A new terror gripped her.

'There was a time when to do that seemed the obvious end to my dilemma.'

'No!' she cried, appalled. 'Please, don't *fight!*'

'I must.'

'Then do not be rash. Don't *seek* death. Please.'

'Even though the alternative is that I shall then return to my wife?'

'Even that.'

'Then you are even more loving and generous than I thought. What gives you the strength, Caroline, when I cannot always find it? Is it Isabel's death? Do you feel you should battle on to compensate for the life she has lost?'

'No.' She saw he needed a serious answer. She did have strength, and it would remain with her even in her greatest agonies. In the last year or two, with Yves to love, she had almost forgotten from where it came. It came from the Rectory.

'Porridge?' Agnes wrinkled her nose up when she saw what Myrtle provided for their breakfast. 'It's only September, Myrtle.'

'Don't you blame her, Agnes.' Margaret bustled into the kitchen. 'It's my instructions. The newspapers say we've got to eat plenty of porridge to keep away the Spanish flu.'

'We don't have to worry out here in the country, surely,' Agnes remonstrated. She hated porridge. 'It's towns and places that have a lot of people sandwiched together that catch it.'

'Mrs Thorn, do I have to remind you you have two young children? Do you want to come marching home from the Wells and pass it on to them?'

Agnes paled. 'I hadn't thought of that.'

Margaret rubbed in her triumph. 'And if I were you, I'd do everything else the paper suggests; make sure you sneeze night and morning, and follow it up with deep breaths, and wash inside your nose with soap and water. I'll be making the household some of those anti-germ masks too.'

Then she relented. 'It's only a precaution, Agnes, but with winter coming on this nasty flu is bound to spread, and it's as well to be prepared.'

'Flu?' Frank came into the kitchen from the Rectory with a face like thunder. 'Don't mention that word to me.'

'Are you here to see Rector about the garden again?' Margaret was puzzled, for she thought everything was settled.

'No,' Frank snarled. 'The cinema. I came to tell him that Swinford-Browne has seized his opportunity. He's closing it down because of the risk of flu.'

She was in a boat, an upturned one, she was sinking. Caroline's eyes flew open to find Luke bending over her, shaking her awake.

'What is it?' She shot up in bed. 'Bad news? Yves?' Yves had left two weeks ago and she had heard nothing since.

'No. And not the Rectory either. It's good news, Caroline. The new British assault has begun. Plumer has attacked the Passchendaele Ridge. Bulgaria has asked for an armistice. Oh, it's all happening.' Luke was excited, stars in his eyes. 'Go to see Felicia immediately and tie her down. I don't want her rushing back to Ypres again. The Belgian army is in action–'

'But the German reinforcements on the way from the east–' It was almost the end of September and she had almost begun to think Yves had been wrong about the timing.

'Diverted to defend Serbia.' Luke perched happily on the side of the bed. 'This isn't perhaps the most proper place to discuss business, but the Germans are on the run now. They're on the losing side and they know it. Ludendorff is running around like a cat with ten tails. This time it's a fight to the finish. It's not going to peter out.'

'How can you be sure?' There had been so many false hopes. Ypres had been fought over continuously since the autumn of 1914. There had been three exhausting

343

battles there already, and even though the salient had never entirely been lost, it was still possible, for the Germans would know that this could be their last chance.

'My guess is Haig's plan is to drive the Germans back, push round on the coast and free Bruges and eventually Brussels. What are the odds that Yves's in the thick of it?'

She felt sick with terror, just as she had been when Reggie had departed. This was worse for in 1914 they hadn't known what it was like out there. Now everyone knew just what fighting on the Western Front was like, and Luke was happily chatting about Yves being part of it.

'Please, God,' she prayed, 'return him safe to me.' Even though when he did, he would have to leave again, and this time for ever.

'What are you doing here?' Felicia stopped in surprise at seeing Daniel waiting for her outside the hospital.

'*Not* very welcoming. I thought we might have dinner if you're off duty now.'

'I am.' Felicia was suspicious. 'This isn't bad news, is it?'

Daniel raised his eyebrows. 'Are you implying that's the only reason I'd make such an offer?'

'Usually, yes.'

Daniel laughed. 'Pure imagination. Not to mention a slur on my noble character.'

An hour later, dining at Rules, Felicia asked politely once more: 'Why are you here?'

'Caroline's afraid you'll scuttle back to Ypres now the offensive has begun again there.'

'I was considering it,' she admitted.

'Then Caroline said "slug" to you. Don't tell me what it means,' Daniel added hastily when he saw the look of thunder on her face.

'I see dear Tilly has been talking.'

'Er – what about?'

Felicia hesitated. 'Promise you won't laugh.'

'On my honour.'

'Out at the Front – well, you know what it's like, and our job was gruesome. One day last summer it was particularly bad. We'd been working for eighteen hours without a break and – to say the least – there was a lot of blood and gore around. Then I found a slug when we at last crawled into our blankets to sleep.'

'Well?' he asked when she stopped.

'I screamed out in terror for Tilly to take it

away. It was only tiredness.' Felicia was defensive. 'Tilly thought it was funny, and after a moment or two so did I. It was an antidote to laugh, I suppose. She said to me, "Now I know you've an Achilles heel like everyone else. Felicia, promise me something." I could hardly refuse. "Learn when to stop," she said. "How," I asked brightly, "will I know when that is?" "You will," she whipped back at me, "for I shall tell you."'

'And now she has,' Daniel said thankfully.

'Yes, I promised, so I must stay here.' She sighed. 'I suppose I've done my bit to atone for Mons.'

Daniel stared at her. 'Is *that* why you chose that part of the line? Because I was wounded at Mons?'

'Yes.'

'It wouldn't work, my love.'

The calm certainty that had been with Felicia all her life that she and Daniel were inseparable suddenly deserted her. He had his own life, his own choices to make, and soon the time would come for decision.

'It will, if we so choose.'

He looked at her compassionately. 'And if I do not choose?'

'You must choose me. Remember what you said to me when you brought me back

346

from France? Choose life, Felicia. Now I say it to you. Choose life.'

'I'm not so selfish.'

'Is it selfish to grant me my dearest wish?'

'Darling Felicia, damn you, Felicia. You know why I won't. We can both choose life, but not with each other. We can't be Abelard and Helöise. Nor, incidentally, have I any intention of going into a monastery after the war, and you shouldn't be thinking of that way out either.'

'I'm not. That decision was made a long time ago.'

'Right. So if – when – I walk away from you, you'll marry Luke.'

'You have no right to ask me that.'

Daniel sighed. 'Look, I don't regard myself as a war-wounded cripple. *My* war work has been in London, it wasn't the five minutes I spent at the Front before a shell put paid, as I thought then, to any hope in my life. Now I know it didn't, and the reason for that is you. You made me see there was life beyond what had happened to me. And there is, even without marriage. Would you want to take away what you gave me?'

Felicia listened, and certainty returned to her. 'I thought,' she said demurely, 'you might like both, with me.'

Daniel surrendered, shouting with laughter. 'I might. Oh, I might indeed.'

Yves returned as the leaves began to fall in earnest, tired and dispirited. The Germans were retreating, but far from defeated. A new assault on the Belgian front was to begin the next day, 14th October, on the River Lys and the Deynze Canal, but he had been sent back to London because of the diplomatic situation. Ludendorff and the German High Command were at odds with the Kaiser and the Reichstag, but the army were still backing their commander. President Wilson's admirable Fourteen Points for Peace a few days earlier had in theory been accepted by the German government, but there was little confidence in their acceptance, since Ludendorff was adamant that Germany should continue to occupy Belgium after the war was over. The enemy had just sunk a passenger steamer off the Irish coast with great loss of life and, worse, intelligence reports suggested that even if the Fourteen Points were accepted and Germany evacuated Belgium, the terms would leave Ludendorff free to devastate Belgium and other occupied land as they retreated to Germany, in order to hold up the Allies from following them there too quickly. Agreed peace therefore looked impossible, but there was no sign of the German High Command being willing to surrender.

'The war will crawl on into 1919,' Yves told her. 'Perhaps a spring offensive might end it.' His voice was tired and without hope, but against her will, Caroline's heart leapt with pleasure at the thought of one last Christmas with Yves. One last Christmas at the Rectory.

If war was doomed to continue, was that so much to wish for?

Thirteen

The maroons boomed out over London. At 11 o'clock French time on 11th November the guns had fallen silent.

'It's over.' Caroline's words sounded flat and unreal, even to her.

It had seemed just another Monday morning in Whitehall until shortly after ten a.m. news had come through Military Intelligence that four years of war were ending this very day. It was impossible to pretend their work still mattered. On the other hand, until those maroons sounded, it was impossible to quieten the instinctive caution that said, wait, this may be one more false alarm. They had compromised by telephoning to Ellen to join them.

She needed no second urging. 'Someone can pinch me to convince me it's really happening,' she'd said.

'Look!' Yves had been standing restlessly by the window, and she went to join him, looking down into the street. A few minutes ago the streets had been almost deserted, but now, like moles greeting spring, every door was opening and more and more people flooding out to join the crowds. What began as little more than a hum, was growing to a crescendo of one deep roaring cheer from Trafalgar Square and Whitehall.

'Let's go.' Caroline was caught up in the excitement. 'Let's *all* go!' Luke and Ellen were already disappearing through the door, but Yves was waiting for her.

She took his hand and pulled him along with her. 'Just for today, let's be happy,' she cried.

They were swept along by the surging crowd into Whitehall, for so long a grey sombre place, but now with the balconies full of red-tabbed high brass, and different coloured uniforms, and the crowds below them waving Union Jacks, colour had returned to it. All buses and taxis were being commandeered by the celebrating crowds; tin hooters were blaring, trays were being banged with zest, and a hundred and one different songs of spring were being hummed, whistled or yelled.

'Where are we going?' Yves shouted into Caroline's ear.

'The Palace, of course. Where else?'

Where else but to go where the people had

gathered when the war began over four years ago, where else to go when four years of slaughter, waste and suffering had ended almost unexpectedly? Despite the increasing military successes in October, despite the surrender of Turkey, and even despite the news two days ago of the armistice with Austria and Hungary, no one truly believed that Germany would have accepted all the Allied terms for peace.

'One last push,' everyone had said. They had said it so often, however, that few had really believed it. Even when the newspapers confirmed some of the wild stories flying round London (Ludendorff had collapsed, he was dead, he had resigned, the Kaiser was dead, the Kaiser had abdicated, Prince Max was in charge, Hindenburg was in charge, no one was in charge, the German fleet had mutinied) they still did not believe it. It was true it was now known that Ludendorff had resigned, the Kaiser had abdicated his throne and left for Holland, and that Prince Max had accepted the Regency and then resigned from it in favour of a Chancellor, but even this news was treated with caution. Ludendorff's understanding of an armistice, after all, had included Germany's right to continue to occupy Belgium, and his obstinacy on this point had been unshakeable. Even though he had resigned, Yves was still naturally concerned that Ludendorff's views might prevail.

No longer, yet there was little to rejoice at in the armistice save that the war was over. The eleventh stroke had chimed, but the known and unknown dead rested silent in the poppy fields of France, in the deserts of Palestine, in the seven seas and wherever the butchering hand of war had stretched.

In Ashden Margaret shifted awkwardly on her knees in the Rectory dining room. They hadn't had family prayers at the Rectory for so long, it seemed strange indeed to be solemnly filing in to join the Rector, Mrs Lilley and Lady Buckford.

'We thank you, Lord, for an end to the suffering of so many people all over the world...'

Margaret listened while the Rector led the prayers, but most of her attention was on a prayer of her own. She was praying for Joe. How proud she'd been to know that it had been a battle in Italy at the River Piave that had forced the Austrians to ask for an armistice. To her it seemed Joe had won it all by himself – and that was a kind of justice, to make up for what the war had done to Fred. Margaret found herself choking, as tears unexpectedly flowed. It must be the relief that it was all over, and she tried not to blow her nose too loudly. Then she heard a loud snort from somewhere, and opening one eye with an apology to the Lord she saw it was Lady Buckford. Mrs Lilley wasn't crying. She had the same set faraway look on her face as ever. Agnes was busy shushing Elizabeth Agnes, who was asking what an armistice was.

'An armistice is when Daddy comes home for ever,' was Agnes' answer, and that kept the little girl quiet.

Margaret thought of Lizzie and what she would be saying to little Frank. Whatever it was, Lizzie most certainly needed a prayer too, but before Margaret could frame her own, the Rector did it for her.

'Lord, let us pray for Lizzie and for Rudolf, far away in Germany...'

At Lake's Farm, Lizzie was alone in the cowshed. To her astonishment, Farmer Lake had given them the rest of the day off, and the Land Girls and POWs had quickly vanished. Even that miserable so-and-so must think there was something to celebrate. Lizzie was in two minds about it. She was glad the fighting was finished with, but the thought of the problems that now had to be faced overwhelmed her, and she found herself reluctant to go back to Frank. Joachim had been working at the farm today, and she'd said to him: 'It'll mean you can go home.'

'*Ja.*' His eyes had been filled with homesickness.

'Your sweetheart must be happy today.' Joachim had showed her the photograph of his sweetheart, a stalwart German *mädchen* with a pleasant face, and soon she would make Joachim a good wife. Not like Lizzie had been to Rudolf, although she loved him. The trouble was she loved Frank too. The time had come to write to Rudolf and tell him about her son. She wasn't any great shakes at writing, and Rudolf would be hurt. He was a kind man though. If he accepted the situation he'd be good to the child. But what about Frank? He'd always wanted a son too, and now he had one he adored. There was going to be no armistice in her problem; it was only just beginning, and had to be faced. Slowly she began to walk back towards her home where Frank and their son would be impatiently waiting for her.

'And for Frank Eliot who has made himself a part of this village with his work at the cinema and on the memorial garden...'
Frank Eliot knew exactly why Lizzie hadn't yet returned. He didn't blame her, for fine words were one thing, and facts another. 'One day when the war ends' had a splendidly far-off ring to it. But now it had ended. What would he do if Lizzie chose Rudolf? It would tear him in two to have to leave his son, and Lizzie too he had come to love, even though she had never replaced Jennifer, his first wife. Had he the strength to leave? He might not have any choice. He could hardly hang around Ashden like a spectre at the feast. He supposed it was but one more blow in a life that had dealt him many. Or would it be one blow too much?

'Let us pray for Joe Dibble in Italy...'
Half past seven the news had come through that the war was over not only in Austria, but everywhere. Their war had been over for a week now, but Joe was going to keep his head down being in a Pioneer battalion, for

the fighting had been bitterer than any he could recall on the Western Front. Mines didn't know there'd been an armistice, and snipers didn't care. Nothing was going to prevent his getting back to Muriel and the kiddies, he vowed. In fact, maybe he'd pray. It must be being brought up in a Rectory, he supposed, because public praying in the army wasn't common – except at gatherings held by the padres. He didn't know anyone who didn't confess to praying privately though.

'Keep me – keep us *all* safe,' he asked God vehemently, as he ate breakfast, if you could call this chow breakfast. He thought of the huge breakfasts his mother used to serve at the Rectory, and wondered if she were still doing it, despite the rations. If not, she would begin again soon. The Rectory would go on for ever, just as it always had. Nothing could change there.

'A prayer for our son George...'
How were they supposed to know when the war was over? George wondered. Carry on as usual were the orders – until eleven o'clock – and by jingo they had. The squadron was still bombing German airfields, the only difference was that the

357

enemy weren't putting up much resistance. No sign of a Fokker in the sky. Where were they now, the von Richthofens and the Udets? Their day was over. And so soon would his be, he realised thankfully, consulting his old pocket watch.

He landed and walked into the mess. No one noticed, such was the hubbub and the drinking going on. His solitary flight in the sky had more to do with armistice than this din. Still, he had to be sociable. Soon the rightful owners would be back in the châteaux so eagerly commandeered by the military and air forces, and signs of war would slowly vanish. It was over.

George suddenly felt giddy with relief as he realised this was indeed so, and he was ready for the pint of beer pushed into his hand. Tonight he'd see Florence, and life would begin once again.

'Lord, we ask you to bring Jamie Thorn back to his family again...'
Jamie hadn't felt much like rejoicing, just a great thankfulness that they could pack up and go home. Stupid, having orders to carry on fighting till eleven o'clock. Some poor sods would get shot all for nothing. He wouldn't be one of them though, for he'd

get home to Ashden if it was the last thing he did. This trench in which he was bivouacking was disgusting; it was a German one now overrun by the Brits, and the way it was constructed showed the Germans weren't good at everything. There was no sound anywhere for everyone was keeping his head down, determined not to be wiped out at this late moment. They'd been ordered not to fraternise with the enemy after eleven o'clock. To hell with that. Nineteen-fourteen was over, and so were these outdated attitudes. As he and his mates looked at each other in wonder when the gup shot round that it was eleven o'clock, Jamie had decided not to wait.

'Come on, mate.' He hauled Jack Wilson over the top with him.

In the distance they could see German helmets cautiously emerging from their lines. Jamie wanted to run to meet them but he couldn't somehow. His legs seemed heavy, like in a dream. He got there in the end though.

'How are yer, Fritz?' He clapped one enormous German on the back.

Funny, he thought of him as Fritz, not the Boche any longer. Not Huns. Just old Fritz, away from his family, like Jamie was. He wouldn't be away from Agnes much longer though. Jamie felt faint at the prospect and almost stumbled.

'What's up, mate?' Jack asked.

'Feel odd,' he mumbled. He swayed again, propping himself up with his rifle. Then he realised Jack, his old mate, was drawing away in horror. What was wrong? The truth struck him with sudden and terrible irony. The men had been dropping dead like flies in the last few days, *and he'd got it.* The sodding Spanish flu.

'*No!*' A great wail tore itself from him. He'd come through four years of war, fought at the Somme, Cambrai, every bloody where. He'd won a fucking medal and he was going to die of fucking *flu.*

'*Lord, we pray for my daughter Phoebe and her coming baby and thank you for the happiness Billy has brought to her.*'
'We'll have to celebrate at lunch, love. I'll be at the Britannia tonight.' Billy kissed her, as the maroons died away. 'Think of me. It's going to be lively.'

'Think of you? I'm *coming*,' Phoebe replied.

'No, love, it won't be safe, not with the baby.'

'Then *make* it safe,' Phoebe commanded. 'The war's over. I'll ask Caroline and Yves to come with me. Oh, I know.' She beamed. 'I'll ask Tilly to take me by ambulance. Even the thickest crowds will let that pass. And if you're really worried, we'll take Felicia too.'

'Lord, we pray for my daughter Felicia…'
'What will you do tonight, Felicia?' someone asked as she dashed to the cloakroom.

'Nothing in particular.'

'But you must, it's *special*. The war's over. Come with us.'

'No, thank you.' She was exhausted. With all the flu patients in addition to the war wounded, life was hectic and did not stop being so just because eleven o'clock had struck and the fighting had stopped. As she walked out of the hospital at lunchtime, a voice said quietly:

'Hello, Felicia.'

'Daniel!'

He grinned, then waved his stick threateningly. 'I've come to take you out to lunch, young woman. And I'm taking you to dinner tonight.'

'There won't be a restaurant seat in London,' she laughed, well pleased.

'I've booked lunch for two at the Carlton

for Admiral Beatty. If he doesn't show up, and we do, the restaurant won't care.'

'I'll have to change.'

'Permission granted.'

'Lord, we pray for Lady Hunney and her family...'

Maud Hunney sat alone in her morning room at the Dower House. John was in London, of course, and no doubt she could join him later in the day if she wished to do battle with the crowds and delays that train travel would bring. John had telephoned the news earlier, and the Rector had called too. He had said he knew how she must be feeling. Did he? Perhaps so, for he was a perceptive man – and, she realised with some surprise, not being in the habit of thinking this way, a good friend. Times had indeed changed, even for her. Before the war the Manor did not think of its rector as a good friend, since it was the patron of the living. Perhaps that too would change now the war was over. That meant no more mothers would be put through what she and most families in the land had endured.

At the end of this war she had one son dead, the other maimed, that was what she was reflecting on. Once, it had seemed vital to have an heir to carry on the estate. It did so no longer, and, though Daniel would inherit, he would not have children. Once, that too would have been a crushing blow. Now it seemed irrelevant, for just to have Daniel was enough. Once, it had seemed important that Caroline Lilley was not the stuff from which squires' ladies were made, despite her capabilities in other fields. Now it was irrelevant, and Reggie was dead anyway. Maud briefly wondered whether she had been right to force her views about Caroline on Reggie. She did not know, but it had seemed right at the time.

Perhaps the Rector had in mind, also, that she was here alone. There was no one with whom she could mark the end of the war – or was there? She hesitated as an idea came to her. It would go against everything she had lived for, and yet the impulse for company, for unity, was overpowering. She pulled the bell-rope, but there was no reply. She was about to do so again, when the obvious reason for the lack of service belatedly occurred to her. She rose to her feet, and walked steadily into the servants' quarters from where there was much noise of merry-making. Here she was a stranger in her own house. Her butler, her cook and the three maids were involved in a wild dance of some sort, accompanied by a tinny gramophone, and they were celebrating with mugs of tea clutched perilously in their free hands.

Maud cleared her throat. 'I wonder...' she asked almost humbly, 'if I might join you for a few moments?'

An aghast silence followed for they had not heard her come in. It was Mrs Coombs recovered first. 'Certainly, madam. May I pour you a cup of tea?'

'That is kind. However, I believe that now the war is over, it would not be unpatriotic to open the cellar door once more. I recall there are at least two bottles of champagne left. That might suffice.'

They looked at her, Maud thought wryly as her butler scuttled to unlock the door, as though the world had come to an end. But it hadn't. It had begun again and now would start the long uphill task of rebuilding. Today was a time to rejoice that the slaughter was over, but tomorrow the cost and the grief must be faced.

'And lastly, Lord, we pray for the soul of our daughter Isabel, who lies side by side with the fallen on the field, for her husband, Robert, in his

364

prison camp, and–' as Laurence's voice broke – '*for our dear daughter Caroline and the hard path ahead of her...*'

How odd to be doing this once more, Caroline thought dizzily, as she clung hard to Luke on the one side and Yves on the other, as they were swept along by the crowd with one common aim: to reach the Palace. The last time she had done this was in August 1914 when Reggie – to her mingled horror and pride – had volunteered, and with him she had joined the crowds outside the Palace the night war was declared, as Britain's ultimatum to Germany passed its deadline. That had been a sombre occasion, but one sound was the same as today: 'God Save the King'. And King George deserved to be saved. He had done a splendid job of leadership throughout the war, an inspiration to those at home as well as in the trenches. He had led the country in so many ways, not least by signing the pledge and locking the cellars at the Palace. It was said that Buckingham Palace lived on the same rations as any of their subjects. The King had travelled to the Front many times, and toured hospitals here and abroad. Queen Mary, too, had indefatigably made her own war effort,

opening canteens, creating war organisations and organising their own allotments
for growing vegetables, and encouraging her
family to do the same.

The King had already appeared once on
the balcony, but the crowds were growing
thicker all the time and he must surely
emerge once more. It was November, not
August as on that earlier occasion, but no
one noticed the cold as they waited. Just
before one o'clock His Majesty came out
again with Queen Mary and his daughter,
and the crowd roared its approval, after he
had spoken a few words.

'Look!' Caroline clutched Yves' arm. 'The
Queen's waving a *flag!*'

For some reason this idiotically small detail
seemed significant, and the crowd seemed to
agree because they roared their appreciation.
The Queen was usually so stately and
forbidding, yet here she was like anyone else,
waving a flag in happiness. She was human
after all. The crowd approved of their
monarchs, as the Belgians did of King Albert
and Queen Elisabeth. Tomorrow Caroline
realised she must face her own problems
again, but today it was wonderful to lose
herself in the unity of the crowd around her
which took on a character of its own,

independent of the individuals composing it.

They returned reluctantly to the office that afternoon, but work had no momentum, as outside the noise of celebration increased rather than decreased. There was one fine moment when over the noise of the crowd came a familiar sound.

'Listen,' said Yves, 'what's that?'

Caroline did listen. 'It's Big *Ben,*' she cried joyously. It had been muzzled for so long. Yves had probably never heard it before, but now its boom rang out once more and that, even more than the maroons, signalled that peace was here. Just as it finished striking the hour, Tilly telephoned to ask what plans she and Yves had for the evening.

'Plans?' Caroline echoed, nonplussed. She glanced at Yves, realising the evening might present a nightmare of discussion on their future – or lack of it.

'Billy's playing at Stratford this evening. I'm taking Phoebe in an ambulance, and we're proposing to make it a family party. You're coming, Yves, Penelope, Felicia–'

'Me,' Luke chipped in on the extension.

A second's pause, then, 'Of course, but–'

'Settled.' Luke hung up.

'Be advised, bring a picnic,' Tilly said briskly.

A glow of pleasure ran through Caroline. The perfect way to spend the evening. 'I don't see the need for an ambulance,' she commented. 'Phoebe's perfectly well. A taxi–'

She was interrupted by hoots of laughter from Luke and Yves. 'Caroline, my love,' Yves explained, 'the crowds are thick now, tonight they will be thicker.'

'And drunker,' Luke added.

'And – er – lustier.' Yves was straight-faced.

'*Lustier?*'

'Tilly obviously realises there will be sights that no well-brought-up Rector's daughters should view.'

'Don't be pompous, Yves.' Caroline hurled her chair-cushion at him, and he shook his head sadly.

'I am your superior officer. Kindly salute when you throw things at me.'

Underneath the banter lay the tension, however, and Caroline was relieved that the evening would provide another escape, however brief.

In the event, not one but two ambulances arrived at Queen Anne's Gate, one driven by Tilly, the other by Felicia.

'How did you manage *that?*' Caroline enquired.

'On the grounds that a poor disabled soldier needed one, as well as Phoebe,' Daniel yelled from the back, and Caroline realised the reason for Tilly's odd pause on the telephone.

'Do you mind Daniel being here?' she asked Luke, concerned.

'Tonight no,' Luke replied magnanimously. 'She has two arms, we'll each take one, and march her into the theatre.'

For all his joking, Caroline conceded Yves had a point about the crowds. The darkness of a November evening had turned the happy crowd into a potential mob. Through the small windows of the ambulance it was obvious that drink was indeed adding its influence to the celebrations, and there seemed to be embracing couples everywhere. Even so, there was a frenetic, almost sinister quality in the air, in people's relentless search for an adequate expression of relief, and she was glad she was inside the ambulance and not outside.

Billy had secured them a large box at the theatre, and miraculously some chicken for supper to add to their individual picnic celebrations, and joined them during the interval. He had brought the house down with his reiteration of the traditional

'Mafeking has been relieved' announcement, quickly followed by a correction, *'Mons* has been relieved'. 'Ladies and gentlemen, Canadian and British troops entered Mons today.' Mons was where the war had in practice begun for the British Expeditionary Force, and it was on his way there that Daniel had been wounded. Caroline glanced at him to see if he was upset by this reminder, but he winked at her.

'That's in remembrance of me,' he whispered, and added even more quietly, 'and all the other poor devils.'

Caroline said very little during the picnic, content just to enjoy being with so many she loved. It was not only she and Yves who had problems to face; they all did in some way. At the very least readjustment would not be easy. Take Penelope, for example. Penelope was always popular with men, but somehow she never met anyone, she had once confided to her, for whom she felt *love*. Perhaps it was her strong personality that made her seek something hard to find among the men of her acquaintance. Caroline remembered how jealous she had been of Penelope when she had been Reggie's girlfriend – until she rejected him. Since then, Caroline had seen Penelope with many escorts; she was cheerful, friendly – but not in love with them.

'What will you do?' Caroline asked her now.

'No idea. Start a driving school, perhaps. Organising seems to be the only thing I'm good at.' Penelope spoke lightly but Caroline detected a tinge of bitterness. 'At least,' Penelope added, 'you never say I'll meet some nice young man and settle down. Nice young men don't want to settle down with rackety women like me, even if I am an earl's daughter. Earls' daughters are expected to come out and then go straight back. That means back into their traditional role, ladies-in-waiting for marriage.'

'I didn't,' Tilly observed amiably.

'No,' Penelope agreed fervently. 'You're my inspiration. I could go into politics, I suppose,' she added. 'That's if parliament ever gets round to allowing women to stand.'

'You can have my seat in the Lords,' her father said generously.

'I don't think my dear brother would like that.' James would be returning from the East with his regiment soon.

'Marry one of those Labour fellows,' Billy suggested wickedly.

Penelope rose to the bait. 'I don't have to marry anyone. I would stand in my own right.'

'You're not old enough yet.'

'True, but it won't be that long, and in any case I won't marry.'

'Why not?' Felicia asked, genuinely interested.

Maybe it was the champagne talking, or maybe it was because it was Felicia asking, but Penelope revealed that in fact she *had* met someone. 'Unfortunately,' she added briskly, 'he's not free, as they say. Pa disapproves, don't you, you fusty old grumpy?'

'No,' Simon replied amiably. 'Not if it's what you want.'

'Well, I don't,' Penelope said. 'He has a child, too, so that's that. Anyway, he's never even cast an admiring look at my eyelashes. No, we have to remember there's a brave new world out there awaiting us women, especially me, Caroline, and Tilly.'

'Not me?' enquired Felicia.

'No, darling, your path is fixed.'

Felicia gave her a black look and Simon quickly intervened. 'That brave new world is going to be your father so far as one of you is concerned.'

'Me?' Tilly enquired.

'The war is over, it's high time you made up your mind.'

'Very well,' Tilly said amiably, attacking her chicken leg with gusto, 'I will marry you.'

'I knew it – *what* did you say?' Simon looked astounded.

'I said yes. With conditions.'

'Naturally.' Simon recovered his sangfroid with some difficulty. 'I'm sure they include complete independence of house and husband. I assume you're only marrying me so you don't have to return to your esteemed mother's roof in Dover.'

Was there a slight note of interrogation in his voice? Caroline wondered, highly amused.

'No, I'm not. One condition is that I can put myself forward for parliament as soon as they get the bill through, which I gather may be quickly. I *am* old enough.'

'Agreed.'

'The other is that I can drive your Rolls Royce.'

'Also agreed. It will save me paying for a chauffeur.'

'And moreover,' Tilly glared, 'I wish you to know I'm marrying you because I love you.'

Caroline was still getting over the shock of

Tilly's acceptance, as indeed Simon himself seemed to be. Yves had a smile on his face that seemed glued to it, Felicia was hugging Tilly, Phoebe was giggling, and Billy was roaring out the music-hall song: 'They hadn't been married but a month or more...'

'Splendid,' Penelope said happily. 'I can leave Pa and set up on my own. Thank you, darling Tilly.'

'Felicia,' Luke began hopefully.

'No!' Felicia banged her fist on the table, and Daniel laughed. 'Will you both stop eyeing me like vultures? I know the war's over, but this evening is Tilly's. I haven't had a chance to think, and anyway my work hasn't ended because the war has.'

Daniel said nothing, Caroline noted, but Luke replied amiably: 'I'll give you until Christmas. And if you say no, I'll marry Penelope.'

'How good of you,' Penelope murmured. 'Do I have a say in the matter?'

The mention of Christmas struck home for Caroline. This was the Christmas she had hoped to spend at the Rectory with Yves. This was the Christmas there would now be happiness and rejoicing in every home, but not in her heart. By then, the sword of Damocles that had been swaying over her head for so long, would surely have fallen, and cleaved her heart in two.

Even Mrs Lilley was looking a little brighter now the war was over, and it had certainly dispelled the usual November glooms. Not so much as Mrs Phoebe's baby would have done. Funny that. Fancy her being six weeks out in her reckoning. Ah well, arithmetic was never Mrs Phoebe's strong point. When Mrs Lilley came back from London and told her you could have knocked her down with a feather, she was so surprised, and whether it had anything to do with it or not, the Rector had been gloomy for days.

Still, that was all over now, along with the war. Even the shortages seemed easier to bear, now they knew everything would soon be back to normal. Margaret thought with pleasure that it was time to be thinking of Christmas, now they were all perking up like little birds after a storm. She wondered how many there would be at the Rectory. Perhaps Sir John might be asked to get them a chicken, if not a turkey. Or a grouse, maybe. Margaret's mouth began to water at the thought. She supposed she should do one last major Food Economy demonstration on Christmas fare. With a sigh, she realised everything was about to fall in place again, just as it always had.

She heard the knock on the front door, but Agnes was out there, so Margaret didn't bother to send Myrtle to answer it. After all, she had to finish chiding Myrtle for wasting too much potato on her potato peelings. The girl had answered back. Now that was a sign of the times, if you like. Then Agnes came into the kitchen.

Margaret cried out in alarm. The girl's face was dead-white and she looked as if she were about to pass out. As she rushed forward to help her to a chair, the telegram fell from her hand. Margaret picked it up and read it. Shock jolted through her. Armistice hadn't meant telegrams were over and done with. Nor grief, nor mourning. Grimly, she hurried to her still-room for the sal volatile, and Elizabeth Agnes came bouncing in after her. She didn't say a word of reproach. The poor little thing was fatherless, after all.

'Caroline, I have some bad news for you – for us.'

St James's Park looked bleak in its winter plumage, as bleak as the news she knew must surely come. She had guessed from today's newspaper that it would be sooner rather than later. She was secretly surprised that Yves had not already left. The timing was not his decision, after all. He was a serving officer in the Belgian army and liaison officer to a king who was about to reclaim his country. What else could she expect other than bad news for Caroline Lilley? A miracle? God did not work in such mysterious ways as that. One plodded on, and then He helped you, in her experience, and yet for all her plodding on in life, here she was about to lose Yves. *Boche napoo, guerre finie,* as the troops were saying everywhere. Caroline too was about to be *finie.*

'Have you read the newspaper this morning?' Yves asked quietly.

'Yes. King Albert has made a state entry into Bruges and reviewed the troops.'

She knew that the Germans were not giving up easily. Even though in Brussels the newspaper reported that their soldiers had revolted, and Belgian armed troops were restoring order, the German army were leaving a trail of wreckage and rape behind them, as they had threatened. They had even deliberately flooded some areas in order to hold up the Canadian and British troops following them to Germany. Any secret hope Caroline might have had that this would delay the King's return to his capital was doomed, for King Albert was not the sort of person to be prevented at this late stage from reclaiming Brussels.

Now Yves confirmed it. 'His Majesty plans to enter Brussels in full state with British, American, French and Belgian army march-pasts.'

'When?'

'On the 22nd. *Cara, carissima,* I must be there.'

'And after that you will rejoin your wife.'

'I have no choice.'

'One always has choice.'

He did not reply. Caroline knew she should feel ashamed, but was too depressed to feel anything save the foretaste of emptiness. Tomorrow the pain would come.

'When do you leave?'

'On the 20th.'

She could not help the cry. 'That's less than a week!'

'Then, like Antony and Cleopatra, let's have one other gaudy night. Only for us we will have a whole gaudy week.'

'How?' she asked dully. 'And don't tell me

to be brave.'

'I don't. For at least where you are concerned, I am not.'

Counting the last dinner, the last day in the office, the last walk in the park, the last of love... How could she bear it?

It took nearly three weeks for the pain to override the merciful numbness that had prevailed this last week. Even their parting had seemed just another parting. Not a word was spoken, not a tear shed that would imply he was not returning. Even when she read the reports in the newspapers of King Albert's entry into Brussels on the 22nd, the pain stayed away. Then on December 7th *The Illustrated London News* carried many pictures of the grand re-entries, and whereas words did not conjure up Yves' image, photographs did. Photographs of the King on his white charger, Queen Elisabeth at his side, and accompanied by Prince Albert, King George V's second son, in RAF uniform. Despite his shyness, Prince Albert had obviously inherited his father's devotion to duty and was well thought of by the Belgian king. Yves was probably in that photograph of the Belgian army, at the end of the long procession of the Allied forces, as they took the salute from King Albert at the Place de la Nation.

Caroline was beginning to feel resentful of King Albert; he took for granted what she would have given so much for – to have Yves at her side. *Everyone* talked about King Albert, she was heartily sick of the sound of his name. If only the general public knew that staunch patriot though he was to his own country, he had swayed to and fro in his belief in the ultimate victory of the Allies. As it was, even Aunt Tilly hadn't lost a minute in accepting an invitation to visit him. She was there now, though she would be back in plenty of time for Christmas.

Yves, at this moment, was almost certainly reunited with his wife. Suppose they now shared the same bed? Suppose war had made a difference? A thousand such supposes flashed through her mind. She had heard nothing from him and she would hear nothing of him. All that was left was a gaping hole. Home at Queen Anne's Gate was no home now. Yves had left, and though everyone did their best to cheer her and distract her, they failed.

'Join me and Felicia for dinner, Caroline,' Luke pleaded.

'Come to the theatre,' Penelope suggested.

'Why don't we go to the pictures?' Ellen asked brightly.

'Do come over, Caroline,' Phoebe demanded. 'I need you here – the baby's due any moment.'

She dutifully obeyed, but nothing helped. Then one evening the telephone rang, and she unhooked the receiver to hear her mother's voice.

'Darling, I know Phoebe's baby is coming along, but I just wondered whether you could spare the time to come down here this weekend. Everything is so sad here, what with Jamie's death, and Mrs Dibble doesn't like to remind Agnes Christmas is only two weeks away. I thought if you came down you might cheer everyone up. She hasn't even begun on the Christmas puddings. She just says that it doesn't matter if they're late, since they're not proper puddings anyway, but that isn't the point...'

Caroline listened to her mother's rambling appeal, and reluctantly agreed. What good could one more grieving person do to help though? On the other hand, just to crawl back to the comfort of the Rectory might be a relief. She would escape a thousand daily reminders of Yves for two days. Escape? She vaguely remembered promising God she would plod on along the road He'd chosen for her. To do that, she should not go to the Rectory for comfort and escape. She would have to offer it something.

She also remembered her earlier conviction that, with Yves gone, the Rectory would prove her salvation. She had forgotten that in her misery, but now it suddenly returned with renewed meaning. She *did* have something to contribute to the Rectory, even if for the moment it was only stirring the Christmas puddings.

Fourteen

Margaret tried valiantly to sing the traditional Sussex carol 'On Christmas Night all Christians sing' and to pretend this was like all other Christmas Eves, now the war was over. But it wasn't, not here in the Rectory, nor anywhere in Ashden. There was too much grieving to lay aside even for the celebration of the Lord's birthday. Even that, she supposed, had been tinged with grief. The slaughter of the innocents. The innocents in Ashden were poor Mrs Isabel and Nanny Oates. Then there was Agnes's Jamie. Agnes was still walking around as if hit by shell-blast and no wonder. What kind of a Christmas was it for her, with the end of all her dreams?

Margaret had done the best she could to make it seem like a real Christmas. She only had the mince pies left to bake now; they were oval-shaped, cut as her mother had taught her, but even they failed to raise the usual anticipation in her. Today, everyone would be gathering under the Rectory roof, including Miss Tilly, Miss Penelope and her father. They hadn't had such a full house since before the war. Agnes was busy making up beds, Mrs Lilley was looking flustered instead of absent-minded, and perhaps by this evening when they all attended the midnight service, the Christmas spirit would come in more generous measure. Most of them had problems, but being all together must help. Poor Miss Caroline had been looking like a white ghost when she came ten days ago, though she was pretending all was well. No mention of her Belgian officer though. No doubt he'd gone back to his wife with not a thought for the girl he was leaving behind him. Then there was Agnes. She was working too hard, for all her abstraction.

'You ought to be with your ma, Agnes, or Mrs Thorn, at Christmas.' Margaret was concerned. 'Not that I can't do with you here, of course.'

Agnes had just said flatly: 'This is my home, Margaret.'

Margaret had shut up quickly, and Agnes obviously felt guilty for snapping for she continued: 'At any rate, it's *almost* as good as a home of my own, the one Jamie promised...' That was all she could manage before she broke down. To Margaret's way of thinking, she'd never fully got her strength back after the birth of little Isabel, and Jamie's death had made life all too much. Margaret felt guilty at her own private joy. Joe would be home from Austria for Christmas, and he and Muriel had chosen to come here for Christmas Day. If it hadn't been for poor Lizzie she'd have been on top of the world.

Lizzie had arrived last evening, clutching Baby Frank, and sobbing her heart out. Agnes and Myrtle took one look, and tactfully withdrew, leaving the kitchen for Margaret to cope with her daughter as best she could.

'What's the matter, love?'

'It's Frank,' Lizzie wailed. 'I told him he's got to go.' She burst out crying again, and Mrs Lilley put her head round the door to see what was up. She hastily withdrew it when she saw what it was.

'I had this letter from Rudolf,' Lizzie hiccuped. 'I never told you, nor Frank I'd written to him. He thinks he can get back here in the spring, and says he understands about the baby. I told him Frank was ever so nice, and that he would like him.'

Bet that cheered him up, Margaret

thought, while uttering clucking sounds of sympathy. 'So you've chosen old Rudolf. Not that I don't agree with you, but what made up your mind?'

Lizzie howled again, and Myrtle popped in with a glass of the medicinal brandy that Lady Buckford kept for emergencies, sent by courtesy of the Rector. A gulp of that, and Lizzie was calmer. 'I love them both, like I told you. But Frank and me are different somehow, and Rudolf and I are the same. Do you know what I mean?'

Margaret did. It used to be called knowing your place, but nowadays it didn't have a name. Not that Frank Eliot was gentry – far from it – but he was an educated man who'd seen the world, and, love Lizzie or not, it set him apart. And her Lizzie had had the sense to see it.

'I'm proud of you, my girl.'

'What for?' Lizzie was astounded. Ma had never said anything like that before. Proud of Joe, proud of Fred even, but her?

'For having the Sussex sense to see where your long-term interests lie, and they're not in Frank Eliot's bed.'

Lizzie giggled. 'I wish I could have Frank in bed, and Rudolf the rest of the time.'

'Lizzie Dibble, I'm ashamed of you.' Two

pink spots appeared in Margaret's cheeks. In her day one might think such things, but never, never did one voice them. It was her own fault for speaking too free, she supposed. All the same, she felt very sorry for Frank. She'd been set against him at first, and looking back maybe that was because he was 'different', as well as being a foreigner to Ashden. Ah well, if there was one thing this war had taught them, it was that foreigners weren't that much different to themselves.

Ah well, Christmas Eve morning and a lot of work still to do. Sir John had provided two geese and a turkey, which was all very well, but what was one to stuff them with? Supplies weren't back to normal yet, and she hadn't got that young Peter Bertram at the butcher's trained to save her a nice bit of suet, the way his father did. Wally Bertram had hung up his cleaver at last when the war ended and decided to hand over the reins to his son, now Peter was coming back from war.

Luckily Mrs Coombs had come over herself from the Dower House with a lump of suet. Before the war, she wouldn't give you the time of day, she was so proud of her position at the Manor. Now she was a regular jaw-me-dead, and Margaret couldn't get rid of the woman. She sat at the kitchen table drinking tea and telling her all about Lady Hunney and how the atmosphere had changed.

'And a good thing too,' Margaret said politely. But she was thinking of that new song everyone had been singing since the armistice: 'What shall we be when we aren't what we are?'

'Mother, what can I do?' Caroline was determined to be bright – made harder by the fact that her mother had long since given up trying to pretend all was well, and Christmas was just one more burden. She had a perpetual puzzled look as though continually wondering why there was one fledgling missing from the Rectory nest. It had its blessings in that she had taken the news of Phoebe's deception remarkably well – which was more than Father had.

'Tidy the drawing-room?' It was almost a standard reply to keep her quiet. The drawing room *always* needed tidying, although since it contained not only the presents awaiting wrapping in tissue paper but Phoebe and her paraphernalia, it was more cluttered than usual.

Caroline had been here since yesterday, having travelled down on the Monday evening. Luke had volunteered to man the office and to travel down on Christmas morning. It was very self-sacrificing of him, but as he said jestingly, he was so confident of Felicia's answer that he didn't mind allowing Daniel the field for another day. Phoebe had arrived by motor car yesterday evening too, beaming and very large. The baby was due in three weeks' time, but Mrs Dibble was still maintaining it would be early.

'I think you decided to have a baby just to get out of household chores.' Caroline cheerfully tidied up around her.

Phoebe grinned and stretched lazily. 'Perhaps I like watching you do them, though.' She ducked, as a duster came whizzing through the air. 'It's like old times, isn't it, being here at the Rectory?'

'You once told me you never did feel at home here.'

'That was before I had a home of my own.'

'O wise young sage.' Caroline bowed.

'Will you move back to the Rectory, Caroline, when your job comes to an end?'

'I don't know. I gather that Lizzie Dibble has decided to remain with her husband, and now the delightful Swinford-Browne has closed the cinema, I can't even take over Frank Eliot's job.'

'You're usually so enthusiastic about work.'

'Just at the moment, sister dear, I don't feel very enthusiastic about anything.' Especially, she smarted inside, about younger sisters who sat smugly awaiting their first-born and lording it over their elders.

'I think Yves behaved very badly.' Phoebe managed to put her dainty foot right in it, as usual.

'No, he did not,' Caroline yelled, red-faced, all good intentions of remaining calm forgotten. 'It was always agreed what the end of the war would bring and so *would you please not talk about it?*'

'Sorry.'

'What on earth are you two shouting about?' Elizabeth came in crossly. 'Didn't you hear me calling, Caroline? Luke is telephoning from your office.'

Instant alarm. What had gone wrong? Was it a summons to return to London immediately, or to say that Luke could not come? And if so... She flew to the telephone, a hundred horrors flicking through her mind.

'Wild horses wouldn't keep me away,'

Luke reassured her. 'I've had an odd telephone call from your own wild horse,
however.'

It took a moment before Caroline realised
whom he was talking about. 'Yves?' Her
heart pounded in a fanfare of joy.

'It was a very bad line from Belgium. I
couldn't hear all he was saying, and then we
were cut off.'

Keep still, heart, she silently ordered.
Keep still, hope.

'What did he want?'

'I gather he's been sent back to England
today. All I could make out was Caroline,
Dover, Town and half-past three, and then
the line went completely. Oh, and Caroline,
tell Felicia not to get married before I get
there tomorrow.'

Caroline's hand trembled as she hung up
the receiver. Why couldn't Yves have rung
her here? She knew the answer. Lines were
difficult, to say the least, across the Channel, and only the line to the office would
have any priority. *Sent* back to England? For
how long? For Christmas? For two days? A
month? Frustration clouded her mind, and
only one thing was obvious. Yves would be
at Dover Town Station at half-past three,
and that was where she must go. *Now*. She

flew to the *Bradshaw* in the drawing-room, leafing nervously through its bulk for the timetables she needed, for she'd have to change trains twice.

'Tell mother I have to go to Dover,' she told Phoebe. 'I'll be back in time for the midnight mass.'

Would she? She didn't know, she couldn't think. Would Yves be with her, or would it be just a fleeting encounter on his way to London?

'Caroline, don't be silly!' Even Phoebe was alarmed and went through to find Elizabeth, who came back hurriedly from her glory-hole, but too late. Caroline was already running for the railway station. If she hurried, she could just get the twelve twenty-four to Tunbridge Wells, which might, if she were lucky with her connection, get her to Tonbridge in time to catch the Dover train from London. She'd arrive there at three-fifteen.

Why on earth had Yves cut it so fine? Was it a sudden mission? The problem was that timetables were almost irrelevant nowadays with so many troop trains and delays, and that hadn't stopped just because the war had. British troops had advanced into Germany to occupy it while they were establishing their political system and that, with returning POWs crowding trains in the opposite direction, guaranteed wartime train travel conditions still prevailed.

Suppose she missed Yves? Suppose he had been planning to go to London after seeing her? At the very least he might come down with Luke for Christmas Day. Even King Albert wouldn't insist he worked then, so Caroline might have her Christmas after all. What matter if her happiness was restored only for a short time? Omar Khayyam, whose *Rubaiyat* she had given Yves in 1916, worked to the philosophy of eat, drink and be merry. Very well, she would, she vowed, though could not quite convince herself that this was wise. All she cared about was that in about two hours' time she would see Yves.

She leapt onto the train just as it was about to puff off once more, and it was only as the train steamed out she saw two familiar figures. Felicia had obviously just arrived and was now in Daniel's arms. She hadn't even had time to call out hello. No matter, she was decidedly *de trop*, and anyway she was en route to a tryst of her own. God had been listening to Caroline Lilley after all.

'I feel we've both come home at long last,' said Felicia contentedly, as they walked down Station Road.

'Are you sure it's a home with me you want?' Daniel asked.

She smiled at him, for they both knew the question was superfluous. 'Oh, yes.'

'And what of Luke?'

'If the boot were on the other foot, would he be asking the same question about you?'

Daniel sighed. 'I must be the most selfish chap alive – and the luckiest. Shall we live in Ashden?'

'No. You want to travel, remember?'

'But I can't–' He grinned. 'I *can,* but it's no life for a married man.'

'I don't want to prevent you from doing what you want.'

'Climb the Himalayas? Go diving in the Seven Seas?'

'Anything you like. And I'll come with you.'

Caroline fumed. Why did trains have to be so maddeningly slow? *Clickety-clack, clickety-clack, Yves is back,* she silently chanted in excitement as the train steamed on. At last it condescended to reach Dover Town station. Why had he said the Town Station and not the Harbour if he had come by ferry or troop ship? She dismissed this puzzle as she hurried over the bridge and into the booking hall. It was the scene of many family reunions, but there was no sign of Yves. Well, she was five minutes early... She tried to busy herself at the station news stand, then by staring at the timetables. Anything to make the time pass more quickly. With the short days, light was already fading and she envied those who had departed to their own homes, reunited with loved ones. How would Yves arrive here? It was a long walk from the harbour. A train? There was none due according to the timetables. A troop lorry from the docks?

Trying not to feel concern, she watched the hands of the station clock creep round to twenty to four, then quarter to the hour. She went to look at the timetable again. Could Luke have misinterpreted what Yves said? Could *she* have done so? Dover Town – suppose there had been a break between the two words: Dover ... I'm going to town. That's how everybody referred to London casually, and Yves had caught the habit. He could have gone straight to Victoria from the harbour and would be in London at three thirty, not here. *That's* where she should have met him.

With growing dismay, she studied the timetable again. She had only five minutes in which to catch the train she had believed she and Yves might return to Tonbridge on, and it was the last that could reasonably be expected, allowing the two changes, to get them to Ashden this evening. Get *her* to Ashden, she sadly corrected herself. Yves might just be late, but in her heart she knew this was not the answer, and slowly she walked back to the London platform.

Even if she saw Yves for a few hours tomorrow, there would be no precious night together.

'I'll answer it, Percy,' Felicia called out. She was busy decorating the Christmas tree in the entrance hall, with Phoebe shouting orders at her from the comfort of an armchair.

'Isn't it wonderful to be home?' Phoebe had said.

'Yes,' she had answered mechanically, but it wasn't that wonderful. The deep joy of her new understanding with Daniel was marred by the thought of having to break the news to Luke tomorrow.

'He'll take it better than you think,' Daniel had said consolingly.

'Yes, but–' She stopped, for she could not put the thought behind the 'but' into words, even for herself.

She opened the front door, and to her astonishment there stood a familiar khaki-clad figure.

'What on earth are you doing here, Yves? And where's Caroline? Mother said she'd gone dashing off to Dover to meet you.' Felicia was alarmed.

His face changed in shock. 'But I told Luke my train would get in at three-thirty here at Ashden.' No wonder Caroline had not been at the station to greet him as he had expected and longed for.

Felicia groaned. 'Luke said it was a bad line. It wasn't even clear whether you were coming to the Rectory or going to London.'

Yves glanced down at his luggage in despair. 'I must go. *Now*. She may be waiting for me alone in Dover. This is terrible.'

'Yes, but–' This time Felicia could frame the thought behind the 'but'; it was too late, however. Yves was already running across to Station Road. The 'but' had been that it would take hours to get back to Dover, with no surety that Caroline would be there to meet him.

'Who was that?' Her father appeared in the hallway.

'Yves. There's been a mix-up,' she explained, and the Rector paled.

'Caroline would surely have the sense to go to Buckford House if she were stranded?' It didn't sound as if he had any confidence about this.

'She's more likely to go to London or try to get back here. Probably the latter, seeing how slow the trains will be tomorrow.'

'She'll telephone, surely. How long is Yves here for, and where is he?'

'I didn't think to ask him – and he's gone rushing back to Dover.'

'They're both as mad as each other,' Laurence said crossly.

What a to-do. Here it was time for Christmas Eve dinner, and no one knew where Miss Caroline was, and no sign of Mr George yet, though he'd promised faithfully he'd be home. At least Miss Tilly was home, together with Lord Banning and his daughter.

'Myrtle, get those potatoes out of the oven,' Margaret commanded. 'They'll be done to a crisp. And next Christmas Eve, mind you get that stuffing done quicker.'

Myrtle obeyed, then straightened up as she dumped the somewhat charred potatoes on to the table. 'There may not be a next year,' she muttered.

'What's that, Myrtle?'

'I really am going to leave soon, Mrs Dibble.'

Margaret snorted. 'Leave the Rectory? You'll never do that, not while the kiddies are here.'

'I don't want you to think I've not been happy here, Mrs Dibble,' Myrtle said fiercely, 'but now the war's over it's time to think of kiddies of my own. Times are changing. A girl's got to look after herself now, and there are no prospects here.'

'Prospects?' Dismay made Margaret curt. 'What do you think you are – a bank manager? You thank your lucky stars you got a job at all, Myrtle.'

'And I don't meet any young men here.'

'There aren't any to meet any more,' Margaret replied soberly. 'There's many a girl in England not going to have a man of her own ever.'

'So you see,' Myrtle came back quickly, 'I'm right to get out and look around.'

Perhaps Myrtle would change her mind,

perhaps she wouldn't. Margaret made herself a cup of tea and thought about it. Once she accustomed herself to the idea that Myrtle was leaving, it wouldn't seem so bad. Just because she, Margaret, would never leave the Rectory, she couldn't expect the same to apply to everybody else. She'd have to train a new girl though. Agnes couldn't manage alone. And come to that, what might Agnes's plans be?

Penelope finished helping Felicia with the Christmas tree, and decided to take a stroll around the village before dark fell completely. Her footsteps took her to the cinema, and she stood outside it for some moments, surprised to see it in darkness and obviously closed up. Then briskly she walked away along Bankside. Where the bombed cottages had been, she had expected to see an empty shell, a scarred hole of rubble, but instead she saw an orderly piece of ground, fenced off and with winter vegetables growing in it. At the moment it also contained Frank Eliot, whom she hadn't seen since he had returned to Ashden after his illness.

'Hallo, Frank,' she said brightly, opening the new wicket gate and going in. 'Growing for England, are you?' she continued.

He grinned. 'Something like that, Miss Banning.'

'I heard you had gone into the cinema,' she continued doggedly. 'I imagined you'd be another Douglas Fairbanks by now, not growing vegetables.' With his moustache and tall, lean figure, he did have something of the Fairbanks look.

'Not exactly a Douglas Fairbanks. More of a Charlie Chaplin. I'm afraid the cinema is no more. Swinford-Browne couldn't wait to get rid of me in gratitude for all the work I did for his hop fields.'

'I'm sorry.'

'I'm not. It's given me more time to create this garden. It won't be a vegetable garden for long. When life is normal again, it will be a flower garden in memory of Isabel Swinford-Browne.'

'I hadn't heard about that either. What a nice idea,' Penelope said approvingly. 'Are you in charge of the project?'

He hesitated. 'Partly.'

'What will you plant–?'

'*I* won't be planting anything,' he cut in abruptly. 'I'm leaving the village.'

'Leaving?' Penelope was taken aback. 'But your son–'

'I hear Rudolf is a good man. He says he'll take care of him.'

'But,' Penelope struggled to cope with this unexpected development, 'what about Lizzie?' Having heard no more from Caroline, she had assumed Lizzie had elected to stay with Frank.

'She says it's best this way, and I agree.'

'What will you do?'

He shrugged. 'Go into hops again, perhaps. Not here, though. I've had enough of Sussex, even if the old hop fields are kept up.'

'Are hops really your life's work?' Penelope asked hesitantly.

'I'm over forty now, rather old for dreams, Penelope – I'm sorry, Miss Banning.'

'Penelope.'

'You have youth on your side, so what's your dream?' Frank abruptly turned the tables, perhaps, she guessed, to ignore the gauntlet she had just laid down.

She longed to answer, 'You, Frank,' but instead she said, 'Some kind of venture of my own. Some business I can run. I'd be good at that. Now tell me yours.' She spoke so firmly he could not refuse her this time.

Unwillingly he replied, 'I'd like to design gardens, huge gardens, small gardens, and then watch them grow.'

'Then why don't you?'

'It requires money,' he said wryly. 'And connections. Pity. I'd be good at it.'

Penelope stared at him. In 1914 she had gone on an impulse out to Serbia. Now she felt a similar impulse. Again it was a risk, but she had the same feeling that it was right. 'That might be no problem.' She was nervous, not because she doubted herself but because she feared his reaction.

He flushed, and started to say something.

'My money, my connections, your creativity. Think about it, Frank,' she interrupted quickly, before he could turn her down.

He looked at her, saw that she was serious, and nodded his head. 'Very well. I'll think. May I call on you in London?' He seemed surprised himself at his answer, and, well satisfied, she strode away.

Frank watched her go. Not for the first time, it occurred to him she had somewhat the look and character of his Jennifer.

Caroline sat despondently on a bench at Tonbridge, waiting for the Tunbridge Wells connection. It was all a terrible nightmare. There was no Yves and she'd missed the

Christmas preparations too. Furthermore she wouldn't be home until eight o'clock at the earliest, and would undoubtedly miss Yves' telephone call from London. She felt very sorry for herself indeed, and for the first time tears began to flow.

'Poor dear.' The woman next to her on the bench drew nearer. 'Lost your sweetheart, have you?'

'Yes,' said Caroline bleakly. She had. Not once, but twice.

About six thirty the doorbell rang again, and Felicia ran to open it in the hope of its being Caroline. It wasn't. In the Rectory drive was a large and unfamiliar army staff car, and on the doorstep were three large male strangers, one in civilian clothes of a very odd type indeed with a three-cornered hat, and two younger men in army uniform, which Felicia belatedly registered was American. All three of them were grinning and had a somewhat familiar air about them.

'Laurence at home, is he?' the older man asked, as she confusedly stood aside to let them in. He then proceeded to pump her hand up and down. 'Where is the old son of a gun?'

404

Attracted by the loud noise, Laurence came out of the drawing room with Elizabeth close on his heels. He stopped short, and stared at the three of them, his gaze going from one to the other. Then two strides took him to the older man, where he proceeded first to pump his hand up and down, and then to hug him.

'Gerald! Taken your time, haven't you?' He was half laughing, half crying.

'Sure have. Gave up waiting for you to come over to Colorado, and when Jake and Pete here came over to bail you folks out in France, I thought why not meet them and go down to see the folks?'

'And I'm delighted,' Laurence said simply. 'How did you know to come here and not Dover though?'

'Dover?' Gerald grinned. 'How is the old battle-axe?'

Lady Buckford descended the stairs in stately fashion. 'The old battle-axe is quite well, thank you, my son.'

No Caroline at the Town station, and no sign of her at the docks. Yves had gone straight to Buckford House but no one there had seen her either and when he telephoned the Rectory, Caroline had not returned.

Someone at the station remembered seeing a young lady wearing a Waac's uniform waiting much earlier in the afternoon, but she'd left alone on the London train. He promptly rang the office and then Queen Anne's Gate, but there was no reply from either. There were two choices. Either Caroline was on the way back to Ashden, or on her way to London and Queen Anne's Gate. He'd understood Luke wasn't going to Ashden until morning so she could be planning to travel with him. What a waste of precious, precious time.

'Pick me a leaf or two of sage, Agnes.' A little sage went a long way but it was useful because it kept green all winter. 'And then you'd better make up those three rooms.' What a to-do! The Rector's long-lost brother and his two sons come to stay, which meant a full house at the Rectory. She didn't know whether she was on her head or her heels.

There was no reply from Agnes who came to with a start as she saw Margaret staring at her. 'Sorry, I was just thinking.'

Once Margaret would have snapped, 'No time to think, not on Christmas Eve.' And certainly not this one, but she didn't do that tonight. There were more important matters.

Poor Miss Caroline didn't get home till eight thirty – and she was alone. Mrs Lilley popped out from the family reunion and had asked Margaret to get her something to eat in the dining room until she felt up to facing her new relations. Margaret promptly whisked out the nice piece of beef she'd kept warm for her. Miss Caroline only toyed with it, however, and seeing that, Mrs Lilley had decided she'd better tell her the truth.

'Yves has been here, darling.'

'What?' Miss Caroline's eyes grew round with horror. 'I thought he'd gone to London,' she wailed. 'Where is he now?'

'He went to find you. He'll be back, Caroline. Do try to eat something,' Mrs Lilley coaxed.

'Where did he go?'

'Dover, of course.'

It was a good job Margaret was still in the room because she was able to slam the door shut to prevent Miss Caroline rushing straight off to Ashden station again. Mrs Lilley took firm control for once, bless her. 'No, Caroline. Wait here, we have some news for you. Isn't that best, Mrs Dibble?'

Margaret nodded.

'He may think I'm up in London,' Caroline said desperately, eyeing the door and her chances.

'You wouldn't get to Dover tonight. Besides, Caroline, we all need you here, and especially tonight.'

'You don't understand – I could get to London at least.'

'And what if Yves comes here? He *will* come, even if it is tomorrow.'

'I'll go to the station then to meet the trains.'

'No, darling, you will spend Christmas Eve here with us, just as you always have. Now let me explain...'

Of all the stupid things to happen. If Yves was only here for a very short time, he might not have the time to come, he might think it was not worth all the anguish of another parting. Caroline tried in vain to eat the unappetising slice of beef Mrs Dibble had proudly put before her, but found it as hard to digest as the news of Uncle Gerald's reappearance. In the end, she quietly slid it onto the fire, and compromised with the potatoes and cabbage. Just as she was wondering how to dispose of the roly-poly pudding, there was a ring at the door, and

Caroline rushed to answer it, almost colliding with Agnes who promptly retreated.

'Yves!' she cried as she threw open the door.

It wasn't Yves. It was George and he was not alone. With him was a shy-looking slender girl whom Caroline vaguely recognised from one of George's photographs. 'Oh, George, how wonderful.' At least *some* nice things were happening for Christmas.

'Meet Florence, Caroline.' The girl smiled shyly.

Caroline shook Florence's hand. 'How lovely to meet you. Er – if you're both staying, I'll ask Agnes to make up the rooms.' What, she was feverishly wondering, had happened to Buxom Kate Burrows?

'George.' Elizabeth came hurrying into the hall, hearing the sound of his voice. 'I thought you'd never get here. Where have you been?'

'Meet Florence, ma.'

'Oh, how rude of me. Are you both staying? I'll ask Agnes to make up another room besides yours. That's if there are any.' Elizabeth was immediately flustered. 'I'm sure we–'

George grinned. 'We only need one,

Mother. Father's been keeping it secret. We were married this morning.'

'We ought to be leaving for church, Caroline.' Penelope had stayed behind with her as she refused to go till the last possible moment in case Yves arrived. That moment had come, and the bells were ringing out to call them to the midnight mass. Even in her own misery, Caroline was pleased to see Penelope looking so happy, not to mention George and Florence. In fact, everyone was save her, she reflected. Even Felicia, and as for Father and Grandmama, they had remained closeted after dinner with Gerald in the morning room, while Jake and Peter overwhelmed the drawing-room with their good humour, loud voices and funny stories. Caroline had done her best to contribute to the convivial atmosphere, hard though it was. Then her conscience struck her as she remembered Agnes, and she tried to rationalise her own unhappiness. Yves had gone to London, and she had missed him. Perhaps he had even left the country by now. After all, she had assumed he was *entering* Britain when he telephoned Luke. Suppose he had come for a mere twenty-four hours and had been leaving it?

410

The peace of St Nicholas' calmed her. Lit by its Christmas candles, the church was full, as had not been the case during the war. Grief could bring people to God; it could also estrange them. Now the odd unreality of the armistice was past, Ashden seemed to be preparing to heal its wounds and reunite as a village, although it was true that yesterday evening her father had told her that the Mutters and Thorns had once again come to blows. Once Father would have been deeply disturbed by this but he had actually laughed about it.

'Miracles need more work devoted to them than either the Mutters or the Thorns are prepared to give, I fear.' Oddly enough it was this humanity on her father's part that made Caroline realise she was once again at ease in God's presence, and this evening she felt her faith restored for the first time since Isabel's death. Her father too seemed to have taken on new fire, and the emotion and passion that had been absent since Isabel's death to be rekindled.

Behind her, her ladyship was no longer alone in the Hunney pew; Sir John was once again at her side, and Daniel too. What's more, Eleanor and Martin had joined them; another rift was obviously now mended,

Lord Grey had said in August 1914 that the lamps were going out all over Europe, but Ashden was replacing them with its candles of peace (even if they flickered occasionally between Mutters and Thorns).

Caroline had offered to help Mrs Dibble with the mince pies, and therefore emerged with Felicia and Daniel into the cold still night ahead of the main Rectory party. She had hoped against hope to find Yves waiting, and at the sight of a tall khaki-clad figure at the lych gate, her heart leapt, then fell again.

'That's Luke, isn't it?' Daniel asked, surprised.

'No. He's not arriving till tomorrow morning,' Felicia replied.

'Then that looks uncommonly like his twin brother.'

Luke strolled up to meet them, and Felicia, overcome with pleasure, ran to meet him, throwing her arms around him. Caroline glanced involuntarily at Daniel to see his reaction. He watched with impassive face.

'I managed to leave earlier than I'd hoped.' Luke's voice was flat with tiredness.

'Have you seen Yves?' Caroline could wait no longer.

412

'No, I came straight here. Is he at the Rectory?'

'I thought he was in London.' It came out as a wail. The Christmas angels were neglecting her badly.

Luke sighed. 'Not so far as I know. It's the fault of that bad line. I'm sorry, Caroline.'

So was she. Yves had obviously gone to London in search of her and missed Luke who was on his way down here. By the time he realised what had happened, it would be too late to get a train to Ashden.

As her mother opened the door of the Rectory, the warm glow from the entrance hall fire cheered her a little. Furthermore, there was a smell of mince pies, which meant Christmas was almost here.

The drawing-room door opened and Christmas presented itself. It was Yves.

Agnes was woken by the sound of Myrtle playing with Elizabeth Agnes next door. Isabel, bless her, was still sound asleep in the crib at her side, but the Christmas stocking had obviously proved too much of an allure for her sister. Agnes realised just how much she was going to miss Myrtle when she left. She had longed for nothing more than to have a house alone with Jamie

413

and have the time to look after the children herself, but now that Jamie had left her alone, she had to decide what to do herself.

Tears of self-pity for her lonely Christmas threatened, but she managed to fight them off. She wasn't alone. She lived in the Rectory surrounded by people who cared about her. Moreover, the war had shown that women could lead their own lives without men, by earning their own living. Plenty had done so before of course, but not women like her. Now she could be independent like Miss Tilly and Miss Caroline, and she might or might not continue in service. Service conditions would change because too many Myrtles and Agneses had had a taste of freedom. If they did return to service, it would be on their terms. This war was fought for all; the men who were lucky enough to come home from the trenches expected a better deal from life, and there was no reason women should be any different. They'd worked just as hard. Anyway, Jamie had fought for *her* independence and she wasn't going to let him down. Not again. Perhaps she'd take up Lady Hunney's surprising offer. Myrtle offered to look after the kitchen, and so Agnes had gone to the midnight service.

Afterwards Lady Hunney had stopped to speak to her in the churchyard.

'Agnes Thorn, isn't it?'

Agnes had been amazed. Lady Hunney never spoke to her own servants, let alone someone else's.

'I was very sorry to hear about your husband.'

'Thank you, your ladyship.' Agnes bobbed and went to move on.

'It occurs to me,' Lady Hunney stopped her, 'that with two little children you cannot live in the Rectory indefinitely.'

Agnes flushed red. 'That's my business, Lady Hunney.'

'I know that, my dear, but I wondered if I might help. There is an estate cottage in Station Road that might suit you and your two children nicely. I would be happy to allow you to occupy it for a very small rent.'

'But the Rectory–' Agnes couldn't think clearly.

'You don't have to live there to work there.'

Times were changing, and even Lady Hunney saw it. Perhaps to live alone was not so impossible after all. Indeed, in the light of Christmas morning, Agnes began to see that it was very possible. It occurred to her that perhaps Jamie had provided a house of their own after all.

Caroline knew she must soon ask Yves when he had to leave, but she kept postponing the question so that she could enjoy the morning service, the unwrapping of presents, and Christmas luncheon. Oh, how *happy* she was. This morning at least there was only one sadness, and that was not on her own behalf.

Daniel had not appeared at morning service, much to Felicia's puzzlement, but afterwards, when walking home with Yves after the main party, he unexpectedly appeared. 'Caroline,' he said jerkily, 'I'm sorry to ask you this, but could you break the news to Felicia that I'm returning to London?'

She was alarmed, for he looked very pale. 'You mean you have to work after all?'

'No. I think it has to be for good, so far as she and I are concerned.' He managed a grin. 'You see why I haven't the courage to tell her myself. I might all too easily change my mind.'

Caroline was both horrified and mystified. Only yesterday Felicia had hinted that all was settled and that she and Daniel would be married.

'Why have you suddenly had this change of heart?'

'Bad words to choose, change of heart. I haven't. Because I wanted it so much, I convinced myself Felicia was right when she said it would work. It wouldn't, I see that now.'

'But what will you do?'

'I shall travel, as I always intended. But alone.'

'You'll break her heart.' It was a cliché, but it could well be true.

'I thought that too – until I saw the look on her face when she greeted Luke last night. Felicia thinks–' Daniel stumbled over his words and began again. 'She will believe that she will never recover, but I know the pain will grow less, and in any case she loves Luke too. You know it's right, don't you, Caroline? She's not yet twenty-three, which is incredible to believe when you think of all she's achieved. How can I take the responsibility of her assurance that she doesn't want children or a normal married life? She's too young to take that decision.'

'I can't bear it, Daniel,' Caroline said miserably. 'For either of you, but most for you, for she has Luke.'

'Nor can I. That's why I want you to tell her, Caroline. You know what suffering is, because you and Yves are parted too. You have Yves this Christmas as a surprise present, but sooner or later the holiday is over, and life must begin again.'

'How can you, Laurence?' Elizabeth cried. The sight of her husband dressed in his jester's costume as narrator of their traditional Christmas game appalled her. She had assumed he would drop the idea for today at least. Even in the excitement of meeting Gerald and his sons, the missing one must be remembered.

'My dear,' Laurence came to comfort her, 'this year of all years we should play the Family Coach.'

'But Isabel—'

'*For* Isabel,' Laurence replied gently. 'Isabel is in our thoughts all the time; she cannot be displaced by a game. And not only our thoughts either. Our Maud had a word with me after the service. She – you will hardly believe this, Elizabeth, when you recall Sir John was as opposed to it as I was four years ago – has arranged to buy the cinema from Swinford-Browne, and to open it up as a commercial venture, and ensure that Isabel's name is firmly connected with it.'

'*What?*' Even Elizabeth began to laugh at that. 'Is she going to manage it?'

'No. Janie Marden is going to try.'

'Oh, Laurence, that is – Isabel would have been delighted.' Janie, the doctor's daughter, was a close friend of all the Lilley girls.

'Maud said she had to fight off a rival offer from Patricia Swinford-Browne by pointing out she was clearly set for promotion in the police force.'

'Thank goodness for that,' Elizabeth said fervently.

'So we may have our Family Coach? It would please Gerald immensely.'

'Yes, Laurence.'

When the players had taken their places in the drawing-room, where all the chairs had been positioned in the usual circle, Laurence announced: 'This year my subject is Good King Wenceslas. Alas, a fall in the forest incapacitated him, and he was forced to make use of–'

'The Family Coach,' came the unison chant.

'I bags the wheels,' Phoebe yelled, getting up to demonstrate.

'No, Phoebe,' Elizabeth began, but she cried in vain as Phoebe took no notice.

'Guess I'll be the cowboy outrider,' Gerald said.

'You will not, Gerald,' his mother said firmly. 'You have clearly forgotten the rules. All players must be inside or part of the coach.'

'Yes, ma.' Gerald winked at his sons. 'Just for once, eh?'

'No, Gerald. Mother's quite right,' Tilly said, straight-faced.

Lady Buckford looked at her. 'That, Matilda, is the only time in your life you have admitted I am *always* right.'

Her three children, her daughter-in-law and grandchildren examined her face for a smile. It did not come. Just when Caroline had given up hope, something else even rarer issued from Grandmother's lips: a laugh.

The trials and tribulations of King Wenceslas and his page exhausted even Caroline, and she was weak with laughter as an hour later the Family Coach rattled its triumphant way back over the drawbridge. Phoebe, on the other hand, still seemed to have boundless energy, and insisted on pounding out the accompaniment to Billy's songs on the piano.

'Our baby will get used to racing around before he's even born, won't he, Billy?' she said happily, when Elizabeth remonstrated again.

Apparently it didn't, for just as supper was served, Phoebe gave a shriek.

'Anyone would think you'd never seen a trifle before,' Caroline laughed as Mrs Dibble triumphantly bore in the fruits of her hard labour.

'It's not the trifle,' Phoebe gasped. 'I think it must be the baby.'

'This staircase is a real Jacob's ladder,' Caroline flung over her shoulder in passing to Yves. 'Just look at all us ministering angels running up and down.'

No midwife could be found on Christmas Day, and Felicia had once again with Mrs Dibble's help put her nursing experience to good use, with Dr Marden's help, since the baby was premature. Mrs Dibble was highly satisfied at being proved right about it's not being six weeks late. At seven o'clock on Boxing Morning, with her 'angels' white from lack of sleep, Phoebe produced Billy's daughter three weeks early.

Caroline took the first opportunity to fall

into bed, and awoke three hours later to find pale December sunshine streaming through the curtains, and Yves patiently sitting at her side.

Her eyes were instantly wide open. 'You're leaving?' she cried. She had delayed and delayed asking him this, and then Phoebe's baby had made it impossible. That he was still at her side seemed enough.

'For what?' He seemed surprised. 'I do not take up my position until the New Year.'

'You're here until then? I have you for another...' she counted busily, 'five days.'

'Here, yes. Then we return to London.'

For a moment she thought she did not hear properly. 'We? So how long are you here for in all?'

'Why, for ever.' And seeing her lack of reaction, added uncertainly, 'If you will have me.'

The words finally made sense in a Boxing Day gift of glory. 'For *ever?*' It came out as a squeak.

'I told Luke–'

'The line was cut.'

It was Yves' turn to be shocked. 'You mean you did not know? All this time you thought I was here but for a day? Oh, *cara, cara.*'

She was in his arms, he was cradling her,

rocking her to and fro, stroking her hair while she sobbed out her happiness against his shoulder.

'Why?' she asked, for it mattered that she should know. 'You have always said it was a matter of honour to return to your wife.'

'And you said, my love, that even I had choice. I did not believe you then, but I changed my mind, thanks to King Albert and your Aunt Tilly.'

Caroline began to laugh. *'Tilly?'*

'I will tell you of King Albert first. He asked me about my plans, and I explained my problem – or rather as I saw it, my duty. I had to tell him, for he had met both my wife and yourself. He thought for a moment and then said at the outbreak of war he had had three choices, each of which could be said to be the honourable one: to stay with his occupied people to encourage them; to fight and lead his free troops against the enemy, or to go to lead the Belgian government in exile to have greater control over Belgian destiny. Faced with three honourable choices, he had followed his instinct, or perhaps one could say his heart. I too had a choice, he said, and I saw he was right. Annette-Marie is my wife in name only, you are my wife in fact. I saw that I am honour-bound to both, and not to recognise that would be to dishonour the love that lies between us.'

Caroline sighed with happiness. 'And Aunt Tilly?'

'She came to visit me. You thought she was visiting King Albert. In fact she came to us to see how things were, I suspect. Why did I stay, she asked indignantly, when she saw how hard I found it to adjust and how unforgiving Annette-Marie was of my absence in the war. I replied pompously that I had promised to look after Annette-Marie for the rest of our lives. And did I wish, she asked sarcastically, to take responsibility for her unhappiness if *she* later decided she loved someone else? Would I insist on remaining with her? I was very angry with Tilly, for I thought I knew that Annette-Marie would *never* find the love of a man acceptable. She told me then that she herself had believed that of herself, assuming life had omitted to provide her with the necessary feelings. She had had to wait until she was over fifty to meet Simon and find she was wrong. Could I take the risk for Annette-Marie, who is not yet thirty, Tilly asked? Suppose she later met a man – or a woman, had I thought of that possibility

– whom she could love?'

'Dear Aunt Tilly.'

'It took some time – and it was hard – but Annette-Marie has reluctantly agreed that I should annul our marriage. That too will take time, but after that you will be the wife of Colonel Rosier, at his Belgian Majesty's Military Legation in London. If you agree, of course,' he asked anxiously.

Elizabeth came triumphantly downstairs with the baby in her arms to show Laurence.

'Our first grandchild.'

Laurence looked at his wife, however, not the baby. He saw that her face was alive and glowing once more. Just as the Americans had injected new life into the war, Gerald's visit might open up new horizons. He and Elizabeth might even visit America if they could afford it, certainly their children might. And as for this little girl – he looked fondly at the now screaming mite in Elizabeth's arms – who knew to what horizons she might fly?

'Yes, my darling Elizabeth. A new life in the house–'

'But she can't replace Isabel,' Elizabeth said immediately.

'No, but we will cherish her memory alongside the living. My love, we have been parted from one another.'

'And now we are together.'

Mrs Dibble, listening outside the door, having lingered for a sight of Mrs Phoebe's daughter, crept away well pleased. The Rectory was itself again.

The publishers hope that this book has given you enjoyable reading. Large Print Books are especially designed to be as easy to see and hold as possible. If you wish a complete list of our books please ask at your local library or write directly to:

Magna Large Print Books
Magna House, Long Preston,
Skipton, North Yorkshire.
BD23 4ND

This Large Print Book for the partially sighted, who cannot read normal print, is published under the auspices of

THE ULVERSCROFT FOUNDATION

Other MAGNA Titles
In Large Print